MENDING VANESSA

Mending Vanessa

An Oregon Romance

ROSEANN COTTON

LUMINARE PRESS
WWW.LUMINAREPRESS.COM

Printed in the United States of America

Luminare Press
442 Charnelton St.
Eugene, OR 97401
www.luminarepress.com

LCCN: 2021920411
ISBN: 978-1-64388-819-4

To my husband and two daughters

Part One

Chapter 1

———— ◆ ————

Neal Youngman rubbed his goatee as he rushed from the office mumbling about an accident to the school secretary.

In another wing of the building, fifth-grade teacher Vanessa Cox rested her chin on her open palms. She surveyed the bare bulletin boards, shelves stacked with textbooks, and upside-down chairs placed on top of the empty desks. Best friend and colleague, Melanie Rhodes, walked in and plopped her butt onto Vanessa's desk.

"Well?" Melanie asked.

"Well, what?"

"Did you pass Willie to the sixth grade?"

Vanessa leaned back, smiling as she pictured the immature boy, the youngest of six children in a dysfunctional family. "Yep. He buckled down the last few months." She patted her shoulder, grinning. "It was a combination of my outstanding influence and him not wanting to embarrass himself by repeating the fifth grade."

Melanie jumped off the desk. "Frank's gonna be so thrilled to hear Willie'll be in his class next year." She tilted her head backward, laughing and brushing aside a stray strand of her blonde hair. She eyed various items still cluttering Vanessa's desk. "Aren't you done clearing out the mess? Everyone else has already left for the staff picnic." She grabbed Vanessa's hand, pulling her from the chair. "The start of a three-month reprieve. Let's go!"

"I'm coming," Vanessa said, snatching her unzipped purse and sweater.

"You won't need your sweater. It's hotter than usual for early June," Melanie said.

They stepped into the hallway. No nonsense vice-principal Youngman approached them. He said nothing at first but stood looking at Vanessa with a grim expression.

Now what? Vanessa asked herself. The stupidest things make him crazy. She couldn't control her mouth. "Are you uptight because one of my pupils dared to put purple and blue streaks in her hair?"

Youngman ignored her remark and bowed his head. He smoothed his gray crew cut with his fingers and took a deep breath. Vanessa sensed he was more serious than normal. "Something's wrong," Vanessa said.

"It's your father."

"My father?" Vanessa raised her voice.

"I got word your father was in an auto accident. An ambulance took him to Providence. I don't know any details."

Youngman grabbed Vanessa as her legs crumpled. He guided her to a nearby bench. She sat for a few seconds before jumping up. "What happened? Never mind. I've got to go!"

"You're in no condition to drive. I'll take you to the hospital," Melanie said. "We'll take my car. Jason and I'll come for yours later." Melanie spotted the keyring peeking out of an inside pocket of Vanessa's open purse and snatched it.

Vanessa grabbed it back. "I can drive myself."

Melanie gripped Vanessa's hand, dragging her toward the exit. "We're wasting time." She unlocked her minivan. "Get in." She blasted the air conditioning on high and zoomed out of the school parking lot.

Vanessa's brain buzzed thinking about all the possibilities. She twisted her engagement ring, tapping her right foot as though that would hasten their arrival. "Can't you go any faster?" she asked in an impatient shrill.

"Do you want us to be in an accident too? I'm driving as fast as I dare."

Vanessa cursed every red light and slow driver that seemed to delay them. "What do you think happened?"

"I have no idea." Melanie glanced at her friend for a split second. "It might not be severe."

"They hauled him off in an ambulance for God's sake! What'll I do if…" Vanessa trailed off, rubbing her clammy fingers back and forth along her forehead.

"Think positive thoughts. We'll be there soon and you can find out."

"Melanie, do you realize my father is my only relative?"

"Don't you have an aunt?"

"Yeah, my Aunt Helene. But I haven't seen her since my grandparents' funeral and that was twelve years ago."

"How come?"

"She's an archeologist and treks the globe on expeditions. She's practically a stranger to me. We've never had much of a relationship. She and Dad had a bitter disagreement, so they rarely communicate."

"What about her husband and children?"

"Never married."

Vanessa lowered her head, silently praying her father's injuries were not serious. Her mother died when she was an infant, and Lyle Edward Cox devoted his life to her for the past twenty-four years. She couldn't imagine life without him.

What seemed an eternity later, Vanessa and Melanie arrived at the hospital. Melanie dropped Vanessa off at the emergency entrance and took off to search for a parking spot. Vanessa dashed through the automated double doors and stepped onto the polished tile floor. She paused, searching for someone, anyone, who would direct her to her father. She spotted the reception desk. Trying to catch her breath, she said, "I'm Vanessa Cox. My father, Lyle Cox, was in an auto accident, and he's here. Where can I find him?" She turned and looked for a sign indicating the direction to the emergency room.

"You can't go into the ER. You'll have to wait in the waiting room like everyone else," the receptionist said in a clipped tone. She gestured to where she was talking about. "There are some comfy, well, semi-comfy chairs over there and some coffee if you'd like."

Vanessa wasn't about to be dismissed. "I demand to see him now."

Looking at Vanessa with her heavily mascaraed eyes, the receptionist reached for the phone. "Okay, I'll call for details on him and see if the doctor will allow you to visit now."

Vanessa paced back and forth, pounding her right fist into her left palm. "Please let him be all right," she whispered to herself. *What happened? What a difference a day makes. Last night he was fine and now…*

Melanie arrived, hurrying to Vanessa. "Any news?"

"No."

"I'm here for you." Melanie offered to get her something to munch.

"No thanks, Mel. I can't eat right now."

Eventually, a portly nurse wearing bright yellow scrubs and a pleasant smile arrived. "Miss Cox?"

Vanessa rushed to her side.

"Please follow me."

Vanessa glanced at Melanie and gestured for her to tag along. Melanie fell into step beside her friend.

The nurse escorted them to a small conference room. A doctor wearing a customary white physician's coat sat behind a table perusing a report. He didn't acknowledge the two women.

"Ahem, Doctor." The nurse interrupted him. "Mr. Cox's daughter is here."

Before the doctor reacted, Vanessa leaned across the table. "What's wrong with him? Is he going to be all right?"

The doctor pushed the papers aside. Gesturing for them to sit opposite him, he greeted the pair. "Good afternoon, ladies. I'm Dr. DeWitt." Extending his hand to Vanessa, he smiled. "You must be the daughter."

Vanessa nodded. Dr. DeWitt's firm, yet warm, handshake decreased her stress level. But only a tad. His graying hair and receding hairline gave Vanessa a modicum of confidence he was experienced enough to treat her father. No interns! Vanessa introduced Melanie. "This is my friend Melanie Rhodes. I'd like her with me."

"Fine, but shouldn't we wait until your mother arrives?" Dr. DeWitt asked.

Vanessa stared downward. Melanie told the doctor Vanessa had no mother.

Dr. DeWitt leaned against the chair back. "A drunk driver ran into your father's car. In the two hours since he arrived, we've run extensive tests and performed X-rays.

He's in no immediate danger, but he's in very serious condition. He endured substantial damage to L1 and L2 of his
lumbar spine, or in laymen's terms, his lower back. There's
also something wrong with both kidneys."

Vanessa's right hand covered her mouth.

The doctor continued. "We are running more tests to
determine to what extent. He sustained many lacerations
on his back and arms."

"He's going to be okay. Right?"

"It's too soon to tell. The next twenty-four to forty-eight
hours will be critical in determining his prognosis."

"May I see him now?"

"I understand your need, Miss Cox," Dr. DeWitt
answered. "Your father is under heavy sedation now and
is not conscious."

Vanessa pleaded.

"All right, Miss Cox, but just for a few minutes. I'm sorry,
Ms. Rhodes, but only one visitor at a time is allowed in the
Intensive Care Unit."

Melanie hugged Vanessa. "I'll call Greg and tell him
about the accident."

"Oh my God!" Vanessa wailed. Her stomach churned
and her knees buckled at the sight of her forty-eight-year-
old robust, athletic father lying unconscious, hooked up
to a variety of machines. She reached for the bed to steady
herself. Dr. DeWitt escorted her to a nearby chair and
guided her onto the seat.

"Do you want a glass of water?" Dr. DeWitt asked.

Vanessa choked back tears as she tried to gain her composure. "Ah, no…no thanks." The doctor handed her a
tissue, and she wiped her eyes. She stood and approached
the bed, touching her father's right hand.

A nurse moved the chair next to the bed. Vanessa lowered herself onto it. "Dad, I'm here. I love you. You're going to pull through this thing. Anything you need, I'll see you get it." She stroked his hand, attempting to reassure him. She reminded him of her August wedding to Greg and how she was counting on him to give her away. He wasn't going to get out of it.

"Miss Cox," the doctor said. "It's time to leave."

"Can't I stay with him?" Vanessa laced her fingers and held them up, displaying her most convincing smile.

"No, I'm sorry. I know this is hard and I understand your concern. But I must be firm. The best thing would be for you to go home and rest. If there's any change, we'll contact you. He won't be able to communicate with you or anybody else most likely until tomorrow." Dr. DeWitt opened the door. "On your way out, please stop at admissions and fill out some forms."

Vanessa reluctantly tore herself away from her father, staring at him the entire time she walked backward from the room. Outside the ICU, she asked Dr. DeWitt again about her father's kidneys.

"We should know within a day or two."

"What if they are damaged?"

"We'll have to determine the extent. If only one is affected, he can function without dialysis. If both are irreparably damaged, then dialysis for the rest of his life is the treatment. And as a last resort, a kidney transplant."

"I'll give him one of my kidneys," Vanessa volunteered without hesitation. "We'd be a match."

"We'll cross that bridge if we come to it, Miss Cox."

Entering the waiting room, Vanessa noticed the daytime activity had decreased. She glanced at her watch. 5:15 p.m. She saw no sign of Melanie. She plopped into a chair. Her body doubled over, rocking back and forth. She didn't bother to wipe the flood of tears flowing down her cheeks and was oblivious to the stares of sympathetic onlookers.

"There you are! I got here as fast as I could!" Greg said as he approached Vanessa, pulling her up into his powerful arms. "How is he?"

Vanessa clung to Greg's comforting body. "I won't know much for at least a day or two," she answered. "Damn it! Why did this happen? He may have sustained irreparable damage to his kidneys. The doctor won't know for sure for a couple of days. He may need dialysis or even a kidney transplant. He can have one of mine."

"Hold on there," Greg said, releasing his embrace. "Noble of you, Van, but you're so young. I don't want you sacrificing your health or future."

"He's my father! Who else would be a perfect match? You won't talk me out of this, Greg," Vanessa warned. "I won't listen. I can't turn my back on him."

"Let's wait and see," Greg said. "Come on."

"I've got to fill out some forms first." She racked her brain to remember pertinent information. She was ready to rip and toss the whole damn stack of papers into the trash. She shoved the completed forms across the counter. "I'll be back here first thing in the morning."

"We'll keep you posted," the clerk said. "Call first before coming tomorrow morning in case the doctor doesn't think it would be advisable for you to visit. Also, visiting hours—"

"I'll be here!" Walking to the car, irritation festered within. *What's with the resistance to my presence I keep getting from these people? I love my father. All I want is to be here for him and help in any way I can.*

Once Vanessa settled next to Greg in his Jeep Cherokee, he asked her if she knew what had happened.

"A drunk driver hit his car. I don't know any other details."
She glanced at Greg before resting her head on his shoulder.
I'm glad I have him to help me through this ordeal. Closing
her eyes, she reminisced about the day she had met Greg
fourteen months earlier. Greg was jogging and had stopped
to observe her struggling to instruct fifth and sixth graders
on basketball skills.

"Mind if I try? I can help these kids learn the basics."

A male, in his late twenties, she guessed, stood an arm's
length from her. His engaging smile charmed Vanessa.
Before she stopped herself, she handed him the ball. During
that first class, Greg had the students dribbling and passing.
Smiles abounded.

"Thanks for pitching in," Vanessa said, as the students
gathered their belongings and left the basketball court. "I
know little about the game, but our vice principal decided
I should teach them anyway. What a mistake!" She raised
her arms in the air. "But, man, you're quite knowledgeable
and have a rapport with the students."

"I better be. I'm the basketball coach at Milwaukie High."

"No wonder."

"I'd be glad to volunteer my services."

"You would? I appreciate that. I'll clear it with Youngman."

"Allow me to introduce myself. I'm Greg Vardanega."

Vanessa extended her hand, grimacing at the strength
of Greg's handshake. "And I'm Vanessa Cox, a fifth-grade
teacher. Pleased to meet you."

During the next six weeks, every Tuesday and Thursday,
like clockwork, Greg took over the class. She scrutinized
him from the sideline, marveling at the pure pleasure and
enthusiasm he exuded. He could be a poster boy for pumping iron or an NBA player with his over six-foot frame. The

basketball tattooed on his left bicep attested to his passion for the game. At the end of the mini-classes, Greg had the group performing basketball skills with commendable proficiency. They gathered around Greg and cheered.

"When I'm a freshman, I'm gonna try out for the team," a freckled-faced, red-headed student had said. "I hope you're still the coach."

Greg grinned and tousled the lad's hair.

As the last of the pupils straggled off the court, Greg sat on a bench, wiping sweat from his face. Vanessa caught him staring at her as he'd done dozens of times. She suspected Greg didn't want to fade out of her life, but he was uncertain if she felt the same way. She solved the dilemma. "I want to show my appreciation for all you've done. How about if I prepare you a home-cooked meal as a thank you? This Saturday?"

The smile radiating from his face would have melted an iceberg.

They began dating shortly thereafter, and eight months later, Greg popped the question. "Vanessa, I've talked to your father about marrying you and he gave me his blessing. So, how about it?"

Vanessa laughed. "What? You're not getting down on one knee?" She tapped his nose with her finger. "I'll overlook your rather informal proposal." Fluttering her eyelashes, she'd said one word, "Yes." And now she would depend on Greg's support to weather through this ordeal.

When Vanessa arrived at the hospital the next morning, Dr. DeWitt invited her into his office. "We've moved your father out of the ICU."

A smile appeared.

"We've determined your father's kidneys are beyond repair and no longer functioning."

Vanessa's shoulders slumped. She'd prayed for a better diagnosis.

The doctor continued. "He's experiencing end-stage renal failure. The only treatments are dialysis or a transplant."

"Did you tell him?" Vanessa asked, sinking into a chair.

"Yes, we've told him and explained the options to him."

"How did he take the news?"

"Better than most folks," Dr. DeWitt answered. "Naturally, he's depressed. It will take him time to adjust to this situation and decide what route he wants to take. If he chooses a transplant, we'll have to put him on a list—"

"Yeah, along with a thousand others."

Dr. DeWitt resumed his spiel. "If a compatible donor surfaces, we will perform the transplant if that's his choice. I'm going to ask your father if he's open to meeting with one of our psychiatrists. It can help patients to talk about their emotions with a trained professional."

"Other than his kidneys, he should recover then?"

"As far as we can tell, yes. The lacerations will all heal. Your father will be recovering for a long time, Miss Cox. We'll work for the best outcome."

Vanessa stood up and announced, "I'll donate one of my kidneys. I'm his only relative other than his sister, and they haven't spoken for years."

"Let's not rush into this," Dr. DeWitt said, shaking his hands back and forth. "Let your father decide, and then we'll go from there."

When Vanessa entered her father's room, she scowled at the army green walls, drab curtains, and sterile atmosphere. "You need some color. Next time I visit, I'm bringing a bouquet."

"My day is brightened now that you're here, my dear. And have no fear, I'm feeling better…I think. My back aches and I'm tired, but seeing you I forget my pains."

"Dad." Vanessa wrapped his hand within hers. "Seeing you alive and talking makes me feel better too." She kissed him on the forehead. "And don't worry, I'm going to give you one of my kidneys!"

Although weak, Lyle's voice increased volumes. "No way, Vanessa! I won't even consider the possibility. I don't want to hear another word about it. I'll be on dialysis for the rest of my life before I let you donate one of your kidneys."

"But, Dad," Vanessa protested, "I want to. And if I'm compatible, I won't take no for an answer." Turning to Dr. DeWitt, Vanessa asked him how soon she could be tested.

Lyle winced as he struggled to sit erect. "Vanessa, you've always been headstrong and stubborn, but this is one time you will not prevail. The subject is closed. You will not, I repeat not, donate a kidney!" He lowered his head back onto the pillow, winded.

"Miss Cox," Dr. DeWitt said. "I advise you to wait and give him time to think about his decision after discussion with me and the other doctors. The testing process might be unnecessary based on what your father decides."

"Vanessa, leave the room," her father said in a firm voice. "I want to talk to Dr. DeWitt privately."

Placing her hands on her hips, Vanessa didn't budge.

"Out!" Her father pointed to the door.

Vanessa moved, forcing a grin and shaking her finger at her father, trying to make light of her hurt feelings. "But I'll be back in a few minutes, so make it fast."

Lyle cast a stern expression directly at the doctor. "Under no circumstances is Vanessa to be tested as a potential donor. Is that clear? I'll die before I allow her to donate."

The doctor checked Lyle's pulse. "I respect your wishes," Dr. DeWitt said. "But are you sure? Your daughter may be a perfect match."

With clear, steadfast eyes, Lyle said. "There is a good reason, one which I will not disclose. It would ruin…never mind. I won't change my mind."

Chapter 2

A few days later, sitting on the sectional sofa, Vanessa snuggled against Greg's bare chest. "I can't understand why Dad is being so stubborn," she complained.

"Stubborn? Look in the mirror," Greg said. "Why don't you give this transplant business a rest, Van? Your father said no. Can't you respect his wishes? I'm tired of hearing you talk about it." He wiped a few beads of sweat from his forehead and pushed Vanessa from his sweaty chest. He reached for a few bridal brochures and handed them to Vanessa. "Why not think about planning our wedding?"

"The wedding is not my primary focus right now."

"Yeah, I noticed."

"I don't like your attitude. What if it were your mother or father?" She stood, tossing the brochures aside. "If Dad's condition means postponing the wedding, then so be it."

"You're stressing him."

"Why is everybody treating me like a villain? I'm trying to help."

"We realize that, but your father said no several times. What is it about no you can't accept? He can be on a waiting list and hopefully, another donor will work."

"Why wait for a suitable donor when I may very well be

compatible? I'm miffed he won't tell me why he doesn't want me to be tested. Seems he's harboring a mysterious secret. I'll try anyway. We'll know then."

Greg rubbed his hands through his hair, forcing himself to remain silent. The phone rang, a welcome excuse to discontinue this conversation. "I'll get it," he said. Moments later, he returned, a smile etched on his face. "That was Melanie. She and Jason are going to the beach. They want us to join them. How about it?"

"I'll pass," Vanessa said. "If I don't visit Dad today, he'll think I've deserted him."

"No, he won't. I'm willing to bet Lyle would encourage you to join them. Come on, Van, I want to go. A day at the beach would be good for both of us. We've been under quite a strain this past week."

"What if something happened to Dad and the hospital couldn't reach me? No, Greg, you go without me. I'll visit Dad, then come back and try to make some plans for our wedding."

"Your father is doing fine," Greg said, trying to persuade Vanessa. "He's due to be discharged soon, isn't he? You'll see him every day."

"I insist you go," Vanessa said, pushing him toward the phone. "Call Melanie and tell her. But count me out."

An hour later, Melanie and Jason arrived, along with Jason's younger sister. Jason hugged Vanessa, then introduced Alicia. The resemblance between brother and sister struck Vanessa…the light brown hair, hazel eyes, identical noses. Alicia's eyelashes and face had a touch of makeup. Her athletic physique mirrored her brother's. "You two could pass for twins."

Melanie turned to Vanessa. "Are you sure you won't come? You need a break."

"I wouldn't be much company. I'll worry about Dad the whole time and I don't want to spoil your fun."

Greg kissed Vanessa goodbye and promised to call her when they returned.

Vanessa sorted through the many wedding brochures and pamphlets she had collected. After a bit, she dropped the materials on the coffee table. She kicked off her sandals, leaned her head against the sofa, and closed her eyes. *I love Greg, but my heart isn't into planning my wedding. Am I procrastinating or is it something else?*

"How are you today, Dad?" Vanessa asked as she entered his hospital room two hours later.

"I can't wait to leave this so-called hotel. The sooner the better."

"Any word yet on a donor? Or are you going to remain stubborn and continue on dialysis?" Vanessa kissed his forehead.

"You're always so impatient, honey," Lyle said. "Anyway, I haven't decided yet."

"I don't understand your attitude. It's a vast mystery to me!"

Lyle squinted when the bright sun glared into his face as Vanessa parted the curtains. "Close them."

She obeyed, then sat on the edge of his bed. "Thought you'd enjoy looking outside. Now, about me donating a kidney."

"I gave you my answer. Where's Greg?"

"He went to the beach with Melanie and Jason."

"Sounds like fun. Why didn't you go too?"

"I rather visit you," she answered, stroking his head with her fingertips.

"I know this ordeal's hard on you, my dear, but you need a break," her father said. "You're neglecting Greg. After all, he should be the main man in your life now. He might lose interest and find himself another gal."

"You'll always be my key man. And don't worry, Greg's committed to me," Vanessa assured him. "I told him to go to the beach. Jason's sister went with them. They can entertain each other."

"After you're married, Greg will replace me, and rightfully so. What's the latest on your wedding plans?"

"I haven't been in the mood lately to think about the wedding, let alone plan it. I glanced through some brochures today, but my heart wasn't in it. The gathering is a small affair. Shouldn't take much time to plan the ceremony and reception. Greg's mother offered her backyard. I have to order a few flowers, arrange for the priest, invite the few guests and…" Vanessa threw her arms up. The pressure to plan the wedding from Greg and now her father irritated her. She approached the window and parted the curtains enough to peek outside. The sight of an array of purple and yellow pansies in the hospital courtyard caused her to smile. She turned to face her father. His closed eyes and rhythmic breathing greeted her. She walked to his bed, smoothed the blankets, and kissed his forehead.

Later that evening, as Vanessa was preparing for bed, the phone rang. She hoped it was Greg.

"Hi," Melanie said.

Vanessa stifled her disappointment.

"You should have come. The weather was glorious. We had such a great time. I didn't even wear my jacket. Only my sweatshirt was enough and you know how cold I always am."

"I'm glad you guys had a great time. Did Greg?"

"Hasn't he called you? We dropped him and Alicia off at her apartment about two hours ago. He told me he planned to call you when he got inside. She was going to take him home."

"He's no doubt at home now. I'll call him," Vanessa said. "Thanks for inviting me today, Mel. Let's plan a lunch date and—"

"How about next Tuesday? We can shop for my matron of honor dress. We can kill two birds with one stone. It'll be good for you to get out."

"Fine. Call you tomorrow." She hung up and immediately phoned Greg. After four rings, she heard his voice on his answering machine. *Why wasn't he home yet? Still at Alicia's?* She slammed the receiver onto the cradle.

VANESSA AWOKE THE FOLLOWING MORNING TO RAYS OF warmth streaming through the opened window. She threw back the sheet and stretched from head to toe. Annoyance with Greg had prevented her from sleeping soundly through the night. The warm water cascading from the shower spigot soothed her. The frustration toward Greg disappeared. As she stepped from the shower, the sound of the phone ringing drifted into the bathroom. She wrapped the towel around her dripping wet body and dashed to her bedside phone, her wet feet leaving a trail of water.

Greg's cheery voice boomed in the earpiece.

Paying no heed to his jovial spirit, she asked. "Why didn't you call me last night?"

Greg ignored her question and told her he'd be there in an hour with a surprise.

Vanessa returned to the bathroom and dressed in her favorite jeans and an oversized sweatshirt. Drying her hair, she was unsure how to react when Greg arrived. He had mentioned a surprise. *Hmmm…*

When Greg tiptoed to Vanessa and wrapped his arms around her from behind, she swung around, admonishing him for startling her.

With a mischievous smile, Greg bent eye to eye. "You'll forgive me once I tell you what I was doing."

Curious and impatient, she asked, "Okay, what's the surprise?"

"Have you ever been to Hawaii?"

"No." Not in the mood for games, Vanessa said, "Just tell me."

"Buy plenty of suntan lotion because we might be going to Hawaii for our honeymoon. And the best part, our trip will be free!" He picked Vanessa up and twirled her around.

"What?" Vanessa couldn't imagine how he secured a free trip to Hawaii.

Greg set her on the sofa. The rapid rate of his voice couldn't conceal his enthusiasm. "A short while after Mel and Jason dropped us off at Alicia's, her boss, Hal Haskins from the Sheraton hotel chain, showed up. He came to offer her the opportunity to help organize a boys' basketball tournament in Maui. Alicia didn't hesitate for one second to accept." Vanessa pictured Alicia jumping up and down and throwing her arms around her boss. "He mentioned his hotel chain is sponsoring one team of local all-stars to travel to Maui and compete in the tournament. And they need a coach to help with the tryouts and practices and then go with the team to Maui. When I told him I was a high school basketball coach, his eyes lit up." Greg paused, smiling as he recalled the moment. "He said they were looking for a coach and would consider me. The tournament is going to be in mid-August for a week. Good timing for our honeymoon!"

"Why were you at Alicia's?"

"She invited me in for a while and I figured why not? She's a nice gal. We had a fun time at the beach. It was pure coincidence her boss showed up while I was there. What an opportunity for me! Isn't that great? Of course, I don't have it in the bag yet, but it sure looks good!" He stood and crossed his arms. "I'm surprised you're not excited."

"I don't know what to say," Vanessa said, leaning forward. "On a honeymoon, you're supposed to spend the time with your bride. What am I going to do while you're occupied with the tournament? Besides, I'm not sure I want to be so far away from Dad."

"Come on, Vanessa. It's only for a week. I'm sure your dad won't object. I'll be with you all night. You can sunbathe or go sightseeing while I'm at the tournament. It'll be fun, and a great opportunity for me. If I'm offered the gig, I'm going to accept."

Vanessa hurled a decorative pillow at Greg. "You're dismissive of me. Looks like you've already decided. Well, don't let me stand in your way. I'm only going to be your wife."

Disappointment etched on Greg's face. "I can't understand your cool reception to Hawaii. I thought you'd be thrilled." He picked up the pillow and sat next to Vanessa.

She exhaled. "I guess I understand why you're so eager, but you should discuss our honeymoon with me first. Anyway, there's a chance we may have to postpone the wedding."

"Postpone the wedding?"

"If I donate my kidney before August, I may not be in any condition to get married let alone travel."

Greg faced Vanessa, placing his hands on her shoulders. "You're not donating a kidney. Your father has already told you no, no, no! Why can't you accept his choice?"

"Listen to me, Greg. Dad is too active. He loves golf. When he realizes how his life will now revolve around dialysis, he'll change his mind."

"For whatever reason, he won't let you. Besides, you may not be compatible. Even if he consents to have a transplant with your kidney, his body could reject it or many complications could arise and he'll end up on dialysis anyway. Then you'd be out a kidney. Can't you see how little sense your stubbornness makes? Your Dad does. You've shown your support and willingness to help him should he want it. It's his decision now, Van. Give it a rest. You're being unreasonable at this point."

Vanessa removed Greg's hands from her shoulders. "Look who's talking. Going to Hawaii whether or not I want to? You're the unreasonable one!" Vanessa folded her arms across her chest and crossed her legs, staring at the clock tick-tocking on the fireplace mantel.

Greg stood in front of her, blocking her view.

She closed her eyes.

"Be rational. Your father won't allow you to donate a kidney, so it's not even an issue. And if you expect me to pass up an opportunity for my career and our future, it will not happen!"

"Well, what makes you think I want to go to Hawaii? Maybe I'd rather go to Alaska to hike in Denali Park and see the breathtaking scenery."

Greg sighed, bending his head upward. "Whatever." He glanced at his watch. "I'm out of here. I have a formal interview with Mr. Haskins at eleven."

She looked at her watch. Only nine o'clock. "What's the hurry?"

"I'm headed to Alicia's. She's going to give—"

Vanessa bounded from the sofa. "You're going where?"

"Alicia's." He advanced toward Vanessa to hug her good-bye, but she pushed him away.

"I thought we could make wedding plans."

Greg laughed. "What the hell? Didn't you say a little while ago we may have to postpone the wedding?"

"So, this tournament and Alicia are more important than our wedding? Or me?"

"For God's sake, Vanessa! Relax. I met her yesterday. She's giving me tips on how to impress Mr. Haskins."

Vanessa picked up Greg's car keys from the coffee table and threw them toward him.

He retrieved the keys from the floor and stormed out, slamming the door.

⸺⸺◆⸺⸺

"You're pacing like a caged tiger," Lyle said within a few minutes of Vanessa's arrival. "Something's bothering you. What is it?"

"Nothing," Vanessa lied.

"This is your father speaking, my dear. You don't fool me," Lyle said. Patting his bed, he told her to come sit by him.

She complied, rubbing her clammy hands on her jeans. "Greg and I argued for the first time."

"Oh?"

"He's being selfish, Dad. He has an opportunity to coach a boys' basketball tournament in Hawaii, which coincides with the week after our wedding. If they select him, he wants that to be our honeymoon!"

"What's wrong with that?"

Vanessa glared at her father. "He didn't discuss it with me."

Lyle rarely disagreed with his headstrong daughter, but on this occasion, he sided with Greg. "It sounds like a great opportunity. You're overreacting."

Vanessa leaped up and paced around the room several times before declaring, "No, I'm not. And besides, I won't leave you while you're still recovering."

"That's almost two months from now. I'll be much better by then."

"What if you decide to undergo the transplant?"

"I wouldn't schedule it before your wedding unless a suitable donor became available."

Vanessa stood beside her father's bed. "Dad, I told you I'm going to donate a kidney if compatible."

Lyle shook his finger at his daughter. "Vanessa Rosemary Cox! I've told you a hundred times! You will not under any circumstances be a donor for me. Sink that into your thick, stubborn noggin."

"Why do you object? I'm your best chance." While Vanessa and her father continued to argue, they were unaware the door was slightly ajar. Standing outside was a woman rivetted by their heated conversation.

Eventually, the eavesdropper could no longer remain silent. She entered the room. Without so much as a hello, she challenged Lyle. "Are you going to tell Vanessa the *real* reason you don't want her to be a donor, or shall I?"

Chapter 3

"Helene!" Lyle sat erect, ignoring the sudden rush of pain as he stared at his older sister.

The years had treated her well. Her radiant yet rugged appearance hadn't diminished. At fifty-one, she was still in great physical shape and had only a touch of gray in her brown hair secured into a bun. Recovering from his initial shock, he greeted her, then demanded, "What are you doing here?"

Helene overlooked Lyle's cool reception. She projected a cheery demeanor while she bent to kiss his cheek. "I'm home from my last dig of relics of a bygone culture. It's time I visited my brother and niece."

"How'd you find out I was in the hospital?" Lyle cast a suspicious eye at Vanessa.

"No one was home at your house. I dropped in at *Pal's*, my favorite eatery when I still lived here. Remember? Still has the best veggie omelets. Anyway, while perusing *The Oregonian*, I spotted an article about an investigation of an auto accident. It mentioned your name. I did a little sleuthing," Helene answered. "I hope your injuries aren't too serious." After a few moments of uncomfortable silence, she said, "According to the article, the police are investigating the accident. They may charge the driver with a DUII." Approaching Vanessa, she pulled her close to her bosom. "You've developed into quite a lovely young woman."

Vanessa hesitated before hugging her aunt. Then, stepping back, she redirected the conversation. "What'd you mean the *real* reason Dad doesn't want me to be a donor?"

Helene's visit opened the wounds caused by the siblings' bitter disagreement. Lyle glared at Helene, his body tensing. His gritting teeth and pleading eyes signaled her to stay silent. "My position on this matter hasn't changed," he said.

Helene shook her head. "It's time you told Vanessa the truth. I swear, Lyle, if you don't, I will! She has a right to know."

"Get out!"

Vanessa stared at Helene, her heartbeat increasing and her breathing audible. What was this long-kept secret shared between the two siblings? Why didn't her father want her to know? "Tell me, what's this big secret?"

Helene focused on her brother. "Do I have your okay?"

Lyle's voice shook. "I'm warning you, Helene. Don't say a word." Vanessa noticed a slight tremble work its way through his body. She contemplated summoning a nurse, but curiosity overruled.

Turning to her father, she implored him yet again. "Tell me, Dad."

"No, I will never tell you."

"Since Vanessa now knows you're keeping something from her, she's going to keep pestering you. A no-brainer." Helene aimed piercing eyes at Lyle.

"Why did you come? Everything was fine. Look what you've done after all these years!"

"You think you're protecting her, but it's about time you told Vanessa what happened. It was wrong not to disclose the truth."

"And you have no right to tell her against my wishes," Lyle said, his chest rising and falling at a rapid rate. "Now leave before I call security. And don't bother coming again. I want nothing to do with you." He turned his head, dismissing her.

"I'm sorry you feel that way," Helene responded. "It's not simple, though. I'm giving you one last chance to tell Vanessa." Helene tapped her foot, waiting.

Vanessa cried out at the top of her voice, "Spit it out!"

Lyle's face turned to stone as he stared out the window, ignoring both women.

"Okay, Lyle, I gave you a chance." Helene faced Vanessa and wrapped her fingers around Vanessa's hands. "My dear," she paused, taking a deep breath, "Lyle is not your biological father. He adopted you."

Chapter 4

Vanessa's scream resonated outside the room and down the hallway. She staggered to the small sink and filled a paper cup with water, guzzling it to quench her dry mouth. Tossing the empty cup toward the wastebasket, she looked at her father. "She's lying, right?" Lyle grimaced, not denying it. Vanessa clenched her fists and pounded his mattress.

With all the strength he could muster, Lyle's weak voice said, "Look what damage you've caused, Helene."

"I'm sorry you feel that way," Helene spoke in an almost whisper. She touched her brother's hand. "I didn't come here to upset anyone. But you should have told Vanessa years ago."

Lyle jerked his hand away. "Get out. Don't contact me again. I have no sister."

Helene plucked a tissue from a nearby box and dabbed her eyes. She looked at her niece, extending her arms.

Vanessa twirled around, facing the opposite wall.

"This isn't the outcome I hoped for." Rejected by both brother and niece, Helene took the cue to leave. Backing away with a crying heart, she departed, tears blurring her vision.

Vanessa approached Lyle's bed, leaning down mere inches from his face. "Why, Dad? Why? All these years living a lie." Lyle had been the ultimate father, and she had trusted him with every breath of her being. "What about my mother? Did she die or is there something else you're keeping from me?"

Her father clutched his chest, his breathing rapid and wincing in pain. In a barely audible voice, he said, "Not now, Vanessa. Later."

Insensitive to her father's physical distress, Vanessa continued to press him. "Do you fathom what I'm feeling? My entire life is one big lie. Is my adoption the reason you and Aunt Helene rarely speak to each other?"

"Yes. I told her to never tell you. She didn't agree with me. We had several heated arguments."

"I don't want to, but I'm forced to talk with Aunt Helene. She's willing to tell me the truth."

"Please don't contact your aunt." He struggled to speak. "I don't know if you'll ever trust me again. But keep one thing in mind. What I did, was out of pure love and consideration for you. You've got to believe me."

"You deceived me. I want you to tell me whatever it is you're withholding from me."

"I toyed with telling you the truth many times over the years. But I believed it would be better if you didn't know the circumstances of your birth. I always assumed my sister would continue to respect my wishes. I was wrong." A deep sigh escaped. "I suspect this revelation might damage our relationship."

"I'm going to contact Aunt Helene whether or not you like it."

"Please don't," begged Lyle. "I promise I'll explain tomorrow. I'm tired. We both need to calm down. You're too emotional now."

"You're damn right I am," Vanessa said through blinding tears. She mumbled something about seeing him tomorrow. Without a goodbye, she grabbed her purse and glanced back at her ravaged father. She bumped into a man wearing a police uniform, losing her balance. The officer grasped her arms, pulling her against his taut chest. Vanessa pushed away, glancing at him before fleeing from the room. The police officer scratched his head as he watched the young woman depart.

Lyle lifted his head and ordered in a weak voice, "Go after her. She's very distressed and in no condition to drive. Hurry!"

When the confused police officer didn't move, Lyle pleaded. "Please! Bring her back or at least try to calm her down."

The policeman pulled out his badge. "I'm Officer JP Monroe and—"

Lyle labored to blurt out. "Go! Go!" He raised his right arm, shooing him away.

Monroe bolted from the room. He saw Vanessa's silhouette just as the elevator's doors closed. He spun around, looking for the stairs. At the opposite end of the hall, he noticed the illuminated stairwell sign. He blasted through the thick door and rushed down the two flights.

As he entered the lobby, he saw the woman pushing open the glass door leading to the courtyard. With a renewed burst of energy, he ran toward her. Catching up to her, he spoke. "Ma'am, may I have a word with you?"

Vanessa continued, quickening her pace to a sprint.

"Hey, is this a marathon?" Monroe asked. "How about slowing down so we can talk?"

His grin irritated Vanessa. Turning on her heels, Vanessa stopped and barked. "Unless I'm under arrest, I have nothing to…" Her annoyance drained from the trailing words as she realized this was the cop she had bumped into.

"The patient in the room you left asked me to go after you because he's worried about you driving." He pointed out the obvious. "You're upset. Is there anything I can do to help?"

"Nobody can help me. I've been living a lie." Looking downward, she said, "The man is my father, or at least I thought he was."

JP's gentle touch on her arm directed her to a nearby bench. Yanking herself free from his slight grip, she turned, rushing toward the street. Lightheaded and consumed by inner turmoil, Vanessa stepped off the curb. She didn't notice an approaching car.

JP lurched after her, grabbing her shoulder as he pulled her to safety as the car whizzed by. The driver honked his horn and shook his fist at her. As Vanessa began to collapse from sheer emotional exhaustion, the officer caught her. She clung to him and sobbed. Eventually relaxing her grip, she allowed JP to guide her to the wooden bench. "I do believe you need a hanky," he said, smiling and pulling an unused cotton handkerchief from his pocket. "Your mascara is not waterproof." He tried to lighten the mood.

Vanessa pulled her compact from her purse and noticed the streaks of black under her eyes. She declined to use the handkerchief and pulled a tissue from her purse. What was more embarrassing, her messy face or her rudeness to this officer who had saved her from a potential disaster? "Thanks for rescuing me. Sorry I was so rude."

"Apology accepted, Miss, or is it Mrs.?" JP held out his hand for a handshake.

"Miss," Vanessa answered, shaking his hand. Noticing the surname Monroe on his name tag, she stood. "I'm heading home now, Officer Monroe."

JP rose. "You seem calmer now, but I'm still concerned you shouldn't drive. May I call someone to fetch you?"

Vanessa stepped backward, tilting her head upward to look at his face. "Thanks, but no thanks," she answered. "By the way, what were you doing in my father's room?"

"I'm investigating the accident. I'm here to ask your father a few questions. Shouldn't you go back and tell him you're better? He was quite concerned."

"I...I can't talk to him right now," Vanessa stammered, bowing her head. "When you return to him, please tell him I'm okay."

"He'd rest easier if you tell him in person. Don't you agree?"

Vanessa sighed, exhaling a deep breath. She walked to the bed of pansies, groaning with bitterness that still gripped her. She shot a glance at the window of her father's second-story room. Lacing her hands together, she admitted maybe she was too harsh. But she continued brooding about the devastating revelation so fresh in her mind. Eventually, Officer Monroe tapped her shoulder.

Monroe's smile was comforting as he wrapped her arm around his. Still on an emotional treadmill, she was powerless to resist. She yielded to him as he escorted her back inside the hospital.

Officer Monroe allowed Vanessa and her father privacy. He remained in the hallway, helping himself to a cup of complimentary coffee.

As Vanessa entered the room, three subdued medical personnel filed out. A plump nurse wearing a pained expression gave Vanessa a sympathetic squeeze on her arm. Dr. DeWitt stood over Lyle, shaking his head in disbelief.

Vanessa approached the bed. She placed her hand on her father's still warm skin, then over his chest that didn't rise or fall. Her eyes widened and her jaw dropped as she realized what she was staring at. But she refused to accept the reality. She cried out, hoping the fury of her voice would cause his eyes to open.

Dr. DeWitt circled the bed and placed a chair near Vanessa. "It'd be a good idea for you to sit down, Miss Cox." Informing a family member a loved one has died, especially suddenly, was an unwelcome part of his job and never got easier.

Vanessa shoved the chair away.

Dr. DeWitt breathed a heavy sigh. "Miss Cox, your father has passed."

"No! You're lying!" Vanessa turned and shook her father. "Wake up!" She buried her head into his lifeless body, wailing. "You can't leave me!"

Dr. DeWitt tried to hold her back, to calm her, but in her hysteria, she was too strong, too wild. She pounded his chest. Backing away, she tripped on the chair leg. She plunged headfirst into the food tray. She and the dishes crashed to the floor.

Officer Monroe could hear the commotion. He rushed into the room, dropping the coffee cup as he reached to assist Vanessa. She felt her head spinning like a top. Before she passed out in Monroe's arms, she mumbled, "It's all Aunt Helene's fault."

Chapter 5

Greg burst through the doctor's office door. In a state of confusion, Greg searched the doctor's face. Dr. DeWitt's expression confirmed the worst. "What happened? I thought Lyle was recovering. How could he be dead now? I can't believe this. It's a bad dream. A nightmare." Greg's stomach churned as he plunked into a chair, shaking his head. Gathering his wits, he asked about Vanessa. "Where's Vanessa? I can't imagine she's taking this well."

"You are?" the doctor asked.

"Greg Vardanega, Vanessa's fiancé. Call me Greg."

"Okay, Greg. I'm Doctor DeWitt. We haven't determined what caused Mr. Cox to die so suddenly. We thought he was recovering, but sometimes, death occurs without warning after traumatic injuries. An autopsy will determine the exact cause of his sudden death." He paused. "I suspect a blood clot. It is so unfortunate. He was so young at forty-eight." Dr. DeWitt looked at Greg straight on with an even more serious tone. "When I told Miss Cox we lost Lyle, she erupted, then tripped and hit her forehead against the food tray and fell to the floor. A police officer helped her up, but she fainted. She spewed words I couldn't make sense of. Once she came to, we had to sedate her because she was so distraught. I'm keeping her overnight for observation."

"Is she bad? And what about a cop?" Greg asked.

"The policeman had arrived to question Mr. Cox about the accident. There was a heated argument between Mr. Cox and his daughter. She took off." Dr. DeWitt recounted the incident as best he could. "When Miss Cox walked back into the room, she assumed her father was sleeping." Dr. DeWitt drew a deep breath. "I can't think of too many things worse than to have your father die right after you argued with him. She may blame herself for his death and impose guilt upon herself. She's going to need a lot of support in the coming weeks. I hope you're up to it. I know she has no mother. Are there any other relatives?"

Greg answered, "Only an aunt she hasn't seen in years."

Dr. DeWitt rubbed his chin. "A nurse saw a woman lingering outside the room earlier today. Hmmm…"

"Could have been, but I doubt it. She doesn't live in town." He raised his head toward the ceiling and ran his fingers through his hair. "How is she going to get her through this tragedy? Lyle was everything to her. And I was very fond of him also," Greg confided, suppressing tears. "I had the deepest respect and admiration for Lyle. I can't fathom the fact Lyle is gone…forever. His passing will impact Vanessa. To what extent remains to be seen." With a bowed head, he walked to Vanessa's room and peeked inside. She was peacefully sleeping. He stood for a few moments, staring at her. He wouldn't awaken her. "I wish I could turn back the clock," he said out loud to no one.

VANESSA AWOKE THE NEXT MORNING, CONFUSED BY HER surroundings. She raised her upper torso, resting on her forearms. Her forehead stung. She reached to touch it, and her fingers felt a small bandage. Flinging off the blankets, she saw the thin hospital gown draping her body. *What the hell?* Then it hit her. The events of yesterday came crashing to the forefront of her mind.

"Oh my God! Dad! Why did you leave me? What am I going to do without you?" Then realizing her father died with her anger seething toward him, she buried her face into the pillow. Her tears soaked the pillowcase. Shock, grief, disbelief, and guilt snuck up on Vanessa, gripping her like a boa constrictor squeezing the life from its victim. She'd never experienced anguish this intense. She'd lost the most important person in her life.

"May I come in?"

Through blurry eyes, Vanessa looked in the voice's direction. She didn't recognize the stranger dressed in a uniform.

"Remember me?" the officer asked. "I'm the cop who rescued you yesterday from a close encounter with a car."

"Oh yeah. What do you want?" She grumbled, pulling the blankets to cover her body.

"Allow me to formally introduce myself. I'm Officer JP Monroe." He stood at the end of the bed, smiling. "Please accept my sincerest condolences. We're investigating the accident. We may charge the driver with criminally negligent homicide or vehicular manslaughter."

"It won't bring my father back," Vanessa said. "I do hope the creep gets what he deserves." She plucked a tissue, blew her nose, and tossed the moist paper onto the floor.

"I'll keep you posted in case you want to appear at his trial if there is one," Officer Monroe said. "If you need information or help of any kind, please call me. Here's my card." He placed it on the shelf near the bed and turned to leave.

Triggered by grief and guilt to lash out at someone, anyone, Vanessa made JP her first target. "I don't appreciate you coming here. Is it your habit to bother people like this? Do you always offer this sort of individual attention?"

"Only the ones who faint in my arms." He winked at her.

After Officer Monroe left, Vanessa thought about her father. What had caused him to die? Was it Aunt Helene's visit and/or her reaction to the adoption news? Could she ever forgive herself for running from him? What was his last thought?

A few moments later, Greg entered the room. He sat on the bed, and Vanessa threw her arms around him, her tears dampening his shirt. He asked, "Are you hungry? Can I get you anything?"

"Adopted."

"What did you say?" Greg asked, a puzzled look etched on his face.

Vanessa looked straight into Greg's eyes. "Dad adopted me."

"What do you mean *adopted*?"

"I found out yesterday. That's why Dad didn't want me to be a donor."

"What? How?" Greg stood, pacing around the room.

"Aunt Helene showed up after all these years. She told Dad if he didn't tell me the reason he didn't want me to donate a kidney, she would. Dad refused so Aunt Helene blurted out the news." Vanessa covered her face with her hands as she began crying again. "Not only have I lost my father, now I may never find out why he adopted me and kept it a secret. And what about my mother?"

"Wow. Are you sure your aunt told the truth?"

"Dad admitted it, but he wouldn't tell me why. So, we argued, and I ran from the room quite angry. That's the last time I saw him alive." She rubbed her eyes. "I blame Aunt Helene for his death. And myself."

Dr. DeWitt heard Vanessa's last comment as he entered the room to check on her. "No, Miss Cox, your father's death didn't result from his conversation with you or your aunt. With your permission to perform an autopsy, we can determine the exact cause. Don't blame anybody. Unexpected deaths happen."

Vanessa agreed to allow an autopsy. She had to find out the cause of his sudden death.

Greg reiterated. "It's not your fault."

Dr. DeWitt examined Vanessa's cut forehead and pronounced her fine physically. "I'm going to sign your discharge papers. You can get dressed. I'll have an orderly wheel you out while Greg fetches the car."

"Good deal, I'm eager to leave."

"I'm sorry about your father." Dr. DeWitt made a few insertions into the computer. "When you've had time to think about it, let the hospital know what funeral home you want your father taken to. I'll be in touch as soon as I have the autopsy results."

Greg helped Vanessa off the bed and gathered her clothes. "I'll meet you at the entrance." He rushed from the room, running after the doctor.

"Doc, I'm worried about Vanessa's emotional state. Would talking to a psychiatrist or grief counselor help? Finding out Lyle adopted her besides losing him is more than I'm afraid she can handle. And she's already feeling guilty."

"I'm sure she does. That's a good idea if she'll agree. She's suffered a double whammy. Medication might help her cope. I'll leave a prescription in the computer." Dr. DeWitt extended his hand. A deep sigh escaped from Greg's mouth as he gripped the doctor's firm handshake.

Vanessa dressed and gathered her belongings. When she saw the business card JP had left, she sat on the bed, staring at his name. When the orderly arrived, she stuffed it in her purse.

Greg assisted Vanessa into his jeep. "How about a pizza? Hospital food's not appetizing." Greg tried to be cheerful.

"No thanks. I just want to go home."

Greg glanced in Vanessa's direction. He took a risk. "I'll try contacting your aunt about Lyle's passing. I'm sure she—"

Vanessa bolted erect. "Don't you dare. Even though she's the only one who can tell me all about my adoption, I never want to see her again. And even if I did, I don't know where she lives. The last I knew she lived in Seattle."

"I disagree. You should try to notify your aunt about her brother's passing. She's his only other relative. She'd want to attend the funeral and pay her respects."

She was in no mood for an argument. Vanessa leaned her head against Greg's shoulder, emphasizing, "I don't want her there, okay?"

Greg revved the motor and sped from the patient loading area.

VANESSA PLANNED A SERVICE FOR LYLE WITH THE HELP of Melanie and Greg. She wanted him to have a memorable, dignified service to honor his life. She opted for a memorial at the Oregon Golf Club in honor of Lyle's passion for golf. The parish priest would officiate at the ceremony. His closest friend and lawyer, Ben Kosta, would deliver the eulogy.

The sun's rays warmed Vanessa as she arrived for the ceremony two weeks after Lyle's passing. The sweet scent from a myriad of floral arrangements perfumed the air. Their vibrant colors were a striking display against the crystal-clear floor-to-ceiling windows. She paused at the large portrait of her father and ran her fingers up and down along the surface with reverence. She prayed she'd endure the next hour, but she used every tissue from the small box sitting on her lap. Unbeknownst to Vanessa, Helene stood in the room's rear, also shedding tears.

When the service concluded, Greg escorted Vanessa toward an adjacent room where a buffet luncheon awaited the mourners. As the pair walked through the doorway, Helene greeted Vanessa.

"What the hell are you doing here?" Vanessa asked. She had rarely seen her aunt clad in anything other than khaki trousers and sweatshirts. Today she wore a knee-length black dress and semi-heeled shoes. A bright, jewel-encrusted butterfly locket dangled against her chest.

"I'm paying my respects to my brother. I'm sorry if I—"

She glared at Greg. "I thought I told you not to contact my aunt," she accused him.

"I didn't."

"I saw Lyle's obituary in the newspaper," Helene said. "Despite our disagreement, he was my brother, and I loved him."

"You killed my father!" Vanessa shrieked, lunging toward her aunt.

Greg stepped between the two women. "Vanessa, you're making a scene. Dr. DeWitt said Lyle died of a blood clot as he suspected. You can't blame your aunt or anyone else."

"I'm not here to upset you, my dear," Helene said in a calm tone. "Before I take off again for a year-long assignment, I wanted to see you before I leave." Helene extended her arms toward Vanessa, then dropped them as Vanessa stepped back and gave her an icy stare.

Helene bowed her head and turned to leave, but stopped. "I understand how distressed you are to have found out about your adoption the way you did. Sorry the truth has caused you additional misery. I'd be more than willing to enlighten you about everything. Please give me the chance."

"Yes, I want to know what happened, but I can't forgive you for causing Dad's death. Please leave."

"I'm saddened you don't want a relationship with me. I want to be a part of your life. I'll be out of the country for a year or two. But I can give you my e-mail address and cell phone number, although I seldom get good reception." Helene forced a smile, her eyes begging.

"Don't bother."

When Helene was out of sight, Greg tapped his foot and shook his head. "You shouldn't blame her for Lyle's passing. It's not like you to be so unkind. And why didn't you accept her offer? You could've found out the circumstances of your birth. Who knows when you'll see her again? I don't believe this. You're making a foolish choice."

"I'll find out the information without Aunt Helene."

Greg exhaled a disgusted breath and joined the guests at the reception.

Chapter 6

The shade on Vanessa's patio offered no relief from the blistering August heat. The can of Bud Light did little to quench Greg's thirst. He looked at Vanessa sitting opposite him on the picnic table bench. Since the funeral, all Vanessa focused on was finding out about her biological parents. Greg tried to persuade her to drop the whole damn thing.

"My God, Vanessa. How long are you going to pursue this silly notion?"

She slammed her glass on the table. A splatter of liquid escaped, scattering drops of iced tea. "I'm going to keep trying." It was infuriating to her. No one was going to stop or hinder her from getting at the truth. Vanessa couldn't help wondering if her mother was alive, and if so, why she didn't raise her. Whatever the reason, she wanted to find out. "Do you know what it feels like that my mother may not have wanted me?"

"No, I don't. But someone did." Greg tried to reason with her. "I've never seen a more devoted father than Lyle."

"You're right," Vanessa agreed. Although it had been two months since Lyle died, Vanessa's grief remained acute. Both Greg and Melanie watched her for signs of depression.

They had attempted to include her in activities. Vanessa refused every time. Her sole purpose in life now was to discover the truth.

"Do you realize next weekend was to be our wedding?" Greg asked. "Are you ever going to plan it, or am I way on the back burner? I've agreed to postpone it for a while, but your refusal to even discuss it bothers me. Come on, Honey. You're still noncommittal. I'm open to having a small, intimate ceremony in front of a judge."

Vanessa's hand fluttered dismissively. "Don't be so dramatic. I'm still committed to you, but I'm having a tough time accepting your attitude toward my search. Instead of being supportive or helpful, you discourage me."

"That's because you don't have any interest in anything but this search. If I want to spend time with you, I have to come here. I'm leaving for Maui in a couple of weeks. I hoped you'd be accompanying me as my wife." He hesitated, adding, "I'm tired of playing second fiddle. You're ignoring our relationship. It's an obsession, and becoming unhealthy for everyone involved."

Vanessa conceded. "I'm sorry I'm neglecting you. But these past two months have been hard. I know you're only trying to help me, but I can't act as though nothing has happened. Don't you realize not only did my father die, but he deceived me my entire life?" Her eyes pleaded for his understanding and sympathy.

Greg reached across the table and gripped her hand. "Come on. We're going to Papandrea's for a pizza. I'll bet you're hungry. I am."

Vanessa closed her eyes, sniffing as she imagined the aroma. Her taste buds salivated visualizing the fresh and generous toppings and the thick crust. "Let's have it delivered."

Greg huffed with irritation. "What's the use? You won't go anywhere with me or anyone else. You've become a hermit. It's time to get out and enjoy yourself." He gulped the last of his beer, then grabbed his baseball cap. "For God's sake. Try to contact your aunt. She's got all the answers. Ask her and get this over with." He trudged out, slamming the door.

"TOMORROW'S THE BIG DAY," ALICIA SQUEALED, BOUNC-ing with excitement. "I can hardly believe I'm going to Hawaii! And the best part, it's free!"

"Yeah, I'm looking forward to it too," Greg said with enthusiasm, peppered with a hint of regret. No matter how hard he had tried, he hadn't persuaded Vanessa to go with him. He resigned himself to leave without her. The coaching responsibilities would keep him busy. And Alicia had prom-ised to help him enjoy the amusements the island offered.

Alicia's excited voice asked, "Are you all packed?"

"Yep," he answered. He'd dropped by to leave his luggage at Alicia's apartment. "Just got a few last-minute items to pack into my carry-on," Greg said, snapping his fingers. "I've got to remember my swimming trunks." He headed toward the door. "Vanessa said she'd drop me off, but I told her I'll take a taxi. Be here around 5:45. Don't want to be late for Mr. Haskins's 6 a.m. pick up."

"I'm setting my alarm for five. I need plenty of time to make myself presentable."

Greg smiled. "You don't need gobs of time to doll your-self up. You're a natural."

Alicia's cheeks pinked up as she thanked him for the compliment. "See you in the morning," she said as he closed the apartment door.

Greg stopped by Vanessa's to say goodbye. He knocked twice, then entered when he heard Vanessa's voice telling him to come in. He had told Vanessa a million times to keep the door locked. As Vanessa approached him and greeted him with a rare smile, a sudden rush of desire surged through his entire body. Even clad in her well-worn corduroy robe that covered everything from neck to toe, she aroused him.

"Greg, I'm so glad you came," Vanessa said. "I have something for you."

Greg followed her into the kitchen, where she offered him a can of Pepsi. "I was going through Dad's dresser yesterday." She raised his left hand and slipped a large emerald ring surrounded by small diamonds on his finger. "Emerald is the May birthstone. Since both you and Dad have May birthdays, I'd like you to have this ring." Vanessa then grabbed his hand and led him upstairs into her father's bedroom.

"Here's all dad's golf stuff…his clubs, balls, and bag. I'm sure Dad would have wanted you to have them." She held up the cleated shoes. "I don't think these will fit you." She sat on the bed and watched as Greg examined the golf equipment.

"The quality of the gear is impressive. It'll make a welcome addition to my sorry assortment of clubs." When he finished admiring the items, he sat down on the bed near Vanessa. He could smell the delicate fragrance of her favorite sweet pea-scented perfume. She wore a sheer nightgown under her robe. The combination was too much for him to resist. He traced his hands gently up her arms to her shoulders and began massaging her. He brushed his lips against hers. Vanessa didn't reject his advances, yet she wasn't responsive.

"Oh, Vanessa," Greg said in a low, soft voice. His hands found their way to her breasts, and he squeezed them. His jeans grew tight as the bulge in his groin grew. He was ready to explode. He untied her robe and slipped it off. Vanessa moaned as he planted a fiery kiss on her lips. She unbuttoned his shirt, then ran her fingers along his chest. Greg pulled off her nightgown. As his tongue licked her exposed breasts, she unzipped his jeans.

"It's been too long." He discarded his trousers. He positioned himself on top of Vanessa as her eyes drifted toward a framed photograph of her father. She touched it every night before she went to bed. It felt awkward engaging in lovemaking with her father's eyes watching her. She abruptly pushed Greg away, crying out, "I can't! This is Dad's bed, and he's staring—"

"What the hell?"

"I can't make love in Dad's bedroom. I'm…I'm sorry."

"I'll carry you to your bedroom." Greg was shouting now. "I'm going to have you tonight." He began lifting Vanessa, but she resisted, punching his chest. Overpowered by his current state, he dropped her back onto the bed. He began kissing her with a forcefulness that both frightened and angered Vanessa. She tried to fight him off, but the more she struggled, the more determined he became.

"This is rape!" Vanessa pointed out, raising her voice. "Get off me now!" she commanded, slapping his face. The blow startled Greg. He came to his senses and removed himself. He'd been irrational and overcome by his desires. In a subdued tone, he said, "I don't know what came over me, Van. I guess I miss the closeness we once had." He stood and stared at Lyle's picture. With one swift move, he slammed it face down. "Thanks to Lyle's death and your aunt's big mouth, your search seems your priority."

"Leave!" Vanessa ordered, her voice shaky but resolute.

Greg dressed in silence and left. But moments later, he re-entered the room and placed the emerald ring on the dresser. Vanessa noted regret etched on his face, but she turned her back to him. She was in no mood to talk. He slowly backed from the room.

The next morning, Vanessa replayed the previous night's debacle in her mind. Despite everything, she loved Greg and still wanted to marry him. Greg's actions were out of character. She blamed herself for their strained relationship and understood Greg's frustration because she wouldn't commit to a new wedding date. She vowed to choose one when he returned from Hawaii.

She busied herself sorting through her father's belongings. "There! That takes care of the dresser and the closet," Vanessa said out loud as she completed boxing up the clothing to donate to the local homeless shelter. After a brief break, Vanessa began clearing the items from his desk. She removed a pile of wrinkled papers. A grin appeared as she recognized the crude handmade cards she had given her father on various occasions. She held up the card she'd made for his thirtieth birthday. It was a male stick figure holding a…golf club? She couldn't quite determine what it was. *I was six.* Warmth filled her heart as she realized her father had saved many of her creative endeavors. On the bottom of the pile was a sealed, unmarked manila envelope. Vanessa used an engraved silver letter opener to open it. She pulled out a single piece of paper. A rush of excitement sailed through her body. She was holding a birth certificate! Hers! She saw her name, birth date, time, and other details typed in the spaces. Father, unknown. Then, her eyes fixated on the mother's name…Rosemary Anna Peterson.

Chapter 7

"My gosh. My middle name is Rosemary! This is my mother!" Vanessa exclaimed. Adrenaline cruised through her veins. Her hands trembled as she focused on the document. "This is the first concrete lead. Now, something to go on!" Vanessa jumped up. She had to go to the county's vital statistics to seek more information. No time to waste! She slipped on her sandals and dashed outside, carrying the birth certificate. When she reached the locked car, she realized in her haste she hadn't brought her purse or the car keys. *Stupid me!* She ran around to the backyard and fetched the house key hidden underneath a fairy statue.

Arriving at the county building in record time, Vanessa scurried toward the entrance, focusing on the precious piece of paper. She bumped into a knee-high stone retention barrier surrounding a fountain and pool of clear water. She lost her balance and plunged sideways into the cool water, hitting her head on the fountain's edge. Warm liquid oozed from a gash above her right eye. Blood! *Bummer.* Trying to stand, she slipped on the many coins covering the pool bottom and fell backward. Out of nowhere, two powerful arms caught her. Vanessa's soaked hands grasped onto the man's shirt. "Thanks."

He recognized the woman at once. "We're going to have to quit meeting like this," the man's cheerful voice joked.

Vanessa stared at her rescuer. He looked familiar.

"I guess I didn't make an impression on you. You don't remember me, do you?"

As she raised her fingers to wipe the blood, Vanessa studied him. "Oh, yeah, Officer…"

"Monroe."

"You must think I'm some sort of walking disaster." She hoped her voice didn't convey her acute embarrassment.

"Miss Cox, isn't it?"

"Yes."

"You should head to ER or urgent care. Looks like a rather nasty gash on your forehead." He pulled out a clean handkerchief and pressed it on the cut. "Hold this in place while I retrieve your purse." He reached into the fountain and fished it out. Most of the contents were wet, but Vanessa didn't care. "The certificate!" she yelled, dropping the handkerchief. She lifted her right foot to re-enter the pool.

JP grabbed her hand. "What certificate?"

"My birth certificate! I need it!" She freed her hand from JP's grip and turned her attention to looking for the document.

A young boy spotted a piece of paper floating on the other side of the pool. He removed his sandals and stepped into the fountain, pulling out the paper. He handed it to Vanessa. "This is it," Vanessa said, thanking the dark-skinned lad and giving him a quick hug. The certificate was completely wet, but it was still legible. Relief enveloped her.

As the small crowd dispersed, JP suggested again Vanessa see a doctor. Blood continued to trickle from the wound, a few drops dotting her blouse. He handed her the hanky.

Vanessa wrung some water from her dripping top. "I need to change out of these clothes first. Glad it's warm or I'd be freezing."

"I'm driving you to the doctor." JP grasped her hand.

Vanessa pulled away. "Unnecessary. Besides, I'll get your car seat wet."

"It's vinyl. It'll dry."

JP was practically a stranger. *But's he's a cop. I can trust him. He was so caring the day Dad died.* She accepted his offer.

JP remained in the waiting room of the urgent care clinic while the doctor examined Vanessa. She emerged wearing a gauze bandage above her right eye. JP inquired about the injury.

"I have a deep, open wound, but not bad enough to need stitches. Shouldn't be any scar. Thank God."

"Good deal," JP said. "I'll bring you home."

"No thanks. Drop me off at my car."

"It would be best if you didn't drive right now. Your head must be hurting."

She was eager to search, but her throbbing head and damp clothing convinced her that was not a wise choice. "All righty, home it is."

When they arrived at Vanessa's house, she thanked JP.

"I'll pick you up tomorrow so you have a ride to your car. It should be okay overnight. I've got connections. I'll make sure no overzealous dude tows it away."

"Thank you, but don't you have to be at work or some-place? I'm sure my friend, Melanie, will take me."

"You're in luck," JP said, smiling. "I'm on vacation this week. No time card to punch."

JP trotted around the car to assist Vanessa out. "I'll walk you inside and make sure you lie down right away."

"You don't have to babysit me. Besides, can I trust you? I hardly know you."

"Would I have rescued you twice just to turn around and do you harm?" JP asked.

"No, I guess not." She thanked him again at the door and scurried inside. She went straight to her bedroom and removed the damp clothing. While debating whether to shower, the doorbell rang. She slipped on her bathrobe, secured it, then hurried barefoot to the door. She looked through the peephole.

JP stood there, her purse dangling from his index finger. She opened the door. "You forget this." JP handed it to her. But the exchange failed. The purse fell to the floor, most of the contents spilling out. JP stepped across the threshold to help Vanessa retrieve the items. His engaging smile was inviting, but she was leery of allowing a near-stranger into her home and emotional realm. But something about him put her at ease.

"Thanks. Clumsy me." When JP did not take off, she didn't want to appear ungrateful or hopeful he'd leave. Offering him a soda slipped from her mouth. "Pepsi or 7-Up?"

"Neither. You lie down and rest."

Suddenly aware of her state of undress, she said, "As soon as I put dry clothes on."

JP lingered, waiting for Vanessa's return from the bedroom upstairs. He surveyed the living room. A neutral beige, with one wall highlighted in a shiny gold hue, covered the walls. Pictures of floral arrangements hung in a random arrangement. A huge vase filled with colorful dahlias stood on the fireplace mantel next to a gigantic clock. He recognized her father's smiling face, beaming from a framed portrait hanging above the fireplace.

"Well, thank you again, Officer Monroe. I appreciate your help," Vanessa said, heading to open the door. Instead of leaving, JP guided her to the couch and motioned her to sit down. He joined her. Vanessa inched away. "Officer Monroe, I'll be fine. You don't need to stay."

"Call me JP."

"What does JP stand for?"

"Jonathan Preston Monroe the Third. My mother began calling me JP, and it stuck." He turned toward her. "Your first name is…?"

"Vanessa."

"Is there anything I can do to help you? What about the birth certificate? It seems rather important to you."

Vanessa hadn't considered allowing anyone to assist her. She wanted to prove to herself she could succeed on her own. Or was she afraid of what she might find?

JP wasn't in a hurry to leave. He ventured. "So, tell me, what do you do for entertainment in your spare time? Sports? Shopping? Movies? Sewing?"

"Lately, I have done little of anything. I've been a recluse," Vanessa confessed. "My fiancé is a basketball coach, so I attend his games during the season. I love to hike, and I was the catcher on a co-ed softball team." She chuckled. "I was terrible. I also belonged to a bowling league where I once bowled a two fifteen, then the next game my score plummeted to one o four. Go figure."

"Bowling!" JP stood up and imitated tossing a bowling ball down the alley. "One of my favorite sports. What's your average?"

"My last average in league was one thirty-five. What's yours?"

"About one seventy. Hey, how 'bout we take in a few lines of bowling? My treat." Vanessa's acceptance surprised her. "But not tonight, though. My head is still throbbing. I'll take a rain check."

"You got it. I still have my ball and shoes somewhere. I'll dig them up. Will your fiancé mind?"

"I don't think so." Vanessa frowned. "He's not here. He's in Hawaii coaching in a basketball tournament all week. I don't expect he'll call me."

"I'm going to leave now so you can rest. I'll come by about two-ish tomorrow so you can bring your car back home."

"Fine. But you can just drop me off because I plan to go inside and look for the information I was hoping to find today. It's important to me."

"Your wish is my command." JP smiled and bowed. "Remember, I'm a cop. I may help you cut through some red tape or streamline the process for you."

"I appreciate your offer, but I don't think anyone except my aunt can give me the answers I want." And as an after-thought in a low voice, she added, "I've got to know who…" she stopped.

"Who what?" JP asked.

"Who my mother was."

"What are you saying?"

"It's a long story. It wouldn't interest you," Vanessa said. "My father adopted me." Her voice sounded harsh, even to her ears.

"So? Adoption is a joyous occasion in most cases."

"You don't understand. I only found out about the adop-tion the day my father died." She cringed, remembering the startling revelation.

"Is that why you were so upset when you ran from the hospital room?"

"Yeah."

JP tried to soothe her. "Is there anything I can do?"

Vanessa regained her composure. "I'm fine. I still become emotional when I think about my father. No need to concern yourself," Vanessa said, managing a weak smile.

"Guaranteed?" JP asked.

"Yes," Vanessa said, rising from the sofa. "I'm okay. See you tomorrow. And thanks for everything." She contrived a more convincing smile.

"You're welcome." He stepped outside into the refreshing breeze of the mid-August afternoon. Vanessa closed the door and locked it.

There was something about Vanessa. Her vulnerability brought out JP's protective instincts.

JP ARRIVED THE FOLLOWING DAY, RIGHT ON SCHEDULE. "How's the head today?" he asked in a cheery voice.

"Better," Vanessa replied, "but it still hurts a little." She touched the bandage. "I'll take it off tomorrow or in a few days."

"Glad you're better. Ready? If so, let's hit the road."

During the ride, JP kept the conversation easygoing. He chatted about the outlandish people he'd encountered on his shifts and his position as the right fielder on the police softball team. Vanessa studied him. She guessed he was in his late twenties. There was no fat on his well-conditioned body. His hair was light brown, matching his eyes. She pegged him as the rugged, outdoorsy type, someone you wouldn't want to challenge. But he also showed a cheery, caring, soft side. "I suppose you're wondering why I was so worried about the birth certificate and what the stuff about my mother is all about."

"I'd be lying if I said I wasn't."

Vanessa summarized the events of the previous two months.

"What a shock for anyone. I now understand why your father insisted I go after you. And it makes sense why you were in such distress when I first encountered you."

"My father died before I could find out anything. Rosemary Peterson is the mother's name on the certificate. My middle name is Rosemary. I need to know the truth. Greg thinks I'm obsessed and wants me to stop searching, but I can't."

"Greg?" JP raised an eyebrow.

"My fiancé."

Vanessa detected a look of disappointment on JP's face. Was it jealousy? No, of course not. Surprise? No, she had mentioned a fiancé yesterday.

"Here we are," JP announced as he parked beside Vanessa's car. Hesitating, he ventured, "If I may be so bold to suggest, why don't you ask your aunt for the info? Might save you some time and frustration."

Vanessa still blamed her aunt for Lyle's death. Crinkling her nose, she said, "No way. Even if I wanted to ask her, she's out of the country. I don't know how to contact her." Stepping out, she opened her purse and pulled out her wallet. She leaned back inside the car, offering him a twenty-dollar bill.

JP waved her off. "Glad to help. Good luck."

Vanessa emerged from the building an hour later, dragging her feet. "Darn!" Another disappointment. No helpful information. But she would try again. She wouldn't give up.

EARLY THE NEXT EVENING, DRESSED IN A PAIR OF LEVI shorts and a bright pink tank top, Vanessa cut up some veggies and tossed them into the wok. She added soy sauce and instant brown rice, her mouth salivating. She could eat stir-fry every day. The sound of the doorbell interrupted her preparations. She turned down the burner before sprinting to the front door.

A man stood in front of her, his face hidden behind a bowling bag. She recognized JP's voice when he asked her if she was ready to go bowling.

"Say what?"

"Don't you remember agreeing you'd like to go bowling sometime?" He set the bag down.

"Yeah, but I didn't think you were serious." Vanessa backed away, self-conscious of her scruffy appearance.

JP didn't wait for an invitation. He stepped inside. "I'm dragging you out to have some fun."

Vanessa brushed her hair back with her fingers. "You're assuming a lot, Mr. Monroe." She emphasized his name.

"Refusing is not an option. I'll wait while you freshen up."

She folded her arms together. "And what if I refuse?"

JP parted the drapes, letting the early evening sunlight flood into the room.

"Hey," Vanessa said, pulling them back together. "I'm keeping the heat out. And I'm not going bowling! I'm cooking dinner." Instead of leaving as she hoped, JP followed her into the kitchen and sat at the table. He started whistling while Vanessa finished preparing the meal. JP ignored her hints to leave. She sighed. It would be awkward to eat in front of him. She dished up a serving and handed it to him. "Hope you like stir-fry."

"One of my favorites."

After they wolfed down the food, Vanessa gave in. She stood, hands on her hips. "Okay, Mr. Smarty Pants. You win."

After she freshened up, they headed to Milwaukie Bowl.

After three defeats, Vanessa admitted she had a pleasurable time. It amazed her that JP, a virtual stranger, had got her out of the house. Both Melanie's and Greg's efforts had failed.

For the next few days, JP was a constant presence. "I will not allow you to remain cooped up inside the house." On Friday evening, she attended his softball game. One of the player's wives snapped pictures of the spectators sitting on the bleachers. "I'll give you a copy of your girlfriend's picture when they're developed."

"She's not…" JP began. "Ah, thanks."

Standing in front of the bathroom mirror late that night, Vanessa smiled. She walked to her room and flopped backward onto the bedspread, stretching from head to toe. JP had provided a welcome breather this past week. But now Greg entered her mind. She missed him. Staring at her half-carat diamond ring, a sharp craving for him to appear engulfed her. She jumped off the bed and pirouetted around the room, anticipating his return and the lovemaking she wouldn't refuse this time.

Later, as was her custom, she lay in bed reading. She was devouring Agatha Christie's *The Tuesday Club Murders*. Her body jerked as the paperback book slipped from her hands and fell to the carpet. She turned off the lamp. As she nestled her head on the pillow, to her surprise, it was JP's image popping into her mind. Not Greg's.

VANESSA FOCUSED ON FOLLOWING THE ROUTINE ON AN exercise video. She fell flat on her belly from a push-up position when she heard a voice calling from the door. She rolled onto her back and saw JP poking his head inside. "May I come in?"

"My word, JP. You startled me."

"You didn't hear the doorbell?"

"No. I guess the music on the video was too loud." She pushed the pause bottom on the CD player.

JP entered, smiling. "You should keep your door locked," he said in a good-humored tone. "You never know who'll wander in."

Folding her arms across her chest, Vanessa glared. "I'll keep that in mind. Now, pray tell, what is the purpose of this intrusion?"

Despite Vanessa's cool reception, he kept smiling. "I'm inviting you to attend my softball game tomorrow. It's a rare Sunday game and also the final one of the season. I'll pick you up at one. Bring plenty of water. And wear a hat and sunscreen. Gonna be hot."

Vanessa grinned. "So confident. Just because you prevailed before, doesn't mean you're going to win this time." She headed toward the kitchen and poured two glasses of lemonade.

They settled on the living room sofa, sipping their lemonades and munching on stale popcorn. "Greg's coming home tomorrow evening. But thanks anyway. I had an enjoyable time watching your team last night, despite your team's crushing loss. Nineteen to three!" She giggled, then punched him on his shoulder.

"You can't win 'em all."

"You're a sports fanatic, aren't you?"

"Yeah. I took part in baseball and football in high school and now watch college games whenever I'm not on duty. But," his mouth twisted into a grin, "my first love is hiking, camping, and being outdoors." He beamed at her with appreciation and joy.

Feeling connected to JP in this shared love of nature, Vanessa reminisced. "My dad and I used to hike the forests within an hour of Milwaukie and along trails at the beach every summer. We'd rent a cabin in Lincoln City for a week in August. I had a blast walking along the beach in my bare feet."

JP told her in a lighthearted tone. "On my bucket list is to one day hike Denali Park in Alaska. The scenery is breathtaking."

Vanessa perked up. "I'll be darn. That's one place I've thought about visiting." She put her hand on his shoulder. "I hope you can achieve your goal someday."

"We'll see."

JP had helped Vanessa out of her doldrums this past week. "I'm more cheerful thanks to you. I hope to maintain this mood." She decided she didn't want him to leave. She headed toward a cabinet and pulled out the *Battleship* game. She challenged him.

He rubbed his palms together. "Bring it on! Loser gives the winner a foot massage."

"I'll pass."

After a fair amount of time engaging in serious strategy and studying JP's "poker" face, Vanessa called, "G-9."

"Sunk!" JP said, plunking down his game. "You win. But it was pure luck. It had nothing to do with the strategic placement of ships, so no cockiness from you."

Victorious, Vanessa leaped up. The game fell from her lap. The red and white pegs scattered onto the carpet. "Oops!" She knelt on all fours. JP joined her. They crawled around, focused on collecting the pegs until their heads bumped together. Their eyes met. JP placed a light kiss on her lips. A flush warmed Vanessa's cheeks. She backed away. JP rose and reached out his arms to assist her up. Vanessa waved him away, rising without help and sitting on the sofa. Dismissing the kiss as though it never happened, Vanessa looked at the carpet. "Looks like we got all the pegs."

JP sat beside Vanessa. A faraway look flashed across his face. He dipped his head downward and said in a softened tone. "I apologize if I took a liberty I shouldn't have. You're the first woman since…Never mind."

"Since what?" Vanessa asked.

"Nothing. It's not important."

Vanessa wouldn't press for an answer. She'd changed her mind about a massage. Removing her sandals, she placed her feet on his lap. "Get busy."

JP performed like a professional. Vanessa closed her eyes. *This is pure heaven. Don't stop!* Suddenly, the tranquil atmosphere came to an abrupt halt. A gruff voice cut through the room, demanding, "What the hell is going on?"

Chapter 8

————— ◆ —————

"Greg!" Vanessa jumped up, smoothing her clothes. She went to him. "I didn't expect you home until tomorrow."

Greg pushed Vanessa aside, his neck veins bulging. He jerked his head in JP's direction. "That's obvious," he said, glaring at JP. "Who is this guy you're so friendly with?"

"This is JP Monroe. And JP, meet Greg Vardanega, my fiancé."

JP approached Greg and extended his hand. Greg clenched his right fist and raised his arm.

JP stepped back. He used his police training to defuse the situation. "I'm the cop who was at the hospital to question Vanessa's father the day he died. We had a chance encounter this week when she fell into a water fountain and injured her forehead." JP pointed to Vanessa's bandage. "I took her to the doctor because I didn't think she was in any condition to drive."

Greg lowered his arm. "I'll take over from here," he said, thumping his chest with his thumb for emphasis.

Uneasy, Vanessa chimed in, "We finished a game of *Battleship*. I won and the winner's prize was a foot massage."

"You looked like you were enjoying it too much." He

addressed JP. "If you don't mind, I'd like to be alone with Vanessa."

"I can take a hint," JP said. He put on his baseball cap. "Nice meeting you, Greg. And Vanessa, take care of yourself. Good luck getting info about your mother." He hesitated. "If you need help, call me. You still have my card, right?"

Vanessa nodded, then started to follow JP to the door.

"I'll escort him out," Greg said.

JP turned to Greg. "Be careful how you treat people. They may not appreciate your attitude."

Greg growled at the cop. "Stay away from her. She doesn't need your help." As soon as JP stepped onto the porch, Greg slammed the door.

Vanessa stood nearby, irritated at Greg's rudeness.

Greg brushed by her and plopped onto the couch. He sat with his arms folded, tapping his right foot, a scowl on his face. "I don't like what I saw. Care to explain?"

Vanessa sat on her knees next to Greg and in her most cheery voice said, "Tell me about the tournament."

"I'm still waiting."

Vanessa would not let Greg make her feel guilty. She poo-poohed the massage. "It was no big deal. Loosen up. You've got nothing to worry about. I doubt I'll see JP again." She cuddled up to him. "I'm so glad you're back." *Or am I?*

Vanessa's closeness melted Greg's hardline attitude. He pulled her onto his lap. "Aw, Van, I'm sorry. I guess I felt jealous. I'm sure you won't be seeing that dude anymore. He can deal with your father's accident at the station." He smiled as he kissed her nose. Vanessa pecked him on the cheek. The quick rise of heat in her body surprised her as Greg pressed his lips against hers. She broke the contact before it got any hotter. "Tell me all about your trip."

He grinned. "The team came in third. Pretty good for throwing a bunch of players together. And," he beamed, "the AD at the community college asked me to fill out an application. The head coach is retiring, and they'll be looking for a replacement. It's a long shot, but I'm excited."

Vanessa leaned back, looking at Greg's enthusiastic face. Full of pride, she hugged him. "That's wonderful. I know how much you love coaching."

"And we could live in Hawaii," Greg added.

The innocent remark caused Vanessa to sit erect. She hadn't considered moving to Hawaii would be mandatory if he got the job. "I'm not sure I want to move there."

Greg laughed. "If they offer me the job, of course, I'd have to live there. It'd be a rather long commute."

"Greg, I love my home here. And I have my search."

Greg pushed her off his lap with more force than necessary. She caught herself before she landed on her butt, then stood as he walked away from her. He rubbed his palm through his short-cropped hair.

"So, it looks like you're not excited at the prospect of starting our married life in an unfamiliar environment. A change of scenery would help your grief. You may find you like living in a warmer climate."

"I'm glad this opportunity may help your career, but you should've discussed it with me before applying."

Greg pulled his shoulders back. "Aw, come on, Van. It never crossed my mind you'd object."

"Well, I do." She hesitated. "I didn't tell you in case I didn't get it. I applied for a scholarship toward my master's degree in education at Portland State." A smile crossed her lips. "I got it!"

Greg leaned against the mantel, silent.

"No comment?" Vanessa asked.

Greg placed his hands around hers. "Congrats," he mumbled, his tone and expression conveying no sincerity or enthusiasm.

"This opportunity will help *my* career. This is another reason I can't live in Hawaii."

"Of course, you can. What's here for you? It seems all you care about is this quest of yours. You have done nothing else, including planning our wedding. You won't do anything with Melanie, your best friend. What are you so worried about leaving behind? Your negative reaction surprises and bugs me." Greg shook his head. "This guy JP. Is he the *real* reason you don't want to leave?"

"That comment was out of line." Greg's snide remark angered Vanessa. She didn't appreciate his insinuation. And she told him so. She stood, facing away from him, and looked around the room. "This is the home where I grew up. And my career is as important to me as yours is to you."

"So, what you're saying is this search for your mother is more important than I am? This opportunity is something that will help me to gain experience in my chosen career so I can provide for you." His eyes narrowed as he spoke, and his tone became harsh. "Look, we can discuss this later. I thought this was going to be a romantic reunion, but you put the brakes on it."

Vanessa's eyes shot daggers at him. Raising her voice, she said, "I hoped for a call from you."

"I was afraid you'd hang up on me. And also—"

"Let's start again," she suggested.

"I agree." Greg hugged Vanessa tighter. Smiling, he asked, "How 'bout we head to the bedroom?"

"Tempting, but I'll pass."

Greg wrapped his arms around Vanessa. "All the way from the airport, I thought about whisking you upstairs to *your* bedroom this time and making mad, sizzling love." He pressed himself against her body.

Vanessa withdrew and backed away.

She saw Greg's eyes reflecting disappointment and forcing a smile on his face. Exhaling a deep sigh, he headed to the door. She knew he wanted to stay, but she figured he didn't want a repeat of the last time they were together. "See ya tomorrow." He disappeared in a flash.

Vanessa popped open a can of diet Pepsi. She tried to figure out why she'd refused to hop into bed with Greg. She always looked forward to their lovemaking. But she resented his assumption she'd want to move to Hawaii. He hadn't considered her feelings or her career. Maybe he won't get the job and moving won't be an issue. The sudden ring of the phone interrupted her thoughts.

Surprised to hear Alicia's voice, she listened while Alicia rattled on, yapping about the divine weather and the third-place tournament finish. "Is Greg there?"

"He's already left," Vanessa said. A heavy sigh drifted into Vanessa's ears. "I'll tell him you called." *Hmmm. Alicia sounded disappointed.*

LATE THE NEXT DAY GREG PHONED. "I'LL BE OVER IN about an hour."

"I'll get busy preparing a nice dinner. Lasagna. And by the way, Alicia called after you left last night. She—"

"I talked with her."

Greg arrived over two hours later. The aroma of the stacked layers of pasta, sauce, ricotta, and melted mozzarella overwhelmed his nostrils. He beelined into the kitchen, anticipating the meal. He grabbed the Parmesan cheese from the cupboard, then swung Vanessa around, planting a smooch on her lips.

Vanessa responded. The kisses got heated as the oven timer buzzed. She pulled away. "I don't want burnt lasagna and I know you don't either." Fluttering her eyelashes, she said, "I'll be your dessert."

Greg grinned and laughed. "You're on." Rubbing his palms together, he said, "I could eat your lasagna anytime, anywhere. Even in Hawaii."

Vanessa ignored the poke. "Why did it take you so long to get here?"

"I stopped by Alicia's to work on a report Mr. Haskins wants. It took longer than I thought it would. We're not finished."

"What report?"

"He wants a detailed summary of the pros and cons of participating in the tournament so he can determine if it was a wise undertaking. He may or may not want to sponsor a team again. The first draft is due tomorrow."

"Why is Alicia involved?"

"My writing skills are lacking. She's helping me write it. And she's doing the typing."

Vanessa changed the subject. "Let's go out on the patio and eat. I'm starving." She picked up the lasagna and motioned to Greg to carry out the salad. The scent of the deep red roses in the garden laced the air. A gentle breeze provided a tad bit of relief from the heat. Greg grabbed a plate and dived right in, cutting a hefty portion for himself.

As they finished eating, Vanessa wiped a smidgen of sauce from Greg's lips. "Tasty dinner, Van. I love your lasagna. It hit the spot." He maneuvered his chair so he was sitting knee to knee with Vanessa. "It's about time to set our wedding date. How about before the new school year begins?"

"Sounds like a plan. A small intimate wedding with our closest friends and relatives. Nothing fancy." She slid her chair, putting distance between them. Vanessa had put off telling him she'd taken the coming school year off. She planned to devote a lot of time and effort searching for answers about her parents. Also, she wanted to concentrate on obtaining her master's degree. In an enthusiastic voice, she told Greg.

He reacted in a way she hadn't expected. "What the hell? What a bonehead move!" He leaned back in the chair. "How are you going to support yourself?"

"I've some savings. The house is paid off and my inheritance is more than adequate."

"And you'll benefit from my income as well. Perfect plan."

Vanessa considered his remark snide and inappropriate, and her shoulders dropped. She resumed the wedding discussion. "Melanie will be my matron of honor. Did you want Jason to be the best man?"

"Why not?"

"All settled. So, how about this Saturday?"

Greg looked at his cell phone calendar. "August twenty-first."

"August twenty-first it is. The ceremony will be in your folks' backyard. Your mother's green thumb has created such a beautiful garden. I appreciate her help. Only six days to pull everything together." With the wedding discussion finished, Vanessa broached another subject. "Guess what? I found my birth certificate. My mother's name is Rosemary.

The same as my middle name. I don't think it's a coincidence." She leaned against the chair's back. "I'm more determined to find the truth. And I will not quit until I find out."

Vanessa could see Greg didn't share her curiosity. "I don't want you spinning your wheels and experiencing disappointment. You may find out something you'd rather not…something that could devastate you even more than not knowing."

"I'm willing to take the risk," Vanessa said. "I hope you'll support me in this search."

"I see how determined you are, but it's hard for me to encourage you. You're going overboard. It's an obsession."

"I've made no progress except for finding my birth certificate. I want to find out who my biological parents are and why Dad adopted me. I'm not willing to give up. Not for you. Not for anyone." She began stacking the dirty dishes.

"Well, I don't want you to get hurt, Van." He pulled her to her feet and embraced her. He glanced at his watch. "Gotta go."

"So soon? I was hoping to head upstairs for your dessert," she teased him, fluttering her eyelids and running her fingers up and down his chest.

Vanessa's flirtatious demeanor tempted Greg. He embraced her and planted a fervent kiss on her lips. The bulge in his groin grew. He led her toward the stairs, then stopped. Holding both of her hands and resting his forehead against hers, he said, "I'm sorry, Van, but I promised Alicia I'd come back as soon as I could so we can give her boss the first draft by tomorrow."

"Can't Alicia write the report?" She pressed her body against his, blowing soft breaths on his neck.

"No. Haskins wants my perspective as the coach."

"Will you come back when you're done?" Vanessa pushed.

He brushed his lips across her forehead, then rushed toward the door. "Count on it! I promise."

Vanessa tidied up the kitchen, then ascended the stairs, humming *I'm in the Mood for Love*. She put on her sexiest nightgown and sprayed a puff of *Pleasures* perfume on her neck. Her father knew this was her favorite cologne. It was the last gift he had given her. Looking at her image in the mirror, she removed the bandage from her forehead. The gash's redness was fading and healing was progressing well. She lay in bed reading more chapters from the Agatha Christie novel, eager for Greg's return.

Chapter 9

Vanessa awoke to the morning light trickling in through the blinds. Daylight! Her body shot up. Where was Greg? She threw off the single silk sheet and heaved her feet onto the floor. She walked from the bedroom. "Greg? Are you here?" she called out several times. No answer. Vanessa went into the bathroom. Her image in the mirror wearing the sexy nighty mocked her. She'd worn it for nothing. She removed it and tossed the sheer garment into the air, then braced her palms on the vanity's intricate tiles.

"He promised," she told the face staring at her from the mirror. "I'll be expecting an explanation."

A few hours later, Greg pounded on the front door, yelling. "Van! Van! Open the door! I've got exciting, wonderful news!"

Vanessa completed a set of lunges. She inhaled and stretched her arms upward, then took a sip from her water bottle. Opening the door, she put her hands on her hips, a grumpy, accusatory expression on her face.

Greg overlooked Vanessa's scowl. "The college in Maui called and wants me to come for a formal interview. I'm one of three final candidates. I'm so pumped!" He jumped upward three feet.

"Why didn't you show up last night?" was Vanessa's response to the news.

"What?"

"You promised to return after you finished the report," she reminded him.

Greg continued talking. "I'm so stoked. I had an informal interview while there, and of course, they observed me during the tournament. I didn't think too much about it because I figured my chances were slim and none of landing the job. Can you believe this?" He picked Vanessa up and whirled her around.

"Put me down."

"Well, what do you say?" Greg asked, his smile stretching ear to ear.

"I say again, what happened that you didn't show up last night?" She crossed her arms against her chest.

A spasm of irritation appeared on Greg's face. "The draft took much longer than we thought it would. It was almost midnight before we finished. I figured you'd be asleep and didn't want to wake you."

"Humph. Some excuse." Her words were cold and exact. Vanessa took another sip of water. "Did you agree to the interview before discussing your decision with me?" she asked.

An exasperated sigh came from Greg's mouth. "You know my ambition is to coach at a major college, but for now, I've got to pay my dues. Starting at a junior college level is the first step."

"When do you have to be there?"

"This Friday."

"Friday! The day before our wedding!" Vanessa shrieked, lacing her hands on her head, her mouth gaping open.

"We can marry when I return." Then, clapping, he suggested, "Come with me. You can see firsthand where I might work, and we can also search for a suitable apartment, just in case. We're only inviting a few guests. If you've invited anyone already call and tell them we've postponed it. When they hear the reason, they won't be mad. I'll bet they'll be happy for me."

Vanessa couldn't accept Greg was willing to postpone their wedding because of a stupid interview five to six hours away by plane. "I'm sure the committee will accommodate you for such a special occasion," she pointed out. "Did you ask him to wait until next week?" Her lips formed into an unpleasant twist.

"No...I suppose I should have told Mr. Yokohama. But I want this job and don't want to take any chances."

Vanessa tightened her ponytail as she started feeling torn. She realized this was an important opportunity for Greg's chosen career. Talk about bad timing.

Silence dominated the room as Vanessa searched for the words to convey her dissatisfaction. Narrowing her eyes, she finally asked, "Did you consider you have me to take into account now? What about my master's degree? This should've been a joint decision. Did you check into any other nearby colleges? What about Clackamas?"

"No openings," Greg answered. "Not even for assistants."

"I've got a distinct impression, Mr. Vardanega, you've already decided." Vanessa watched Greg's expression. He looked at her and frowned. "This is a step I need to advance my career." His words cut deeper this time. His aspiration meant more to him than she did. And what about *her* career? Did she love him enough to put aside her ambitions and accompany him all around the country, hoping one day he'd land that perfect position?

"I don't want to lose this opportunity. Alicia thought it was a fantastic chance to jumpstart my career. She couldn't congratulate me enough!" He stepped away from Vanessa and eyeballed her. "I thought you'd be happy for me and share my excitement." His voice rose a little at the end, almost condemning her.

"Alicia?" Vanessa asked, putting her hands on her hips. "When did you tell her?"

"We were working on the report when Mr. Yokohama called me last night on my cell phone, about eleven."

"How come so late?" Irritation brewed like coffee in a pot.

"Hawaii is three hours behind us. He forgot."

"You seem to spend an enormous amount of time with Alicia. Is she going to handle your absence if they hire you?" The voice spewed out sarcasm.

"Aw, come on, Van," Greg said, pulling Vanessa toward him. "I told you Mr. Haskins wanted the final draft by today."

"Are you working at the office or her apartment?" She pressed, raising a suspicious and challenging eyebrow.

His jaw tensed. "Her place."

Last night she'd prepared herself for a romantic interlude. But he had spent the evening working on a report with another woman. His no-show, still fresh in her mind, bothered her. And she didn't buy his excuse it was too late to return.

"It was all work."

Greg's nonchalant attitude only worked her up more. "Working with Alicia at her apartment is a huge deal to me," Vanessa said, raising her voice. "I bet Alicia wants to be more than a friend." A slight flush of embarrassment crossed Greg's face. *Did I hit a raw nerve?*

Dodging Vanessa's clear accusation, he said, "Please think about this. And don't worry about your search for your biological roots. You can do it in Maui. For all you know, you weren't born locally."

"Wrong. The birth certificate showed I was born here in Milwaukie at Dwyer Community Hospital. It's now Providence."

"I don't care you're obsessed with finding who you are. Fine with me. When it stands in the way of me getting my foot in the door, then I have to look at this differently." He walked in a circle, rubbing his hands in his hair.

"Differently?" Vanessa repeated the word like a dagger.

"Sorry, I was thinking out loud." He heaved a sigh. "Is there any reason you can't do this search from Maui?" He paused. "I didn't think so. You can find a job there and since we'll be married, it will all work out." He smacked his hand in his palm like he was wearing a baseball glove. "Yes, it will." His voice grew more emphatic.

"I'm sorry you feel this way, Greg. Finding info is as important to me as this job is to you." Vanessa's voice shook. Tears threatened. "I'm not trying to sabotage your coaching ambitions. But I also have a career." He was so wrapped up in *his* career, he wasn't considering *hers*. "Getting my masters will help *my* career. That's a valid reason I don't want to move to Hawaii. It would cost me losing out on this opportunity."

"Why'd you apply in case I got the job? You didn't consult me either."

Vanessa glared at him. "I sent in my application last March. Dad encouraged me." She closed her eyes momentarily. "I planned to teach during the day and take night classes and finish up next summer term. But now I'm free to attend classes full time and will complete the courses a few months sooner."

Greg steered the conversation back to the wedding. "I assume you still want to marry me."

"Of course, I do," Vanessa said. "But right now, I'm angry. I can't accept you're choosing to whip off to Hawaii rather than stay for our wedding. How can you judge me for not caring enough? Call Mr. Yokohama and ask if he can wait till next week for the interview." Vanessa pulled Greg's cell phone from his shirt pocket. "Call him."

"Whatever." Greg scrolled to Mr. Yokohama's phone number. He pressed the numbers and when Mr. Yokohama answered, he explained the situation. Greg nodded several times. "I understand. I'll see you Friday." Words Vanessa dreaded. She felt the heat of disappointment combined with bitterness. She turned away.

Greg approached Vanessa from behind. She kept the distance between them. Greg's smile was on full display, and he ignored Vanessa's irritation. "Friday's the only day all committee members can meet. If I land the job, no, *when* I get the gig, we'll rent an apartment on campus. It'll be close to the library. Convenient for your research. And you can apply for a teaching position, assuming your certificate is valid in Hawaii."

"What about my scholarship?" She faced him. "And the wedding?"

"How 'bout we go to the courthouse when I return? My parents, Melanie, and Jason are the only people we need to invite."

Before Vanessa responded, the doorbell rang. Greg walked to the door, Vanessa on his heels. Standing on the porch, JP looked past Greg. "I've got news for you."

Chapter 10

Vanessa stepped in front of Greg. "Is it about my mother?" The prospect excited her.

With annoyance seeping through his voice, Greg asked, "What's the news?"

Vanessa couldn't contain her hope. "You found info about my mother, right?"

Then she noticed JP wore his uniform. Her heart sank. It must be business.

"Possibly. The primary reason I stopped by is to tell you the status of the investigation into your father's accident." He leaned forward, glancing past the couple. "May I come inside?"

"Where are my manners? Of course," Vanessa said, stepping aside.

"You could've called her or had her come to the station." Greg spat out the words.

Vanessa frowned at Greg's recurring rotten attitude toward JP. Greg slung his arm around her shoulders, preventing her from moving.

The trio stood near the entrance.

"Mr. Demers, the man who caused the accident, pled guilty to criminally negligent homicide. He's remorseful.

He waived a jury trial and will accept a plea bargain."

"What does that mean?"

"He'll have a bench trial with only the judge. He'll read over the plea bargain and decide if it's too harsh, too lean, or just right, then sentence Demers in a few weeks. Demers wants to end this nightmare. He knows his lack of judgment to drive intoxicated caused the death of another human being. He's going to carry the burden with him for the rest of his life, regardless of what his sentence is. And that can be a worse punishment than jail time." JP paused. "His wife had asked for a divorce. He became distraught and his response was to drink. His wife reconsidered, and they're going to seek counseling."

Vanessa stepped away from Greg in a huff. "Is that the news? Shucks. I was hoping you had info about my mother."

JP continued. "I want to add Mr. Demers wants to apologize to you." His expression invited her to accept. "You can also write a Victim's Impact Statement that tells how his actions affected your life."

Vanessa's response surprised everyone, including herself. "I'm inclined to forgive him. Writing a statement won't bring Dad back, but I'll think about it."

Greg butted in. "I can't feel sorry for the guy. What he did has caused a major upheaval in my—our—lives. I'm glad he pled guilty and will serve jail time or whatever. It will be over and we can move on. Right, honey?" Greg squeezed Vanessa's shoulders so hard she grimaced.

JP pulled a folded piece of paper from his shirt pocket. "This is the other reason for my visit. During my break, I searched for info on Rosemary Peterson and came across an old police report. It describes a house fire that occurred about the time you were an infant. It mentions Rosemary Peterson."

Vanessa snatched the paper from JP's grasp. She skimmed through the report about the fire. The lone female occupant was a twenty-four-year-old female named Rosemary Peterson. Investigators determined the victim fell asleep with a lit cigarette. Smoker's carelessness.

Greg stood beside Vanessa. "It's no doubt nothing."

The other two stared at him as if he grew horns.

"Rosemary is the name is on my birth certificate," Vanessa reminded him.

Greg glanced at his watch. "I promised a couple of incoming seniors to open up the gym and help them practice their free throws and three-point shots. I'm still the official coach at Milwaukie High." Addressing JP, he asked, "Don't you need to go give out a few parking tickets or arrest a poor chap for jaywalking? Time to go, Officer." He waited until JP moved toward the door. Before JP left, Greg grabbed Vanessa and ground his lips into hers. When finished, he gave her a slight push.

JP's eyes narrowed as he sized up Greg. Vanessa stepped between them. "I'll keep you apprised of the defendant's case," JP said. He turned to leave.

"Wait!" Vanessa faced JP. "I'd like to pursue the info in the report. Can you stay for a minute and direct me on the best approach?"

Greg's mouth tightened into a stubborn line. "You don't need his help." Opening the door, he gestured for JP to take off. Now.

Vanessa's eyes spewed invisible daggers toward Greg. "Don't be so rude. I'm going to ask a few questions. Now vamoose, Greg."

"Okay, okay, I'm gone, but no foot massages!" He cast a warning glare in JP's direction.

Vanessa shoved him onto the porch and shut the door. Leaning against it, she closed her eyes, drew a deep breath, and exhaled. She wasted no time quizzing JP. "Not much new info in the report. Did it mention anything about a baby? Did it give her address? Her age? The date of the report?"

"Hold on." JP laughed. "I don't recall reading anything that will help much. I thought it was coincidental the female who died in the house fire had the same name as your alleged mother. We could research the death notices or obituaries on that date. But," he cautioned her, "don't get your hopes up. Most likely another dead end."

"I'll check anyway."

"Greg wasn't too happy I came here."

Stealing a glance in JP's direction, Vanessa said, "I'm surprised you came in person. Greg was right. You could have called me to the station or phoned."

"Giving you the info in person was an excuse to see how you're doing."

Vanessa was sure her heart skipped a beat, but she wouldn't admit it.

"Did I come at a bad time?"

"Kind of. The interview committee chose him as one of three final candidates for a coaching job in Hawaii. He has the formal interview this Friday. Our wedding was supposed to be Saturday."

JP's eyes faded into disappointment.

Vanessa continued. "Can you believe the bad timing? I insisted he phone Mr. Yokohama to see if he would change the interview date. He said this Friday was the only time all five committee members could take part. So, he's jaunting off to Maui. He wants me to go with him." She puffed out a breath.

"Are you going?"

"No. I'd go if it were for our honeymoon. I don't want to live there."

"Did you tell Greg?"

"Yep. And it's creating a problem between us. I told him it should be a joint decision. If he's offered the job, one of us will have to give in for the sake of the other." She lowered her head and massaged her tense neck muscles. She thought it unlikely the committee wouldn't offer him the job. "And in this case, there's no compromise. We'll live either here or there. I got a scholarship to pursue a master's degree. If I move to Hawaii, I'll lose it." She leaned against the fireplace. "I took a year off teaching to pursue the degree rather than take evening classes."

"Do you want to be in administration someday?"

Vanessa looked at him as though he lost a few brain cells. "Heck no! I want to remain in the classroom. I love being with the kids. Many teachers get a master's degree for increased pay and advanced expertise in specific areas, such as special education." Her eyes narrowed. "I'm going to miss the students."

"You should let this search rest." The sentence slipped from JP's mouth. "Your father loved you more than life itself. He devoted his entire life to you. Isn't that enough?"

Now JP was also suggesting she abandon the search. *No way.* Her words tinged with stern resolve, she spat out. "I don't plan on giving up. I've got many unanswered questions. I'll search without help from anyone."

JP stood face to face with Vanessa and saluted her. "Okay. Reporting for duty. I'm your official assistant." He tried to lighten the mood but also cautioned. "Keep in mind you may never find out anything. Or the truth could be more devastating than you imagined."

"Greg said the same thing, but I'm willing to take the chance."

"Okay, I'm behind you one hundred percent," JP said. "I'll help you any way I can, but only off duty and no official means or I could lose my job." He winked at her. "Now, I'd like to see a smile on your lovely face."

She focused on the word lovely, and her heart fluttered. Her lips curved into a grin.

Later that evening, Vanessa rubbed moisturizer onto her flawless complexion. *Lovely?* JP's compliment lingered in her mind long after his departure. She stared into the bathroom mirror, running her fingers along her cheeks. Another smile graced her face. She ran the hairbrush bristles through her long tresses, humming Barry Manilow's hit tune *Can't Smile Without You.* The ringing phone interrupted her.

Greg's anxious voice bellowed through the phone line. "Are you coming with me to Hawaii? Need to buy the tickets."

"No."

"I wish you'd reconsider. It might do you well to get away for a few days. And you can scout around for an apartment."

Vanessa remained firm. "I'll stay here. But I'm planning to take you to the airport. You don't need to take a taxi."

"No need. I'm spending the night at my folks' and Mom said she'd drop me off at the airport. I'm going to miss you, Van," Greg said. He made kissing sounds.

She avoided offering the same sentiment. "I'll keep busy. I'm planning to look for info on Rosemary Peterson. JP's going to help me." Oops! She regretted mentioning JP.

Greg ground out words between clenched teeth. "You don't need his help. Stay away from him."

Vanessa didn't want to argue on the phone. "Okay," she agreed.

Greg wouldn't let his irritation drop. "You're more interested in searching than you are about this coaching job. You haven't once wished me luck or showed any signs of support."

Vanessa became defensive. "The same goes for you. You've given me no help to find the truth or congratulated me for receiving the scholarship."

"Search without JP's help. I can tell he's got the hots for you."

Two can play this game. She shot back. "And I suppose you couldn't write the report without Alicia." She was on a roll. "You're too busy pursuing *your* career to care about *mine.*"

"This job is about our future. I'm going to do what I can to enhance my chances of landing a Division I coaching job. It's obvious what's number one in your life right now," Greg exploded. "And it isn't me. You're obsessed with knowing your roots, and your search is becoming too much. Nothing of benefit to us as a couple will happen. I'm going to pack a few things now. See you Saturday or Sunday, depending on when I can book a return flight."

"Wait, Greg! Don't hang up!" Vanessa kicked her left shin for striking back. "I want you to do well in your interview. I know coaching at a higher level is your goal. I guess I'm bummed out it's the day before our wedding. Now we need to reschedule."

"I tried to change the interview date, but couldn't."

"You could've booked a flight Friday night and made it back in time for the wedding. But you didn't try." Vanessa didn't buy his defense.

"I suppose that was an option, but too late now. We'll still get married. How about a week later, the 28th?" Greg was jiggling the few coins in his pocket and tapping his foot.

"Fine. Now, remember, I want you to discuss any potential offer with me before accepting."

"They may want an answer before I leave."

"I'm sure they'll give you time to discuss everything with your future wife. Promise me you will."

"Love ya." The dial tone wafted into her ears.

JP STOOD BESIDE VANESSA, BREATHING IN THE SUBTLE scent of her perfume as she again read the report at the police station. "This report reveals nothing of use. All it tells me is a woman named Rosemary Peterson perished in a house fire on September 20, 1986. My birthday is March second. I would have been six-and-a-half months old. It doesn't mention a baby or anyone else. Seems they closed the case with no more investigation."

"Appears that way," JP guessed. "It's 2010. After twenty-four years, no one is going to care or spend staff time on any investigation. No doubt the insurance company closed the file ages ago. The fire and police departments as well."

The mysterious fire and death intrigued Vanessa. Was the fire victim, Rosemary Peterson, her mother?

"It's almost five. Records closes in a few minutes. Time to leave." JP ushered her toward the exit. "I'll help you research the obituaries in old newspapers at the library. Who knows? We might find some next of kin if we can find the right Rosemary Peterson." He cautioned her yet again. "Don't get your hopes up."

Vanessa considered Greg's reaction if she allowed JP to help. "Thanks, but that won't be necessary."

JP dismissed her refusal. "Tomorrow's Friday. My shift ends at three. I'll pick you up around three-thirty."

Chapter 11

---◆---

"Well, that's that," JP said the following day. They had perused the back issues of all the local newspaper obituaries dated after the time of the fire. A deep sigh escaped. "I hoped there'd be info mentioning Rosemary and her relatives. I want to search through the deaths at county records if you don't mind."

JP glanced at his watch. The five o'clock closing time approached. They wouldn't have time to accomplish anything before staff shooed them out. "We can take another stab at it. But not till Monday."

"I'll go there myself on Monday." Greg would be home by then. She wasn't about to cause any more friction between them. "Looks like this Rosemary Peterson was an ordinary person who didn't generate any interest."

"Like the rest of us lowly peons," JP said. He touched her shoulder as he guided her from the building.

JP drove the long route to Vanessa's house. He idled his car behind Vanessa's Toyota parked in the driveway. Vanessa opened the door and faced him. "Thank you for your help, my official assistant." She patted his hand.

JP asked in a hopeful tone. "Are you sure I can't help you on Monday after my shift?"

"You've already done more than you should." She stepped from the car and closed the door. JP stared at her as he shifted to reverse. Vanessa advanced only a few steps toward the concrete pathway before her feet abruptly halted. "JP!" she yelled as she did an about-face.

JP slammed the brakes.

"There is something you can help me with. The victim's letter or whatever you call it. I don't have a clue what to say. Could you give me some tips?"

JP's eyes lit up. He wasted no time agreeing. He killed the engine and escorted her to the front door.

"I didn't mean now. How about tomorrow?"

"Sounds like a plan. What time?" He tried to act casual despite his racing heart.

"Around six. I'll fix you a home-cooked meal afterward. Anything you don't like?"

"Anything but liver or other organ meats." JP stuck out his tongue, shaking his face side to side. "I'm easy to please."

"I cook a mean lasagna."

JP's appetite kicked into gear a day early. He grinned. "I'll bring a bottle of wine, but feeding my ugly face isn't necessary."

"My way of thanking you." She gave him a friendly hug, but JP held on. When he puckered his lips and leaned his face towards her, she turned her head. *I'm engaged.* But she allowed herself to remain within his arms. They stayed intertwined for several moments longer until a voice surprised them.

"I hope I'm not interrupting anything," a female jested, standing a few feet behind JP's back. "You two love birds should at least wait until you're inside the house. Eh, Greg?" Smiling, Melanie nudged JP. "I dropped by to tell you I got your message about postponing the wedding. Chosen a new date? I need to..." Melanie's voice trailed off when JP turned to face her. She stepped back, her face knotted in a questioning expression.

Vanessa broke the awkward silence. "Mel, this is JP Monroe. He's...he's a policeman who is helping me search for my biological parents."

"I'll call you later, Van." She gave a brief wave and retreated.

"No, don't go, Mel, is it?" JP interjected.

"Melanie."

"Don't take off. Stay and visit with Vanessa. I was leaving anyway." Facing Vanessa, JP said, "See you tomorrow." He rushed off.

Aware of Melanie's unease, Vanessa said, "Come inside. I'll fix us a tall glass of iced tea with a pinch of lemon."

"Can't," Melanie answered. "On my way to pick up Jason from work. His truck is in the shop...again."

"You've been my best friend since seventh grade. Nothing gets by me where you're concerned." Glancing down the street at JP's departing car, Vanessa said, "You're wondering what the hug was all about, aren't you?"

Melanie denied her curiosity. "No. It's your business."

"It meant nothing. I hugged him out of gratitude."

"Whatever you say."

Vanessa embraced her dear friend. "I would never lie to you."

"Okay. Guess I was reading too much into what I saw." Melanie headed toward the steps. "Catch ya later."

"Greg and I have moved the wedding to the twenty-eighth. I'll verify it again when he returns. Say hi to Jason."

A FEW MINUTES BEFORE SIX SATURDAY EVENING THE familiar sound of the doorbell echoed throughout the house. Vanessa paused as she passed the hallway mirror to fluff her hair and smooth wrinkles from her spaghetti strap dress.

Clad in Levi shorts and an orange T-shirt emblazoned with the Oregon State mascot, JP bowed when Vanessa opened the door. He handed her the wine. "From my mother's stash of four bottles. Hope you like Pinot Noir. It goes well with lasagna."

Vanessa stepped aside and JP entered. "This is fine. I'm no wine aficionado."

JP drew a deep breath. "Dinner smells delicious." He rubbed his palms together.

"Let's go to the kitchen while I put the final touches on the antipasto platter. An assortment of provolone cheese, salami, olives, and cherry tomatoes."

JP reached for a cubed piece of cheese.

Vanessa playfully slapped his hand. "Not yet." She glanced outside. "I thought it'd be nice to eat on the patio, but it's too hot." She pointed to the cupboard. "Would you mind setting the table?"

"Not at all."

JP gathered the plates, utensils, and napkins. "But don't expect a table set according to Emily Post guidelines."

"I'm informal."

"So, have you thought of what you want to say to Mr. Demers?"

"A little. Will the statement influence the sentencing?"

"Most sentences are a result of a plea bargain or strict sentencing guidelines." He grabbed an olive. "They allow the victim or the family to express the physical and/or emotional damage caused by the crime."

"Like me losing my dad, my only relative." As an afterthought, she said, "Well, except for Aunt Helene."

JP hesitated but took a risk asking Vanessa about her aunt. "Why haven't you considered contacting your aunt? She no doubt knows everything."

"Yeah, right," Vanessa responded. "I have no clue where she is and don't care. She's as guilty as my father for not disclosing my adoption."

"She finally told you despite your father's strong objection," JP said. "And I suspect your adoption was the reason for their estrangement."

Vanessa mellowed. "I suppose you're right. I guess it takes someone emotionally removed from the situation to take an objective view." A heavy sigh escaped. "I might try getting hold of her whenever."

"Sorry you're not able to find out any more information on the fire that killed Rosemary Peterson. Maybe she isn't even your mother," JP said.

"Possibly," Vanessa agreed. "But it's too much of a coincidence her name should be on my birth certificate. And the baby's birth date is the same as mine. Don't you agree?"

"Yeah."

Vanessa turned the oven knob off. She pulled out the lasagna and placed the dish on the sunflower-shaped trivet.

Eyeballing the warm, bubbly dish, JP said, "My empty stomach is growling. I'm ready to dig in." He took the wine bottle from the drainboard and set it on the table beside the bouquet of pink dahlias.

JP's curiosity overtook him. "What did Melanie say after I left?"

"She acted as though she didn't care. But I knew she wanted an explanation. I told her I was grateful to you for all your help, and I was showing you my gratitude, which I was."

He challenged her. "Is that the only reason you remained in my arms? I got a strong vibe from you."

Vanessa denied his assumption. "I'm engaged. Greg will be home tomorrow. The wedding is on for the twenty-eighth. I shouldn't have allowed myself to remain that close to you. I can't be carrying on with some other guy."

"You should give serious thought about your commitment to Greg before tying the knot."

"I've got the distinct impression you're trying to convince me not to marry him," Vanessa said. She glanced at him for his reaction as she placed a hefty portion of lasagna on JP's plate.

"Perceptive of you," JP said. "It doesn't seem like you two are one hundred percent committed to the marriage."

Vanessa jumped up. "Another thing that happened because of Mr. Demers. The postponement of my wedding! I'll write that down for my statement while it's fresh in my mind. Be right back." She shoved back her chair and raced upstairs to the desk in her father's room for a notepad. JP leaned against the chair's back, his arms dangling at his sides.

When Vanessa pulled on the top drawer, a small paperback bible jammed it. "Darn!" She yanked several times on the knob until the force freed the drawer, hurling her body and the drawer onto the thick carpet. She shoved the scattered contents into a pile, then reached for the notepad. A faded, wrinkled piece of paper with the name Rosey on it caught her eye.

Vanessa's scream soared downstairs. JP nearly choked on a bite of salami as he rushed to the bedroom, two stairs at a time. Vanessa was sitting on the bed staring at the piece of paper. She thrust it into JP's hand. "Read it."

JP read out loud.

Lyle,

There's no way I want to keep the baby and I don't want my parents raising her. I don't think they want to anyway. Since you're willing and already caring for her, she's yours. I'm relinquishing my parental rights. I'll sign whatever documents so you can adopt. I know you'll raise her well and give her the love she deserves. Are you crazy? No way would I marry you. I made a mess of my life. You deserve better. Don't contact me or bring the baby near me. Thanks for everything.

So long and take care. Rosey

Vanessa grabbed back the note, waving it back and forth. She circled the bedroom. Her mind was like a butterfly, fluttering back to the text on the paper. "This note is from my mother! I know it! Rosey was no doubt her nickname." She plopped onto the bed, trying to grasp the significance of the words she read over and over.

"This adoption mystery is getting more intriguing," JP said. "The name Rosemary, Rosey, whatever, has popped up too many times to be a coincidence. You can conclude this note clinches this Rosemary person *is* your mother."

"Wow! She didn't even care one twit about me. And my grandparents didn't either." Her hands covered her face. The words finally sank in. Her excitement melted away, replaced by torment. Vanessa stared across the room.

JP wrapped his arms around Vanessa and drew her close to him. She shivered as she buried her head against JP's chest, repeating, "She didn't want me and neither did her parents. They rejected me."

JP lifted her chin and stared into her pained eyes. "But your dad did." He wiped a tear from her cheek and smiled. "Let's go eat the lasagna before it gets cold."

"I'm not hungry."

"Sure, you are." He led her from the bedroom.

Vanessa toyed with her meal but her appetite was non-existent. JP helped himself to a second helping. "This was delicious. I'm tempted to take leftovers home." He cleared the table and rinsed the dishes while Vanessa retreated to the living room. She no longer had any desire to work on the Victim Statement. Her mind only focused on the note. "I'm afraid I'm lousy company. I appreciate your willingness to help me with the statement. I don't think I want to write one now. Thanks for coming." She hoped JP would get the hint she wanted to be alone.

"I'm not leaving while you're in this mood." He challenged her to a *Battleship* game.

"No thanks." It was only eight but her mind demanded a temporary respite from realizing her mother tossed her aside like a bag of trash. And the note prompted more questions. What relationship did her father have with this Rosey person? Why did her dad want to marry her? And what happened that her mother's life was so bad she wouldn't keep or *love* me? She stared at JP, her eyes begging for answers he couldn't give her.

"I'm heading to bed. Greg'll be home tomorrow and I need to be in a better mood. He'll no doubt gloat he told me finding the truth might be upsetting."

"Has he called you?" JP asked.

"No, but I didn't him expect to."

"Why not?" His face crinkled. "Never mind. Have you changed your mind about living in Hawaii?"

"No," Vanessa answered. "Greg wants the coaching job and despite my objection, he's determined to accept it if offered. I'm expecting a problem then." Letting out a deep breath, she leaned her head against the sofa back and stretched her legs.

"You've convinced yourself you're obligated to marry him and can't back out. This marriage could be a mistake you'll regret," JP warned. "As I said already, I don't think your heart is one hundred percent committed. Seems you don't love Greg enough to move to Hawaii. You're using *your* career and search as an excuse."

"Oh, yeah?" His words cut her like a knife.

"I want you to be happy. I don't want you to get hurt again. Your father's death was a tragedy, and I care enough about you that I don't want any more heartache in your life."

"I appreciate your concern, JP." Vanessa blushed. "You managed to help me out of my doldrums this past summer when no one else could. I'm grateful." Suddenly, she realized she wanted JP to stay a while longer. His presence comforted her. She stood, stretching her arms toward the ceiling. "How about a glass of the wine you brought? I could use a few sips." Without waiting for a reply, she headed for the kitchen, then moments later cried out, "Ouch!"

JP leaped up and rushed to her side. "What happened?"

"I poked my finger on the corkscrew. Careless."

JP examined the wound. "Where's your first aid kit? I'll doctor it up in no time."

"Don't be dramatic." Vanessa smiled. "I'll nurse myself."

As she stepped to open a nearby drawer for a bandage, she slipped on a water spot. JP darted toward her. His strong arms caught the weight of her body and whisked her upwards. His after-shave lotion intoxicated Vanessa. A ripple of exhilaration cruised through her veins. She tilted her head away from JP's. As he strode across the kitchen carrying her into the living room, the pattern of his "rescues" hit her. "You're always rescuing me from some mishap."

"I'm your knight in shining armor." He set her down on the sofa. Instead of releasing her, he stroked her neck and gazed into her eyes. Vanessa let out a whimper as JP's hands worked their way around her figure, touching every curve. JP leaned closer and planted a fiery, passionate kiss on her warm lips. She found herself responding, but guilt enveloped her when a vision of Greg flashed in her mind.

She wiggled from his grasp. In a shaky voice, she said, "I'm engaged to Greg." She rose, staring at her father's portrait, unable to meet JP's eyes. She forced herself to face him. "You can't expect anything more when I'm getting married to another man. I'm not a two-timer. I've got morals."

"Marrying Greg is not written in stone. My gut instinct," he said rubbing his abdomen, "tells me you're torn."

"What makes you think I no longer want to marry Greg?"

"Can you tell me it doesn't bother you he doesn't support your search? And he took off two days before your wedding for a job interview and hasn't called you. You're having second thoughts."

Vanessa opened her mouth to deny his assumption, but her voice refused to cooperate.

"Look me in the eyes," JP dared her. "Tell me you love Greg with your whole heart and soul."

Vanessa's silence spoke volumes.

Taking a deep breath and moving oh so close to her, JP continued. "I can't get you out of my mind and want to be with you every waking moment. I only wish you felt as strongly for me as I do about you." JP wrapped his hands around hers. "I didn't think it was possible to feel this way again since Cheryl..." He sighed.

"Who's Cheryl?"

The sudden ringing of the phone miffed Vanessa. She made no move to answer it.

"Could be important."

An annoyed sigh escaped. She leaned and reached for the phone resting on the end table. Moments later she turned around, a dazed expression on her face.

"What's wrong?"

"Greg. He flew home today and he's on his way here. They offered him the coaching job and he accepted."

Chapter 12

———◆◆———

JP stood. "I'd better be going. Shouldn't be here when Greg arrives." Pulling Vanessa from the sofa, he placed his hands on her shoulders. "I've fallen in love with you. Unfortunate for me, you're determined to marry Greg. I wish you would change your mind and give me a sign there's a chance I can steal into your heart." He stared at Vanessa, his eyes filled with hope.

Vanessa stroked her engagement ring, a gesture showing she couldn't—or wouldn't—change her mind. JP drew her into his arms. He brushed his lips along her face, unwilling to release her. He rested his forehead against hers. "I can't believe this is the second time I…" His voice, tinged with sadness, trailed off. At long last, he tore himself from her and backed away. As he reached the door, he gave her one last heartbreaking gaze. "Hope you find the answers you're searching for. Much happiness."

Had JP walked out of her life forever? She sat for a while, pondering what had happened. *Why am I so torn?* The aching of her cut finger demanded her attention. Sighing, she forced herself to go into the kitchen to medicate and bandage the wound. The unopened wine bottle still sat on the table. As she reached to put it and the glasses into the cupboard, she heard Greg calling her name. She left them on the counter and went to greet him.

"There's my girl!" Greg stood facing her, a grin as wide as the Grand Canyon. He lifted Vanessa off the ground and twirled her around. He kissed her on the lips. "Glad I'm back?"

"Ah, of course. Welcome home," Vanessa said, as he set her down.

Leading him to the sofa she said, "Tell me about the job."

Greg circled the living room, too enthusiastic to sit. "My contract is for three years. Already met two players. I'm sure we'll have a terrific rapport. I'm so looking forward to this opportunity." He did a little jump in the air. "It'll give me the experience to apply at a Division I school, at least as an assistant."

Vanessa stood. "I see how enthused you are. But you seem more interested in your career than teaching and guiding the athletes. I hope you're not putting your goals ahead of the program." Placing her hands on her hips, she added, "I expected you to discuss any offer with me before accepting."

"Don't worry your attractive head," Greg assured her. "I've got my priorities straight. I plan to run a successful and reputable program. It'll help me as well as the team if I get positive results. I have to report for duty soon. Practice starts in a month. Our first game is the first week of November. Can you be ready to go a few days after our wedding? Remember, it's a nice honeymoon destination. I've got my eye on a cozy apartment for us not too far from the campus."

"Are you serious? With no input from me?" Her annoyance grew stronger.

Greg took her hands into his. "People don't apply for jobs they don't want. So, when offered, of course, I'm going to accept. I thought you'd realize that."

"What about this house?" It held so many fond memories. Vanessa couldn't fathom leaving it behind.

"Rent or sell it," Greg suggested. "Melanie or a realtor can handle all the details."

It didn't matter she was overreacting. Vanessa wondered if she could allow a stranger to move in. The answer was no. It had been home for twenty-four years, her entire life. She couldn't accept packing up and leaving only two months after her father's death. The pain of missing him was still acute. It would be intolerable to add giving up the memories the house held.

Reading her expression, Greg was gentle yet firm. "Look, Van, I know it's hard for you to leave, but you didn't think you were going to live here forever, did you? What did you think you were going to do? Set up housekeeping with your father?"

"No, but I didn't plan on him dying this early. I figured Dad would still be here until he died years from now. I could still come and visit." She sat, tears moistening her eyes.

Embracing her, Greg tried to reason. "I didn't think this house situation would be an issue. And what about when I get a job somewhere else? We'll probably never live in Milwaukie again."

As she had predicted, this job offer was creating a problem. "So much has changed since our engagement. I can't fathom leaving this house. And I want to find out all the unanswered questions about my birth."

"There's no reason you can't search from Hawaii," Greg said. "None."

Remembering the note she found earlier, Vanessa jumped up and retrieved it. "Read this."

"What does this mean?" he asked.

"It proves Rosemary Peterson is my mother." Vanessa swung her arms upward in triumph. She considered this discovery progress toward the truth. "Now all I have to do is discover more information about her...who she was, where she came from, what relationship she had with my father, and how she died in the house fire."

"Are you sure this note proves this woman is your mother?" Greg's tone sounded skeptical.

"Almost one hundred percent," Vanessa said. "The note convinced JP too."

"JP?" Greg raised his eyebrows.

"Yes, he was here when I found the note inside Dad's desk."

"You mean you're still hanging around with that guy?" he asked, his eyes projecting an icy stare. "I can't figure out why you need his help. He's got the hots for you and wants to move in on my woman." His voice was thick with insinuation.

Vanessa squirmed as she denied Greg's accusation. "He's only trying to help me," she lied, and added, "something you're not willing to do."

"That's right!" Greg said, raising his voice. "I want *me* to be the focus of your life, not some silly urge to find your parents!" He turned toward the kitchen. "I need a glass of water."

Moments later he returned, holding the wine bottle and two glasses. He thrust them within inches of her face before slamming them onto the coffee table. "Was this intended for us?" Greg asked. "Or is the wine and lasagna from a cozy dinner you and JP were having? Good thing I called before I got here. I might have caught him being more than helpful, like administering another foot massage."

"I invited JP over to help me write a Victim's Impact Statement because I have no idea what to say. I thought he'd enjoy a home-cooked meal. He brought the wine," Vanessa said, her voice unsteady. She wiped her clammy hands on her dress.

"It doesn't look like you two drank any," Greg said, holding up the glasses. "They're clean and the bottle is still sealed."

"I poked my finger while I was using the corkscrew. It started bleeding. JP was going to bandage it when you called. So, he left." Vanessa waved her injured finger in front of him.

"Where's the statement he was helping you write?"

"I wasn't in the mood to write anything after I found the note." She folded her arms across her chest. "Is this an interrogation, Greg?"

Greg sighed, easing up. "You're right, Van. We should be able to trust each other, don't you think? I guess I was feeling threatened."

"No need to," Vanessa assured him. "Now, about our wedding and the move. Exactly when do you start the job?"

"A week from Monday, on the thirtieth."

"What? Only nine days from now! How do you expect me to have everything packed and arrangements for the house taken care of in that amount of time? And plan a wedding? Impossible!"

"We're still on for next Saturday the twenty-eighth. Right? Enough time to notify the few guests. I'm sure Mom will be glad to throw together a few dishes for the reception. People move all the time on short notice. You can come back later and close things. Or you can join me as soon as you've finished. No big deal."

"It is a huge deal to me." She positioned herself inches from his body, hands on her hips. "I'm not prepared for such a move. Did you discuss with the interview committee the hardship of moving so soon? Did you think about my needs or feelings when you agreed to accept this job?"

"Van, please understand. Basketball season doesn't wait for anyone. It will start right on schedule. The college needs its coaching staff in place and working with the team long before the opening tip-off. I need time to get it all together."

"Why did they wait so long to hire a new coach?"

"They had a long-time coach until a month ago. He was going to retire after this upcoming season. But doctors diagnosed his wife with cancer. He decided to retire now. They had to set the wheels in motion and hire his successor as soon as possible. When I was over there for the tournament, we had a mutual liking for each other, and they encouraged me to apply."

Vanessa sat back in the lounge chair, grudgingly accepting his explanation. "This is all so sudden, Greg. This is not what I had in mind, the move, that is. The thought of leaving here is hard for me to wrap my head around. I haven't had time to think it all through."

"Vanessa," Greg said, "consider this move as a fresh start. A blessing in disguise. No one's left here for you anymore. I can't believe you're so opposed to moving. And to Hawaii! Paradise!"

It was clear to Vanessa this coaching job enthused Greg. He would not change his mind, no matter how much she objected. "I'm going to bed. It's been an emotional evening. Let's talk more tomorrow."

Greg wrapped his arms around her from behind and kissed her neck. "Yeah, I'm tired from the long plane trip, but not enough to carry you upstairs to *your* bedroom and make mad passionate love to you. Come on." He reached for her hand.

Annoyed over Greg's cavalier dismissal of her feelings, Vanessa was in no mood to accommodate him. "Not tonight." She put distance between them, then jerked as the door slammed on Greg's way out.

Chapter 13

———◆———

The next day Vanessa skipped church. She busied herself pulling clusters of defiant weeds. By noon her T-shirt clung to her skin. Time to quit. She poured herself a glass of ice water and flipped on the oscillating fan sitting by the sliding door. She flopped onto the chaise lounge, satisfied with the progress she managed. As she surveyed the assortment of dahlias and rose bushes her father had cultivated, her thoughts drifted to Greg. She wondered if he'd call or show up today considering his abrupt departure last night.

After dinner, Vanessa dragged out her father's golf equipment from the closet. She remembered she'd promised Greg he could have the items.

"The last of Dad's things," she declared out loud. She picked up his picture, holding it tight against her chest. Her heart ached for her father. She hoped the pain of his death would one day become more bearable. Well-meaning people told her in time it would. Hard to believe.

"May I come in?" Vanessa looked up to see Greg standing in the doorway. He'd shown up. Placing the picture on the dresser, she pointed to the equipment. "You still want it?"

"You bet." He noticed Vanessa's fingers wiping a stream

of tears from her face. He handed her a tissue and pulled her close. She leaned her head against his chest.

"Will I ever stop hurting so much?"

"I can't give you an answer. Remember how much Lyle loved you."

"I will. But I still can't imagine why Dad let me live a lie. I don't understand why he never told me about the adoption."

He wrapped his hand around Vanessa's and led her downstairs to the living room, easing her onto the sofa. "We need to talk." She noted his serious tone as she blew her nose. "Have you thought about the wedding? Started to plan?"

"There are only about twenty guests. Not too much planning to do. Your parents agreed to set up their backyard for the ceremony. It's a perfect setting with all those beautiful flowers and the ornate water fountain. Your mother is also going to make my and Melanie's bouquets."

"Okay. Go on."

"Melanie will order a sheet cake from Costco. Your parents also volunteered to have a barbeque. Fr. Juliano will officiate."

"It's only six days till Saturday. Too late to send invitations. You'll have to call the guests."

Vanessa stood and exhaled a deep breath. "Me? How about you calling too?"

Greg leaped off the couch, wide-eyed. "No way. I'm focused on this job in Hawaii, for my career and our future. If I'm not mistaken, most grooms don't offer any input. Our role is to show up at the appointed time and place."

With an increased pitch in her voice, she spat out. "In this case, you're going to help call. We can split up the list." Gathering a pad of paper and pen, she handed it to Greg. "Make a list of your buddies and give them a buzz."

"If you hadn't spent so much time fooling around on your stupid quest, everything would be done by now."

Avoiding eye contact, Vanessa said, "I guess I've put my search ahead of planning the wedding. But there are a few clues that need research."

Greg ran his fingers through his hair three times in rapid succession. His frosty stare fixated on Vanessa. He sneered rather than spoke. "Drop the search and focus on the wedding!"

Vanessa stared at Greg with hard eyes that didn't blink. Greg pushing her too hard bothered her. Her arms extended upward, and she exhaled a hearty breath. "Let's go to the courthouse instead."

"That's what I wanted. A quick ceremony. I was willing to go along with all this wedding hoopla to please you."

"Maybe you don't even want to get married because you've already tied the knot to your career." She saw his reaction, first in his clenched jaw, then the tension of his muscles.

"Don't give me that crap! *You're* married to your ridiculous search!"

"You damn selfish jackass! If marrying you means moving to Hawaii and stopping my search, I'm not sure I want to be your wife." She knew from the look in his eyes her words struck a raw nerve. She turned, staring at her father's portrait.

Greg parked himself in front of her. "What the hell are you saying?"

Vanessa backed a few steps away. "It should be clear."

"You're dumping me?"

Greg was a sweet, caring man when she met him. She didn't know what had crawled inside him and turned him selfish and self-absorbed. She saw him for the first time in a way that made her realize they weren't a good fit. "You're no longer the man I fell in love with, the man with whom I planned to stay with till one of us graduated to the next life." Vanessa turned her back to him. She felt Greg's hands grip her shoulders, firmer than she thought necessary.

"Don't touch me," she said, moving away.

"If that's the way you feel, I will not beg you to reconsider. Seems we're both in agreement to end our engagement. I'm tired of your obsessive search and your unwillingness to support my career." Then, the final dagger. "I wish you accepted this opportunity as Alicia did. She's glad I got the coaching job and congratulated me."

There was nothing more Vanessa wanted to say. He made his feelings clear.

Greg walked to the door. As he reached for the knob, he paused. "Aren't you forgetting something?" He focused on her left hand.

She slipped the engagement ring off her finger. She flung it with all her strength in his direction. In that instant, their relationship shattered into a million pieces.

Greg leaped to catch the ring as it sailed over his head. "Good grief, Vanessa! It could've fallen into the heat duct." Snatching up the gem, he examined it, then stashed it into his shirt pocket. He shook his head as he fired off one last expression in Vanessa's direction. Irritation? Relief? Regret? Vanessa wasn't sure.

Vanessa moved about the house in a daze. Nausea churned unrestrained in her stomach. She ran to the powder room where she lost what little she ate for dinner. She plopped onto the sofa. The heated exchange haunted her, replaying like an echo. Her head swarmed with half-formed regret for what happened between them. To the life they set out to make together. She didn't know if she was relieved, sad, angry, or a combination. She rested her head on the armrest and closed her eyes, tears streaming down her face.

Vanessa awoke hours later, warmed by the morning sun's rays. Massaging her aching neck, she climbed the stairs to the bathroom. Through narrowed eyes, she peered into the mirror. Bloodshot eyes and swollen eyelids stared back. Disrobing, she stepped into the shower, the warmth of the cascading water soothing her tense muscles.

Refreshed and with a touch of makeup, Vanessa's outlook improved. A sense of relief enveloped her. The breakup freed her to concentrate on her quest without Greg's annoying objection. And she had no desire to uproot and move to Hawaii. A trace of guilt emerged as thoughts of JP swirled in her head. She admitted she wanted his help. She was confident JP would jump at the chance, especially now since Greg was out of the picture. Vanessa fetched JP's business card. She had no idea what she was going to say, but she hoped to speak with him before he left on patrol. "Is Officer Monroe available?"

The receptionist paused for a few seconds. "To everyone's shock, he handed in his resignation yesterday, effective immediately. He did not explain. Said he was relocating."

The words boomed in Vanessa's mind as the phone slipped from her hand. Had she lost JP also?

Part Two

Chapter 14

The losses of Greg and JP added more heartache. Sorrow grew more profound as summer turned into fall, and Vanessa spent each day inside the lonely, gloomy house. She quit communicating with friends. Voice messages went unanswered. If someone knocked on the door, Vanessa didn't bother to answer. She stopped going to her normal haunts because she might encounter someone she knew. She rejected her scholarship and didn't enroll in graduate school. Her only interactions were with strangers when she ordered food and paid the bills so the city didn't turn off the utilities.

The holidays came and went. And as spring arrived, Melanie and Jason intervened. They insisted she seek professional help. Despite Vanessa's objection, they made an appointment with Dr. Norman Adams, psychologist extraordinaire, according to Melanie. "You're going. I'll handcuff and drive you there if need be," Melanie threatened with a mischievous smile.

A WEEK LATER, A RELUCTANT VANESSA DROVE INTO A tree-lined parking lot. She double-checked the address

Melanie had scribbled on a piece of notepaper. The doctor's office was sandwiched between two other businesses, a bakery and a hair salon. The aroma of freshly baked bread invaded her nostrils as she stepped out of the car. Vanessa decided to wander next door after her appointment and treat herself to a calorie-laden cupcake or cookie.

Vanessa inhaled a deep breath and entered the office. A middle-aged receptionist with a pleasant smile looked up from the computer. She welcomed Vanessa and handed her a form to complete. Shortly, the doctor greeted her, and she followed him into his office. Dr. Adams's shoulder-length gray hair, beard, and faded jeans gave her a negative first impression. It didn't take long, however, for Vanessa to develop a warm rapport with him. She liked his cheerful, caring demeanor. She relaxed and opened up to him. After six Friday sessions, the doctor suggested Vanessa involve herself in an activity that appealed to her. She told him she was a teacher and loved working with children. Dr. Adams smiled, uncrossing his legs and leaning toward Vanessa. "I've got a suggestion. My widowed sister runs a foster home. Six kids. I think she'll welcome someone to help tutor them. Interested?"

Vanessa stood and walked over to the window, staring outside at the trees covered with pink blossoms. "May I think about it?"

"Of course."

Vanessa considered Dr. Adams's suggestion all week. To her surprise, she looked forward to this opportunity. At the next session, she told the doctor she'd like to take a stab at the tutoring. "Helping the children might benefit me as well. You've helped me realize it's about time I did something worthwhile instead of moping around my house."

"Luellen and my brother-in-law raised quite a few foster kids through the years. Never had children of their own. When Perry died several years ago, Luellen continued fostering. She's sixty-two now but has the energy of folks half her age. My daughter, Ellie, lives there and is second in command as she emphasizes to everyone."

"Are you sure Mrs....what's her last name?" Vanessa asked.

"Steiner. But I'm sure she'll insist you call her Luellen."

"Are you positive she wants help?"

"I've already cleared everything with her in case you decided to give it a try. And the state okayed the arrangement as well." He jotted down the address and handed the paper to Vanessa. "Can you meet her tomorrow at ten?"

"Let me check my busy schedule," Vanessa chuckled, pretending to leaf through a small calendar notebook. "Yes, I'm free."

So here she was, ready to meet Mrs. Steiner and six children. Vanessa parked curbside in front of the three-story stately Victorian mansion. It reminded her of a dollhouse she had as a child, with the wrap-around porch and white wicker chairs spaced in a perfect row. She stood admiring the house and landscaped yard before advancing along the stone path. Focusing on the decorative eaves, she tripped on one of the six wooden stairs, snagging her pants. "Bummer." She rapped on the door's stained-glass window. Within moments, a young woman greeted her. She had an engaging smile and welcomed Vanessa with a firm handshake.

"I'm Ellie, Mrs. Steiner's niece. You must be Vanessa." She stepped aside and gestured for Vanessa to enter. "You can put your jacket and purse on the credenza. I'll get my aunt."

Vanessa surveyed the sizeable foyer. Six children's photographs hung on the papered walls. A variety of indoor plants rested on top of the wooden bench seat that stretched the entire length of an enormous picture window. Scratches appeared along the oak banister. Vanessa grinned when she noticed a bookcase full of children's books and games. Subtle updates caught her eye, but the original integrity remained intact. A woman with short-cropped hair peppered with streaks of gray appeared. She wiped her flour-covered hands on an apron. "We're making chocolate chip cookies. Baking is a Saturday ritual." She extended her hand. "I'm Mrs. Steiner, but please, call me Luellen."

Mrs. Steiner's friendly handshake warmed Vanessa. "Pleased to meet you." Vanessa followed Mrs. Steiner into the parlor. She sat next to her on the couch covered with plastic to protect the upholstered needlepoint pattern. The older woman's smile was contagious. Vanessa liked her at once. Luellen and Vanessa worked out the details. Mrs. Steiner gave Vanessa a briefing about the four girls and two boys. The soft aroma of the sweet treats teased Vanessa's nostrils.

Mrs. Steiner stood. "Come meet the children."

Vanessa followed Mrs. Steiner into the spacious, updated kitchen. All eyes focused on the stranger.

One girl stepped forward and curtsied. "My name is Nancie. I'm ten and the oldest girl." Vanessa curtsied back.

Lilyrose, about eight Vanessa decided, offered her a still-warm cookie.

Taking a bite, a delightful pleasure flooded Vanessa. The cookie crumbled, and the chips melted inside her mouth. Her taste buds tingled. "Mmmm. My compliments to you bakers."

Wiping a smidgen of chocolate from her lips, a girl with an engaging smile said, "I'm Alana and my birthday is in five days. I'm going to turn seven. I want a Sleeping Beauty cake."

Placing her hand on a boy's right shoulder, Mrs. Steiner said, "This is Kevin. He's eleven." The youngster pushed his thick eyeglasses upward on his freckled nose, then stuck out his hand. Vanessa embraced it.

"I'm delighted to meet all of you," Vanessa said. "I'm looking forward to helping you with your schoolwork."

"Ugh," Kevin groaned.

"Wayne is in another room watching the annual college men's basketball tournament. He's thirteen and a diehard sports fanatic." A hooray drifted into the kitchen.

"His team must have scored," Ellie said.

"Five children. Is there one more?" Vanessa asked.

A young girl peeked out from behind Ellie. Vanessa's heart went out to this youngster with a shy and withdrawn demeanor. She decided to become her special friend. At four years old, Stephanie was the youngest. Abuse at the hands of her parents had scarred her.

DURING THE NEXT FEW MONTHS, VANESSA EMBRACED her new venture, endearing herself to the children. With Mrs. Steiner's approval, Vanessa included Stephanie in many activities away from the home. In late June Vanessa took her to the beach for the child's fifth birthday. It was Stephanie's first time. The youngster removed her shoes and frolicked in the sand. She picked up several broken seashells and stuffed them in her pocket. Running toward the waves, Stephanie asked, "Can I run into the water?"

"Okay, but the water is cold, even in June," Vanessa said. "Wade in only up to your knees. The waves are sometimes strong and a sneaker wave could knock you down." Vanessa took off her sandals and joined her. She took Stephanie's hand, and they ran into the water together.

"It's freezing!" Stephanie shuddered, but then splashed Vanessa. She stopped when she saw Vanessa's "don't you dare" expression.

On the way home, Vanessa glanced at the exhausted sleeping child. The joy displayed by Stephanie touched Vanessa's heart. The abuse her parents had inflicted on Stephanie sickened Vanessa. Drug addicted, they had both overdosed. She had a renewed sense of purpose in helping Stephanie overcome her emotional scars. And now, almost seven months since their initial meeting, it was time to get a Halloween costume.

"That's a colorful drawing, Steph!" Vanessa said, applauding the young girl. "I like the face you drew on the pumpkin."

"You think so, Miss Vanessa?" Stephanie asked.

"Of course," Vanessa assured her. Vanessa taped Stephanie's drawing to the refrigerator where everyone could admire it. Stephanie marched, swinging her arms like a soldier in a parade, proud of herself.

"Don't forget," Vanessa reminded her, "we're going shopping for your Halloween costume. Do you have any idea about what you want to be?"

"Yes. I want to be a teacher like you," she answered. A cheery smile spread across Vanessa's face.

"A teacher for Halloween sounds okay, but what kind of costume would you wear?"

"Hmmm…I don't know," Stephanie answered, pulling on her braids. "Well, how about if I dress up like a princess?"

"Sounds like a plan to me. We'll go to Fred Meyer's right after school tomorrow and hunt for the perfect princess costume. Halloween is a couple of weeks away. There should still be an excellent selection." Vanessa bent to the girl's eye level, patting her nose and kissing Stephanie on the fore-head. "Now, get ready for dinner," she said as she took her coat from the wall hook. Vanessa had grown fond of the children. She hated leaving when the after-school tutoring sessions ended each weekday.

In the evening Vanessa relaxed on the sofa painting her toenails a bright hot pink. She couldn't recall the last time she'd pampered herself. Humming along with her favorite Barry Manilow CD, she jerked at the sound of the doorbell. She peered through the peephole. Melanie and Jason were waiting on the porch. Melanie presented her with a bottle of wine as the couple walked past Vanessa without explanation and headed to the kitchen. Vanessa trailed behind them and stood by as they grabbed three wine glasses and a corkscrew. A curious flush came across Vanessa's face.

"Let's get comfy in the living room," Jason suggested. Sitting next to each other, he and Melanie looked at each other.

Vanessa slipped on her shoes. "What's going on?"

"First, we're glad you're not so depressed," Melanie said. "We've stopped worrying about you."

"Thanks. I am too. But you didn't bring wine over to celebrate my return to the land of the living."

"You're right," Melanie said. "We have two things to tell you. One is very exciting; the other might upset you."

Jason spoke. "We don't know which one to tell you first."

"Tell me the bad one, so I can put it behind me." She hoped her suspicion of the good news was correct.

Jason took a deep breath and wasted no words. "Greg married Alicia."

Surprise registered on Vanessa's face before she could hide it. Her face fell faster than a rock thrown into water. Her lips parted and her eyes opened as far as she could stretch them.

Melanie rushed to Vanessa and took her hands. "I hope we didn't ruin your evening. We figured it was about time you found out. We told Greg he should tell you, but he hasn't bothered."

Vanessa closed her eyes for a moment, processing the news, then smiled at Melanie. "Our relationship went south, beginning with Dad's death. Thinking back, there were subtle signs. I remember Greg comparing our reactions to the coaching job in Hawaii. He told me how supportive your sister was. I haven't talked with Greg since the night I threw the ring at him." She heaved a sigh. "Our breakup pained me as you're both quite aware, but I'm okay now. It was the best decision." She could tell her pragmatic comments relieved Melanie and Jason.

"I was afraid you'd blame me for introducing them," Jason said.

"Don't be apologetic, Jason. Greg and Alicia are a better match than we were. She's behind his career and Greg no doubt revels in her support. They'll be happy," she predicted. "When and where did they marry? And you went to the wedding and didn't tell me?"

Melanie and Jason exchanged glances. "Greg flew in from Hawaii. They had the ceremony at Greg's parents…in the backyard on August twentieth, two months ago."

"Almost exactly the date one year ago Greg and I would have married. And the same place. What a coincidence. Or was it by design?" Vanessa shook her head. "Never mind. It doesn't matter."

"Sorry. We should have mentioned the wedding long before tonight but didn't want to upset you. You sure you're okay?"

Greg's marriage didn't faze her. She'd long since stopped caring or thinking about him. "There are family ties since

Alicia's your sister, so it might be awkward. Since they're in Hawaii for now, it's not an issue. Now, enough about Greg," Vanessa said. "I hope the other news is what I think it is."

Melanie and Jason looked fondly at each other, holding each other's hands. "How would you like to be a godmother?" Jason asked, unable to suppress his huge grin.

"You're having a baby!"

Both nodded.

"What I suspected and hoped!" Vanessa leaped from the chair with genuine joy. They were so much in love. She couldn't envision any news more exciting than this for her two best friends. Embracing them, she squealed, "I'm so happy for you! When's it due?"

"In mid-June. It won't even interfere with the school year," Melanie grinned. "I'll be able to complete the year, barring any unforeseen complications. And I'll have two-and-a-half months at home with the baby before the next school year begins. Perfect. Couldn't have planned everything better if we'd tried."

"When did you find out?"

"The stick turned pink a couple of weeks ago, and the doctor confirmed it yesterday." Melanie smiled. "We're getting used to the idea of being parents, and we couldn't be happier. You're going to be the godmother, right?"

"What a silly question. Of course."

Jason uncorked the wine and filled the wine glasses. They clanked them together. "A toast to the newest Rhodes!" Vanessa said.

Later, Vanessa lay in bed thinking about the exciting news Melanie and Jason had shared. She was overjoyed for them but envied their ideal relationship. She longed to be as happy as they were. And when JP's image invaded her mind, she closed her eyes. Tears trickled down her cheeks and dampened the pillowcase.

⸺◆⸺

"THIS COSTUME IS PERFECT FOR YOU, STEPH," VANESSA said. "You made a splendid choice. You'll make a lovely princess."

"Think so?" She held the silky pink dress with sparkles adorning the top against her body, admiring it.

"Without a doubt, sweetheart." Vanessa bent down to hug her. "Now, do you need any help with reading or anything else before I leave?"

"Nah. I'm done. Besides, today is Friday. I don't want to think about school for two whole days."

"You don't fool me," Vanessa laughed. "You love kindergarten. Admit it."

"Yeah, I do. What time will you be here tomorrow?"

Two years after her parents' deaths, Stephanie still experienced abandonment issues. Vanessa avoided situations that might trigger those feelings. But for this one time, she decided to forgo their usual Saturday excursion. She wanted to take a solo hike in the forest to seek added solace and reflect on the direction of her life.

"Steph," she said, placing the girl's hands in her own. "I won't be coming tomorrow. I've got to do something by myself."

Stephanie's frown bothered Vanessa. "Chipper up. I'll be here on Sunday morning right after church, and we'll go somewhere."

"Promise?"

"Of course!" They high-fived. "Think of something fun, and we'll do it." Vanessa hugged Stephanie again. She opened the bedroom door, turned around, and blew her a kiss. "See you Sunday."

"Bye, Vanessa," Nancie and Alana said as they ran up the stairs. Kevin chased them to get the comic book they'd "borrowed" from him.

Ah…the shenanigans of the six foster kids. She cherished every moment spent with them, especially Stephanie.

EARLY SATURDAY AFTERNOON VANESSA DROVE TO A favorite hiking spot mid-point between Milwaukie and the coast. She and her father came here when she was a child. They spent the day walking on and off the trail, admiring the various flora and fauna. The sight of a small squirrel scampering across their paths or climbing a tree had thrilled Vanessa. She would chase after the small creatures, but never captured one. Her father took immense pleasure in her delight and determination.

Vanessa zipped the fleeced-lined jacket and put on her wool hat. Inhaling the fresh air and the fragrance of the old-growth fir trees blocking the sky, she began hiking at a semi-rapid pace. She smiled as the pleasant memories spent with her father floated through her mind, yet she mourned. *Why did he die? And why had Greg been so unwilling to support my search for my biological parents?* But most inexplicable was the abrupt departure of JP. He hadn't contacted her since he'd taken off fourteen months earlier. She assumed he wasn't aware she hadn't married Greg or he would have contacted her. *Wouldn't he? After all, he said he fell in love with me.*

Absorbed in her thoughts, Vanessa stepped too close to the edge of the trail. The October rains had saturated the ground. It gave way. A panicked scream rang through the air as she tumbled down the steep slope. She extended her arms, attempting to grasp anything that would halt her rapid downward spiral. Mercifully, the descent ended. Lying on her back, Vanessa felt the dampness seeping through her jacket as her battered body trembled. She tried to steady her breathing as she assessed the situation. Not good, but "I'm alive!" Her relief drained as she realized a dislodged moss-covered log pinned her left foot. She struggled to lift herself and shove it off her foot. It wouldn't budge. Trapped!

Her mind screamed out as the pain deep within her foot throbbed and burned as if on fire. She was alone, with no hope of immediate rescue. No one knew her whereabouts. Hopelessness and self-pity gripped her. She almost wished she would close her eyes and never wake up. *What do I have to live for? There's no one for me except Stephanie. Oh my God!* The thought of the young girl who had given her life purpose these past seven months forced her to emerge from her pity party. With this motivation, Vanessa considered her options. There were none. She'd left her cell phone locked inside the car. And even if she removed the log, could she walk?

Darkness would arrive within the hour. If no one found her by then, she figured she wouldn't survive a chilly night in this Oregon forest.

With renewed determination, Vanessa tried again to move the stubborn log. It continued to hold her captive. Refusing to succumb to her increasing panic, she sporadically yelled, "Help! Help!" Her cries drifted through the eerie silence, heard by no one other than chirping birds and other small—or large?—creatures.

As dusk arrived, Vanessa knew her chances of rescue diminished. "Dear God," she prayed out loud, "if I don't survive, please bless Stephanie with someone who will love her as much as I do. I can't bear the thought of another abandonment for her. Please..."

A barking sound echoed in the distance. She tried to lift her head and scream, but her battered body went limp. Her eyesight blurred. Feeling in her body drained away until all was black.

Chapter 15

"Wagner is barking and wagging his tail," burly Jared Devlin said. "He's found something." It couldn't be a deer. The dog's barking would have scared one away. Jared followed the black Labrador, rifle cocked and ready just in case. He had difficulty keeping pace. He focused on the dog so he didn't lose sight of him in the semi-darkness. Wagner made a quick left turn and disappeared down a slope. Jared stopped to catch his breath before proceeding down the slippery incline. A football field length below, Jared saw Wagner pacing back and forth, his barking loud and urgent.

Looking through his binoculars, Jared's hunting partner, Zach, yelled from above. "Whatever it is, it's not moving. And it doesn't look like an animal. See what's there. Be careful." He headed downward, his leather boots tromping the crunchy leaves and mud caking the crevices in his soles.

Jared inched closer toward the object. He crouched down and set the rifle on the damp ground.

"What is it?" Zach asked as he reached Jared.

"A woman! She's…she's dead!"

Zach pushed Jared aside. "What the hell?" He leaned down, placing two fingers on the woman's neck. He detected a weak pulse. "She's alive! Let's move the log off her."

The men mustered all the strength they had but couldn't budge it. "We can't give up!" Zach said. "Try again." Their neck veins bulged and grunts flooded the air. With a rush of adrenaline, they succeeded to shift the log enough to free the foot. A collective gasp spewed from their mouths when they saw a mutilated foot hanging out of a ripped tennis shoe. Zach's insides curdled like sour milk. Jared gagged as he turned away from the unfortunate victim.

Jared recovered first. "Dare we move her in case she has more injuries? Zach, call 911 on your cell phone."

"No signal. Hope I can get one if I climb back up." Zach's boot soles caked with mud hindered his ascent, but he reached the top, his breath panting. He got through to 911, but static made it difficult to communicate. He shouted into the phone.

"Emergency and location," a garbled voice said.

His booming voice would have awakened the dead. "Name's Zach Tomlinson. We found an unconscious woman with a crushed foot!" Zach kept rotating his position, trying for a clearer connection. "I'm off Highway 26 about a half-mile west of Red's Country Store. On a gravel road."

Zach heard the dispatcher's rapid typing. "Leave your cell on."

Help should arrive soon he reassured himself. He yelled to Jared. "I'm worried the paramedics might miss the turn-off. I'm taking your pickup to the entrance."

"Good idea." Jared pulled off his heavy jacket and covered the woman.

Zach scraped the excess mud from his soles with a twig and raced toward the truck parked several hundred yards further into the forest. He located the keys hidden under the frame. Gravel and dirt sailed into the air as Zach maneuvered the rig on the narrow road and sped toward the highway. He positioned the pickup facing the opposite direction for a speedy entrance back into the woods. The ambulance arrival couldn't be over ten minutes, fifteen tops. He shouted into his cell phone. "I'm waiting at the turnoff to flag the paramedics. Tell them I'm wearing a camouflage jacket and matching cap."

Zach picked up handfuls of gravel and bombarded several small fir trees. Finally, sirens blared in the distance. He ran onto the highway, waving his arms.

"Follow me," Zach said. When they reached the site, both vehicles skidded to a halt. Zach half ran, half slid downhill.

The two paramedics, Dan and Clem, grabbed a stretcher and their medical equipment. They took a deep breath before proceeding downward.

Jared pointed to the injured foot.

A skilled medic, the injury was one of the worst Dan had ever encountered. Turning his head, he faked a cough. He feared gangrene would develop and cut off the flow of blood. He injected the victim with an antibiotic, then stabilized the foot. After determining there were no other injuries, he and Clem placed the woman on the stretcher.

"Is she going to survive?" Jared asked, stroking his beard and reaching for his jacket.

"Don't know," Dan answered. Standing up, he brushed the mud off his knees, then discarded the latex gloves into a plastic bag. "We'll need your help to haul this stretcher up to the ambulance." Slowed by the saturated terrain, the four men struggled to keep their footing.

"Too bad I'm not in better shape," Dan mumbled. "Better cut down on my wife's chocolate chip cookies and the potato chips."

Wagner reached the road with ease and paced, barking the entire time. Huffing and puffing, the men reached the top. After placing Vanessa inside the ambulance, Dan placed a call to St. Vincent's. Before leaving, he asked Jared and Zach if they could identify the young woman.

"No," Jared answered. "My dog found her about forty-five minutes ago. We thought she was dead. Assuming she drove here, we'll try to find her car."

Clem was already rummaging through Vanessa's pockets. Nothing. "If she had a key, it probably fell out, she left it hidden outside her car, or…foul play."

"In case you find anything, we're taking her to St. Vincent's." The paramedics lost precious minutes maneuvering the ambulance. The sirens pierced the spooky silence.

"This is the only way accessible to vehicles in this part of the forest," Jared stated. "The car has to be close by. Unless…"

"I'll head down the road toward the highway on foot with Wagner," Zach said. "You drive the truck and go to where the road ends, about a mile or so. Pick us up on the way back."

Jared saluted his buddy. "Gotcha." He jumped inside the pickup and turned the headlights on high beam. He scanned the roadside for any sign of a car or tire tracks. Reaching the road's end with no success, he maneuvered the truck to turn around. The ditch created by the spinning tires prevented traction. "Shit!" He put the rig in reverse, backed up several feet, then switched to drive and floored the accelerator. "Whew!" he exhaled as the pickup zoomed over the damp, muddy ground. A minute later, the headlights shined on Zach and Wagner.

As Jared approached them, Wagner began sprinting back and forth, his barking non-stop.

Jared braked and popped his head out the window. "He's on to something!"

Wagner disappeared behind a group of tall Oregon grape bushes. "No," said Zach. "He's doing his business." The men caught up with the Labrador. He stood on his hind legs, leaning against a dark green four-door Toyota.

Both men circled the car. "This has got to be the woman's," Jared said.

"How the hell did we miss it before?" Zach asked, scratching his head. "Let's see if we can find any info." He checked for an unlocked door.

Jared ran back to the pickup and grabbed a flashlight. Zach peered into all the windows, looking for something belonging to a female. Nothing. It was showroom spic and span.

Zach scrutinized again. "This car is too clean, don't you think?"

Jared nodded and retreated a couple of steps. "Touch nothing."

"Why? I was going to try to—"

"Stop! Someone may have left the woman out here to die." He grabbed Zach's sleeve. "What if someone wiped it clean on purpose? Now our fingerprints are the only ones there."

"Didn't think about that," Zach said. "Let's write the license plate and call the cops when we turn onto the highway. They can identify the registered owner. I can't imagine what it would be like for our families if our whereabouts were unknown." Zach pictured his wife sick with worry trying to calm his nine-year-old twin sons. "Got anything in the pickup to write the plate number?"

Jared returned with a pencil and a crumpled napkin.

Wagner jumped up and down, as though expecting praise for his discovery. Jared wrapped his arms around

Wagner's neck and rubbed their heads together. "Finding the woman and the car. He's the real hunter!"

"You got that right," Zach agreed, petting Wagner. "Now, let's head out so we can call in the plate number."

"I'd like to drop by the hospital," Jared said.

"Yeah, me too."

Panting from the long run from the parking lot, Zach leaned on the reception counter. "How is the woman?"

"Who?"

Jared pushed Zach aside. "An ambulance brought an unconscious woman here about an hour ago. Name unknown. Is she okay?"

The woman pushed her hair behind her ears, then pressed a few keys on the computer. "The doctors are assessing the extent of the patient's injuries. It may take quite a while."

"We'll wait," Jared said. For a Saturday evening, the emergency room waiting area was more crowded than usual. He and Zach found seats on opposite sides of the room. Jared rested his elbows on his knees, bowing his head. Though not a religious person, he prayed for the young woman. Zach helped himself to a complimentary cup of coffee.

After almost two hours, a nurse leaned toward a dozing Zach, tapping his shoulder. Zach jerked awake. He squinted, focusing on the wall clock. After midnight. Only he, Jared, and a middle-aged couple remained in the waiting area. Zach rubbed his tense neck muscles. "Do you have any info about the lady yet?"

"Doctor Borene will talk with you."

Zach looked across the room. Soft snores drifted from Jared's throat. Zach sauntered to his buddy and gently nudged his leg with his boot. "Wake up, Sleeping Beauty."

Jared's eyelids flickered. He yawned and stretched.

"Come this way." The nurse pushed a button and double doors swung open. She led them to a small private office. A gray-haired man wearing army green scrubs greeted them.

"I'm Dr. Borene. Are you the patient's relatives?"

"No," answered Jared. "We're the guys who found her, or at least my dog did. We called for the ambulance. How is she?"

"She's alive."

"We phoned the license plate number to the sheriff's office and told them the medics were taking her to this hospital. Is she identified yet?"

"They confirmed her identity. Thank goodness you called in the plate number. Now I'm hoping the police can notify her relatives."

"Do you think she'll recover?" Zach asked.

"I can't discuss or divulge any information." The doctor cited the federal HIPAA rule. "We'll do our best."

"Let's head home," Zach said, tapping his buddy's shoulder. "I'm not in the mood for hunting anymore this weekend."

"Me neither," Jared said. "Wagner's been cooped up inside the truck long enough." He pulled his crumpled orange OSU baseball cap from under his jacket. "It will surprise our wives to see us home earlier than planned. And empty-handed. But wait till we tell them what we found." He asked Dr. Borene what would happen if the hospital could not locate the woman's relatives.

"We administer treatment to the patient whatever the circumstance," the doctor answered. "It's fortunate you fellas happened along and found her. I'm certain she wouldn't have survived. When notified, I'm sure her family will want to thank you. Leave your names and phone numbers at the front desk."

"We don't need any thanks," Zach said. "But I'll give mine in case the cops need us for anything else."

"You guys are number one folks," Dr. Borene praised them.

Zach noted the expression on the doctor's face. "I can tell he's worried."

"Yeah, me too," Jared said.

Chapter 16

D r. Tom Jacobs wore a grim expression as he addressed his colleague. "The foot is crushed and the tissues are dead. And gangrene has developed. The x-rays and culture confirm clostridia infection. This is critical. There's no option but amputation to save her life."

Dr. Borene touched his gray mustache and examined the wound again. In his thirty-plus years of medicine, this was one of the worst injuries he had ever faced. The log fractured all five phalanges and metatarsals beyond repair. The area was swollen, the skin shriveled and blackish green. Secretions discharging from sizeable blisters gave off a pungent odor. The foot was dead.

"I concur, Tom," the doctor said. "This could be fatal within forty-eight hours. We need to operate, but it's after midnight on a weekend. Is adequate staff available?"

"Bad time for such a surgery, but we're prepared for emergencies and this qualifies. I'll alert the personnel, and we'll set up for the operation."

It troubled Dr. Borene no one had located the patient's relatives. He hesitated to amputate without their knowledge or input. But he was a doctor, not a detective, and his first concern was treating his patient.

An orderly arrived to transport Vanessa to the operating room. As he wheeled the gurney, he greeted the nurse sitting behind the counter at the nurse's station. "Hi, Diane. Just got on duty?"

"About an hour ago. Hope it's a slow night."

"Pretty busy earlier, but it's slowed down. The usual except for this poor lady. The docs are going to amputate her foot. What a shame."

Diane glanced at the patient. "She's young."

"Yeah. Mid-twenties I'm guessing."

"Any relatives here?"

"Not that I know of. I don't think they've located any yet. We admitted her as a Jane Doe. Had no ID on her. The cops gave us a tentative name and address. It should be on her chart."

"Is the name on her ID bracelet?"

The orderly lifted the woman's wrist. "Yeah, Vanessa Cox. Gotta go. Can't keep the surgeon waiting."

Diane tightened the band around her ponytail, then pulled the chart from the slot. She confirmed another nurse recorded the name. A few steps away, she stopped. *Vanessa Cox.* The name evoked a sense of familiarity. *Could it be?* She ran from behind the counter and caught up with the orderly. Diane stared at the patient. Her heart sank. It *was* Miss Cox, her son's fifth-grade teacher two years ago!

Diane checked the progress of the operation. When Dr. Borene emerged several hours later, she wiped her clammy hands on her uniform pants. She inhaled a deep breath. "How is she?"

"I'm optimistic she'll recover. I'm concerned about what her emotional state will be when she finds out we amputated her foot." He couldn't suppress a yawn. "Have any relatives shown up?"

"No." Diane sat, resting her chin on her palms.

"Too bad. I was hoping the police located her family by now."

"Miss Cox was my son's fifth-grade teacher."

Dr. Borene leaned over the counter, his exhausted body perking up. "Can you tell me anything about her family?"

"Her father died over a year ago. I'm not aware of any relatives. I believe she lives alone." Diane rubbed a tear from her face. "She's a wonderful teacher. My son adored her. Such a rotten shame."

"If you're right, that explains why no one answered at the address the police went to." He proceeded to recovery. "I'm going to check on her before heading home." Another audible yawn escaped.

MRS. STEINER FINISHED BRAIDING STEPHANIE'S HAIR. "Why didn't Vanessa come yesterday? She promised."

Mrs. Steiner couldn't answer the question. She didn't tell the child she'd called both Vanessa's home and cell phones many times, leaving messages. "I'm sure there's a valid reason she didn't show up. She always looks forward to being with you. We'll call her this afternoon after you're home from kindergarten."

Mrs. Steiner couldn't help noticing Stephanie's tired eyes.

"I know Vanessa wouldn't forget me!" declared Stephanie. "She loves me."

"Of course, she does. Never think otherwise. Something happened to prevent her from coming yesterday."

"Where could she be?"

"No idea." Mrs. Steiner took Stephanie's hand and led her toward the eight-seat table. "You need to eat breakfast." She pulled out a chair and gestured for Stephanie to join the other five children. "Ellie, make sure Stephanie eats. The school bus will be here in half an hour."

Ellie pushed her loose eyeglasses up her nose and nodded. She put a bowl of Rice Krispies and a piece of toast in front of Stephanie. The girl took a bite, then put the toast on the plate and pushed it and the cereal away.

"I'll eat it," Wayne said, reaching for the food.

"No, you won't." Ellie's forbidding expression meant business.

Mrs. Steiner phoned Vanessa for the umpteenth time. After twelve rings, she put down the phone, tapping her fingers on the desk. Pacing back and forth, she convinced herself she had no choice. She bit her lip and dialed the non-emergency line.

"Milwaukie Police Department," a voice said. "How may I assist you?"

Mrs. Steiner identified herself. "I want to report a missing person," she said.

"Let me connect you with Sgt. Christensen."

"Mrs. Steiner, is it?" the sergeant asked her. "What can I do for you?" He leaned back in his chair, tapping a pencil on a yellow notepad. When Mrs. Steiner explained the reason for her call, he jerked up. He was all ears. Could this be the woman the hospital had contacted the PD about?

"Are you a relative?"

"No. She's a volunteer at my foster home. Vanessa is very reliable. She didn't show up yesterday and no word today." She wiped her moist hands against her apron. "Something's wrong."

"Does she drive a green Toyota?"

"Yes."

"What else can you tell me about Miss Cox?"

"She's a teacher, single, twenty-five. No relatives except an aunt." Mrs. Steiner seated herself onto the padded desk chair.

Sgt. Christensen scribbled the information.

"Do you know where she is? Has something happened to her?"

"There was an unidentified woman brought to St. Vincent's Hospital Saturday night. Victim of an accident. Through the license plate, we identified her. We've been trying to locate her family since then, but no luck."

Mrs. Steiner's voice raised an octave. "What happened? Is she okay?" Her heartbeat raced as she stood erect. Choking back tears, she asked, "What's wrong with her?"

"I can't disclose any information."

Mrs. Steiner cried out. "I've got to go to her! What hospital did you say?"

"St. Vincent's. Thank you for—"

Luellen disconnected and eased herself into her chair, attempting to gather her composure. *At least I now know why Vanessa didn't show up yesterday.*

Ellie entered the room, eyebrows drawn together. "Aunt Luellen, Stephanie won't eat anything. What do you suggest?" Ellie noticed her aunt's worried expression. "What is it?"

"Vanessa's at St. Vincent's. She was in an accident." She spat out the words as her eyes glared at the potted plants lining the windowsill.

Ellie grabbed the corner of the desk to steady herself. "What happened? Is it serious?"

Mrs. Steiner blinked and focused on her niece. "The

sergeant wouldn't tell me her condition." She stood. "I'm going to the hospital. She should have someone with her."

"What about Stephanie?"

"We'll have to explain Vanessa's in the hospital, but not now. We need to know more info before we say anything." Mrs. Steiner flipped through the yellow pages for the hospital's phone number. "I'm calling about Vanessa Cox. Can you tell me her condition? Is she alive? Is she stable? Critical? Can she have visitors?"

"Unless you're a relative, I cannot give you any information."

"Why not?"

"The HIPAA rules don't allow us to divulge anything about a patient except to relatives."

"Vanessa has no relatives. You mean no one can find out what's wrong? This is crazy."

"I'm sorry." The receptionist sounded sympathetic. "I'll connect with you Dr. Borene's nurse."

Mrs. Steiner sighed. "Okay. Patch me through."

Ellie's eager eyes questioned her aunt the moment Mrs. Steiner hung up.

"Ellie, the doctor's nurse said I could come this afternoon and meet with the doctor. I can't find out her condition until then."

"Crazy law."

"It's going to be hard concentrating on anything."

"Poor Stephanie. Functioning at school today is going to be hard."

"Let's be upbeat and tell her we'll try to find out what happened by the time she gets home." She clasped her hands together. "Pray it's nothing serious."

"Stephanie's going to ask questions and refuse to go to school."

"You're right, but we can't let her know she's in the hospital yet. She'll insist on going there. The other children will no doubt worry too."

After Stephanie arrived home from school, Mrs. Steiner told her about Vanessa. The youngster grabbed Mrs. Steiner's hand, pulling her toward the door. "Let's go right now to the hospital." The other children chimed in, begging to go as well.

"I'm sure the hospital won't allow a bunch of kids. For now, I'll take Stephanie." Whining ensued. Mrs. Steiner's stern expression silenced the group.

Before Mrs. Steiner turned off the motor, Stephanie left the car and ran ahead to the entrance. She stood on her tiptoes in front of the reception counter. "Where is she?"

The lady's lips, covered with a deep red lipstick, smiled. "Who are you here to visit?"

"Vanessa!"

Mrs. Steiner arrived and explained the situation.

The receptionist checked the computer. "The patient's still in the ICU. I have to get authorization for visitors. I'll page Dr. Borene."

Stephanie's mouth tightened into a stubborn line. "I want to see her now!" Mrs. Steiner pointed to a corner filled with children's toys. "Let's wait over here, young lady."

Almost an hour later, the doctor appeared and introduced himself. "I'm Dr. Borene."

"What took you so long?" Stephanie stood mere inches from him.

Dr. Borene bent and shook the girl's hand. "I was with a patient."

"Vanessa?"

"No."

Mrs. Steiner approached the doctor. "What happened? How is she?"

"What is your relationship with Miss Cox?"

"She's a volunteer at my foster home. She's been especially close to this young lady. When she didn't show up for her scheduled outing on Sunday, we got worried. I called the police and found out she was here." Mrs. Steiner rubbed her cheek where a tear escaped. "We're her family. She has no relatives except an aunt. Whereabouts unknown." She pleaded. "Can you tell us anything? We need reassurance, or at least the opportunity to help."

Stephanie opened her mouth to speak. Mrs. Steiner clamped her fingers around the girl's arm to keep her quiet.

Doctor Borene's gaze moved from Mrs. Steiner to Stephanie, then sighed. "I can tell you she's in terrible shape. She has a severe foot infection."

"Does she need a blood donation?"

The doctor smiled. "We always need donations."

"Can't I take a peek?" Stephanie asked in a low voice. Mrs. Steiner looked down at her and released her tight grip.

Dr. Borene caved. "How about I walk you to the ICU and you can look through the window? But only for a few minutes. You can't talk to her. She's asleep."

The two followed him down the stark hallway, past several rooms with open doors. Stephanie waved at the patients.

Stephanie stood on a step stool and gazed through the ICU window at Vanessa. Her jaw dropped. "She looks awful."

Mrs. Steiner covered her face. "Please tell me what's wrong."

The doctor pulled Mrs. Steiner aside. "We haven't told Miss Cox about her injuries. She's been unconscious or sedated since her arrival. Once she knows, she can tell you."

"Sounds serious."

Doctor Borene nodded.

"The past year has been horrible for Vanessa," Mrs. Steiner said, shaking her head. "I pray the injury won't set her back. Thank God for Stephanie. They'll help each other." She sighed. "How long will she be here?"

"It's hard to tell, but a lot depends on her progress. I predict about a week or two."

"Is it all right if we visit?"

"I prefer you wait until she's out of ICU. I want her to know about the injury before visitors come. She'll need time to come to terms with it."

"I don't like the sound of what you're saying," Mrs. Steiner said. "It's something terrible, isn't it?" Dr. Borene's silence validated her fear. "Stephanie will want to see her even if it's through the glass. We'll come again tomorrow."

The doctor knelt at eye level with Stephanie. "I'll bet a cheery card from you will put a smile on Miss Cox's face."

"I'll draw a picture of me wearing my princess costume." Stephanie's face lit up.

"Thank you, doctor. The children will be eager to make cards for Vanessa. I like your suggestion. I'll bring the cards with me."

By Tuesday Vanessa was out of the ICU and in a private room. She had drifted in and out of consciousness many times since the operation. She had a fuzzy awareness of someone attending to her left foot. Her eyes flickered open. She lay still while her eyes became accustomed to the dim room. She raised her head a few inches and took in her surroundings. A nurse hummed as she adjusted an

IV. The nauseating scent of antiseptic caused a sour taste to rise in Vanessa's throat. A vase filled with pink carnations sat beside the bed.

"Who are you? Where am I?"

"I'm nurse Loretta." Her warm smile calmed Vanessa. "I'll be your private nurse, at your beck and call," she said, bowing. "I'll try to carry out your every desire. Well, maybe not, but I like to keep my patients happy and comfortable. Dr. Borene will be here soon." Vanessa stared at the prominent purple streak among the strands of the nurse's brown hair.

Vanessa tried to raise herself but realized it was futile. She bit her lips to keep from crying out when a sharp pain stabbed her left leg. Then she recalled the painful experience. She pinched herself to ensure she had survived the ordeal in the forest.

"Hello, Miss Cox. I'm Dr. Borene. I'm glad to chat with you." He shook her hand, then placed a stool beside the bed. "You've been a guest here since Saturday night."

"Guest? Not funny," Vanessa said. "The last thing I remember is the terrible pain in my left foot and thinking about Stephanie." Vanessa tried sitting up, but her weakened body wouldn't cooperate. "I've got to see her! I promised her I would take her out on Sunday. I've got to explain."

"Not to worry," Dr. Borene said. "Stephanie is okay. She and her foster mother came several times." He pointed to a bedside shelf. "They brought these handmade cards the children made for you. And the flowers."

"What day is it?"

"Tuesday."

"Tuesday! You mean I've been here since Saturday night?" It took her a few moments to digest the news before she reached for the bedside phone. "I must call Stephanie." Her head spun. "Yeow. What is wrong with me? I'll bet it's my foot. I remember excruciating pain there."

"Do you recall anything about your accident? The police stopped by to question you."

The image of herself plunging down the slope and the subsequent ordeal invaded her mind. She didn't want to think or talk about it. She closed her eyes. Within minutes, she drifted to sleep.

Several hours later, Vanessa awoke. The rare autumn afternoon sun rays shined through the window shades. She squinted and pressed the nurse call button.

"Good afternoon, Miss Sleepy Head. What can I do for you?" nurse Loretta asked with a pleasant smile as she puffed Vanessa's pillow.

"Please close the shades. The sun's shining in my face. Thanks. Is Dr. Borene able to come and tell me about my injuries, and when I can leave this joint?"

"I'll check."

Fifteen minutes later Dr. Borene arrived accompanied by a police officer.

Vanessa's lips pressed together, and her eyes narrowed.

"He's here to ask you a few questions about your accident. It won't take long. Right, officer?"

The police officer took the hint.

"Why are you questioning me?"

"To make sure there was no foul play."

"Trust me, it was my stupidity." She quizzed the cop about her rescue. "Who found me and when?"

"You can thank a dog for finding you."

"A dog?"

"Yep. His owner and a friend were hunting in the area and the dog no doubt picked up your scent. He led them to you." Satisfied the incident was an accident, he thanked Vanessa and turned to leave.

"You're from Milwaukie PD?"

"Yes."

Vanessa wondered if he knew JP. "Did you work with…? Never mind." *JP doesn't care* her mind taunted her.

Dr. Borene raised the back of the hospital bed and moved a stool close to Vanessa. It was time to reveal the harsh reality of her injury. The expression on the doctor's face worried Vanessa. An uneasy sensation rippled throughout her body. Dread glared from her eyes.

Chapter 17

———◆———

"You're going to tell me something terrible, aren't you?" Vanessa asked.

Dr. Borene hated telling a patient bad news. Taking a deep breath, he stared into her eyes, mincing no words. "We had to amputate your left foot."

"What the hell?" Vanessa yelled, lifting her head.

"The damage was so severe we couldn't save it. Gangrene developed by the time you arrived here. To save your life, we had no choice. I'm sorry."

Vanessa tossed the blanket aside. Her eyes froze over like the surface of a small pond. She saw her left leg was shorter, the end wrapped in a sterile dressing. And where her foot should be…nothing. Outside the room, her piercing scream boomed throughout the second floor.

Two nurses rushed in. Dr. Borene put two fingers over his lips, signaling them not to intervene. He allowed Vanessa to vent. When he started to explain, she placed her hands over her ears, swaying side to side. Her insides were in turmoil. A mess. The emotional agony was now visible on her face. She covered it with her hands, repeating the doctor's words through her mind, trying to make sense of them. "This can't be! How could you do this to me? No one even asked. You had no right! I hate you!"

"I understand how upsetting this news is. You were unconscious and your injury was life-threatening. We had no other choice." He forged on, trying to give her hope. "Dr. Hutchinson, a doctor on staff who is tops in his field, can fit you with a prosthesis. With physical therapy and a lot of hard work, you'll be able to adjust and live a normal life."

Losing her foot was another blow. It wasn't fair. She had a right to be angry. She hadn't asked for this. It arrived like a plague she never wanted. Burning rage flowed through her body like a deadly poison. She needed to blame someone. Anyone. Her first target was Dr. Borene. She punched his arms, the only part of his body she could reach. Her upper torso rocked back and forth and the tears cascaded full force, drenching her face.

Nurse Loretta offered her a tissue. Vanessa grabbed it and ripped it into a million pieces.

"Leave me alone! Get out! All of you!" She rubbed her runny nose with the back of her hand. She flopped her head onto the pillow, facing the wall, her body shaking.

Dr. Borene administered a sedative into her IV. Within minutes, she calmed and conked out.

Several hours later, Vanessa awoke to a semi-dark room. She lifted her head, blinking. The clock's hands pointed to five twenty-five. She yawned and stretched her legs. Something felt different. Then she remembered. She sat up and peeked under the blanket. The sight of the elevated, bandaged leg both terrified and saddened her. Self-pity engulfed her. *I've lost everything. Dad, Greg, even JP. And now a part of my body. Why? Why? Why?*

"Miss Cox?" Dr. Borene's familiar voice startled her.

"Go away."

"We need to talk."

"Forget it." She pulled the blanket over her face.

"I know you've suffered quite a shock, but everything will be better in time. Trust me."

"Why should I?"

"I'm here to help you and answer all your questions but I'll come back tomorrow."

As he stepped into the hallway, Stephanie greeted him. "I'm here to visit Vanessa."

"Hi, young lady." He acknowledged Mrs. Steiner. "I don't think Miss Cox is up to visitors."

"She'll want to see me," Stephanie said. "I brought her a pumpkin cookie from us kids."

"Two visitors are waiting in the hall," Dr. Borene told Vanessa.

Vanessa removed the blanket from her face. "Tell whoever it is not now."

"A young girl named Stephanie brought you a treat."

"I don't want anyone to come in here." She turned her head, staring at the window.

"But—"

"Did you hear me? No one!"

The doctor bent eye level with the child. "Sorry, she can't see anyone right now," he fibbed.

"She'll see me." Stephanie stepped toward the room. Mrs. Steiner took her hand, holding her back. The tears and wailing came with the force of a thundering waterfall.

Vanessa lifted her head, listening to the sound of Stephanie's outburst. She raised herself halfway and rested on her elbows. She could hear Mrs. Steiner trying to console the child. *What was I thinking?* "Stephanie!" she called out.

In a flash, the youngster bolted to the side of the bed. She climbed up and pressed her upper body against Vanessa's chest. The pumpkin cookie crumbled.

Vanessa wasted no time. "They amputated my left foot."

Mrs. Steiner stifled a gasp. She offered as much comfort as she could without breaking down. "You will beat this, dear. I insist you stay with us while you recuperate. You'll have lots of company."

"Yay!" Stephanie loved the idea. "But what does amp… amputate mean?"

"The doctor cut off my left foot."

"Why?"

"I hurt it too bad."

Stephanie peeked under the blanket. "What a big bandage! Where did they put your foot?"

"Hmmm. I don't know."

"I'll take care of you. Nancie and the other girls too, but not Kevin and Wayne." Stephanie yapped on and on about Halloween and the picture book she was reading until Mrs. Steiner told her time to go home. A smile surfaced as Vanessa waved goodbye, her mood improved. She summoned a nurse. "Is Dr. Borene still here?"

"He's finishing up a report before he heads home. Do you want to talk to him?"

"Yes."

Dr. Borene arrived, exhaustion etched on his face, yet willing to speak with Vanessa.

Vanessa mumbled an apology for her outbursts. "I don't hate you. Finding out about my foot was a shock. I lashed out."

"Understandable."

Vanessa wanted to know every detail. She bombarded the doctor with questions. "How much did you amputate?

What does my leg look like where you cut it? Will I have to use a wheelchair or crutches? What—"

"Whoa. Slow down," the doctor interjected.

Dr. Borene answered Vanessa's questions till she couldn't think of any more.

"My leg is now called a stump? Sounds terrible." She shook her head. "When will I be able to walk?"

"As soon as the site of the amputation heals, we can fit you with the prosthesis. That should be about six weeks. In the meantime, you'll use crutches and/or a wheelchair. Nurse Loretta will bring you some literature about the prosthesis process tomorrow."

"I'm aching at this moment where my foot was. It feels like a burning, twisting sensation, with throbbing pain. How come?"

"You're experiencing phantom pain. It may last several months or years but normally disappears without treatment. It's not harmful. The intensity will vary. You can determine how much pain you can tolerate and take medication as needed."

"Dr. Borene, I'm wondering. What do you do with amputated limbs?"

"We send them to a biohazard crematorium where they're destroyed. Or we may donate them to a medical college to use in dissection or anatomy classes."

"What if the patient wants to keep the limb?"

"On those rare occasions the patient wants it for religious or personal reasons we provide it to them."

"Ugh. Not for me," Vanessa said, crinkling her face.

A medical assistant delivered the evening meal. Dr. Borene shoved the stool aside and patted Vanessa's shoulder. "I'll check on you tomorrow."

"Doctor, one last thing." She lowered her head. "How do I use the bathroom?"

"Buzz for help. You need to be mobile soon to prevent blood clots. You'll have to keep wearing the cuffs wrapped around your legs."

Blood clot. The cause of her father's death. Her heart twisted and her breathing came in sharp pants. She tried to maintain control. *Inhale, count to ten, exhale.* The unease ebbed away.

"What's wrong?" Dr. Borene asked.

"My father died from a blood clot. Recalling the day overtook me. Don't want the same thing to happen to me."

"Keep on the cuffs, and you should be fine." He turned to leave, pointing to the food. 'Eat."

Vanessa forced herself to consume a sufficient helping of the chicken noodle soup and applesauce. She sipped the tea to wash down a few bites from the stale roll, then pushed the tray table aside. Her lips quivered as she pondered her future. She must accept and overcome her disability. Wallowing in self-pity and disappointing Stephanie was not an option. A smile appeared, thinking about how the young child always cheered her up when she needed a lift…like JP did. *Where was he?*

A WEEK AND A HALF LATER, VANESSA BEGGED TO GO home. Convinced Vanessa had become adept at caring for her stump, Dr. Borene discharged her.

"I'll make an appointment for six weeks from now to determine if your leg—"

"You mean my stump," Vanessa said, glancing at what remained of her leg. "I'm used to the word now."

"I like your attitude," the doctor said. "Follow my orders, and your stump should heal by the time Dr. Hutchinson starts the prosthesis procedure. You'll also start physical therapy."

"Yes, sir!" She saluted Dr. Borene. "I'd like to say it's been a blast as your guest, but I'd be lying. No offense intended, but I'm glad to be out of here. Thank you for everything."

"Doing my job."

Vanessa appreciated he'd gone above and beyond.

———— ◆ ————

MRS. STEINER CONVERTED THE MAIN LEVEL COMBINA-tion library/sewing room to a bedroom for Vanessa. Vanessa made it clear she was not about to be babied. "I'm not helpless," she told everyone. "I need to become independent and adjust to the crutches. So, if I refuse your help, don't take it personally. And as much as I appreciate your help, I plan on returning to my house as soon as possible."

"Understood," Mrs. Steiner said. "But in the meantime, all of us will help you as needed. And don't worry about Halloween. Ellie's going to take the kids trick or treating."

"I got my princess costume ready. I'll share my candy with you." Stephanie grinned.

"That's thoughtful of you, but I won't eat too much," Vanessa said, rubbing her tummy. "Got to watch my weight."

"Ah, you're skinny. I hope you're here for a long time. I want you to stay forever."

"So do I," Nancie said. The other children dittoed her sentiment.

"Thank you." Everyone, even thirteen-year-old Wayne, had gathered in the room to welcome her. A lost body member is something they had never seen before. They flooded Vanessa with questions.

"Does it hurt?"

"Can I see your leg?"

"Will you walk again?"

"How come they cut off your foot?"

"I'm sorry for you. Are you mad?"

"Kids, I appreciate your caring. I'm improving. And yes, I'll walk again." Vanessa said this to convince herself as well as the children.

Clapping to gain everyone's attention, Mrs. Steiner said, "Lunchtime. Vanessa needs to rest after she eats."

Stephanie lingered and wiggled onto Vanessa's lap.

"Comfy?"

"Yep."

Vanessa stroked Stephanie's long hair. "You've been so helpful." This girl was instrumental in pulling and encouraging Vanessa out of her emotional misery. There'd been a learning curve for Vanessa, with lots of gains and losses, and also bouts of discouragement, self-pity, and even despair.

"When you get your new foot, we can go to the park and zoo," Stephanie said. She hugged Vanessa. "Hey! Can I live with you at your house? I could help you every day." Sitting erect, she blurted out, "You could be my mommy."

Mommy. The word sounded like music to her ears. Stephie was an integral part of her life. She couldn't imagine life without her. She thought of her adoption. What if…?

Mrs. Steiner entered the room, carrying a food tray. "Stephanie, go eat."

"I want to adopt her," Vanessa said when Stephanie was out of earshot.

"Do you think that's a good idea? Have you thought this through?" She placed the turkey sandwich and apple on a coffee tray.

"Ah, no, it just occurred to me."

Mrs. Steiner pushed a chair next to Vanessa. "There's a lot of things to consider. You must be confident in your ability to support yourself and Stephanie. A mother has to say no, reprimand, and teach right and wrong. You'll have to deal with issues that come up. How are you going to handle every possibility besides dealing with your disability?"

"I want her in my life." Vanessa wasn't prepared to dismiss the idea. "Dad, a single parent, adopted and raised me okay."

"Are you still interested in finding out about your adoption?"

"Of course. I'm not giving up. I'll resume searching as soon as I recover enough."

"I'd be willing to help you," Mrs. Steiner offered.

"Thanks." Vanessa welcomed the offer, but she'd prefer JP's help. *Like that would happen.*

"Anyway," Mrs. Steiner said. "Promise me one thing."

"What?"

"You won't mention adoption to Stephanie."

Vanessa shrugged her shoulders. "I know I'm facing an uphill battle, but I love her and I know she loves me. I can't believe the state would rather sentence her to a life in foster care than place her with a loving parent. Besides, nowadays, many single parents adopt. I'm going to try."

"For now, drop the adoption idea and concentrate on your rehabilitation. In case your plan doesn't happen, you'll only disappoint her. Heaven knows, she's already experienced too much disappointment and trauma in her young life."

"All right, I promise." Vanessa raised her right hand. She sighed. "Right now, I have three goals, Luellen. Adopt

Stephanie, find out who my parents are, and function with my prosthesis."

"When you get the list in the right order, we can try to make adoption happen. I'm not sure you're ready to be a mother."

Vanessa's cell phone sounded the familiar ringtone. She looked at the caller ID. Greg. Vanessa's face washed blank with surprise. She froze, her hand hovering above the phone. Greg hadn't spoken to her since the day over fourteen months ago when she'd thrown the engagement ring at him.

Mrs. Steiner pointed to the food and headed to the kitchen. "Eat."

"Hello, Greg."

"Hi, Vanessa. Jason told me what happened and gave me your number. How are you doing now?"

"Getting better."

"Great."

This is awkward Vanessa thought. "Ah…how's the coaching?"

"We won fifteen games last season. Not bad for my first year. The team's practicing for the upcoming season that starts next week. I'm sure we'll win even more games this year. Got a six-foot-nine transfer."

So what? "How's Alicia?"

"She loves Hawaii and supports me one hundred percent. Talk about a perfect match."

Vanessa's lips curled at the inferred slight. Then she straightened herself and pretended she hadn't heard his remark.

Greg plowed on. "We both love the climate. Nice year-round. Don't miss the rain. By the way. Find out about your mother?"

"Not yet."

"Too bad. You were so obsessed with your search. Is your buddy JP still hanging around? He was more than willing to offer his help." The sarcasm in his voice didn't encourage an answer, so she didn't bother. The silence hung like a dark cloud.

Greg cleared his throat. "Well, sorry about what happened. Take care."

"Next time you think of me, don't bother calling. Bye."

She disconnected. She breathed a heavy sigh as her head rested against the chair and her eyes closed. JP's image flashed into her mind. *Hmmm.* She wondered for the umpteenth time where he was and why he left with not so much as a goodbye.

Chapter 18

Over the next two months, Vanessa worked hard with her physical therapist and adjusting to the prosthesis. The children gave her encouragement when she wanted to give up and laughed with her when she stumbled over obstacles. "They helped me keep me out of the dumps. A little too eager," Vanessa chuckled as she chatted with Mrs. Steiner. "I grin watching Lilyrose and Alana argue over who would fetch whatever I need."

Vanessa struggled to stay busy now since she could move on her own. "Everyone's back at school after the Christmas holidays. Time to be on my own and return home. I'm getting spoiled."

Mrs. Steiner patted Vanessa's hand. "We've all loved having you here." She continued to fold a load of towels. Vanessa helped. "The kids have thrived under your tutoring as well. You've learned a lot about football thanks to Wayne's explanations."

"I now know what a touchdown is."

"Explaining sports to you lets him feel important. His self-esteem is better. Your tutoring is a godsend. Nancie's reading has improved. You've convinced all of them learning is fun. Stephanie's benefited the most. She's still suffering from the emotional scars, but she's happiest around you. She's come out of her shell, but I worry she's still unable to control her temper and she's experiencing occasional nightmares."

"We've bonded so well I'm afraid of what will happen when I leave," Vanessa said. "I still want to adopt her." She clapped, sitting erect. "Hey! I wonder if the state would allow me to be her foster mother."

"You're not ready yet." Mrs. Steiner picked up the stack of towels and headed for the linen closet.

The line of Vanessa's mouth tightened. Mrs. Steiner was right, but she didn't have to say so.

The children begged Vanessa to stay longer when she told them she planned to return to her house by Valentine's Day. "Hey, I'm not abandoning you. I'll be coming as I did before my accident."

⋯⋯⋯⋯⋯◆⋯⋯⋯⋯⋯

VANESSA THRUST HERSELF INTO FIGURING OUT THE BEST way to navigate the house. Climbing the stairs proved a challenge. It took her several days to become accustomed to the absence of the noise and lively activity of six children. She already missed them, especially Stephanie. Within a week, boredom overtook her. She couldn't sit there staring at the walls or reading all day. She cared little for television. How many game shows or soap operas could she watch? And tending to the garden wasn't an option in chilly February. It was time to resume her quest.

Her mind flashed back to the painful day Aunt Helene revealed the adoption and her last conversation with her father. There would be no escape she'd fled the hospital room madder than a raging bull the last time she saw him alive. She stared at her birth certificate, Rosey's note, and the police report about the fire. So far, the only connections to her bio mother. Her lips quivered and as she blinked, a few tears leaked, blotting the document. She wasted no time wiping them from the paper with her sleeve cuff.

The next morning, Vanessa stuffed the envelope containing the papers inside her purse. If she had to lose a foot, she was thankful it was her left one. Driving was manageable.

This first trip on a blustery late February day was one of many she made to various public agencies. Every time she thought she'd found a lead to her parents, it turned out to be another dead end. She questioned if the search was worth the effort and frustration. She reflected on how the events of the past year and a half had such a far-reaching effect on her life. Last year, she relished the love of her father and Greg. Now she was twenty-five, single, and disabled. And JP. *Where was he? What was he doing? Had he met another woman?* Each time she stepped inside the police station, she casually asked about him. With personnel changes and promotions, there was only a few staff that had any connection to him.

This novel way of life was not of Vanessa's liking or choosing. She found comfort knowing she wasn't alone. Dr. Adams, the children, Melanie, Ellie, and Mrs. Steiner helped her confront her feelings and wouldn't allow her to become defeated and broken. Those weren't options.

"YOU'VE ADJUSTED WELL TO YOUR PROSTHESIS," DR. Hutchinson said. "I'm pleased. Have you followed Tony's instructions?"

"Yes. I walk extra between the parallel bars to get my gait right. And I experimented to find the best way to adjust the pads on my stump. I decided if I didn't, I'd only be hurting myself. I've been a model patient. Ask him."

"Tony's kept me apprised of your progress these past six months. Your positive attitude has been instrumental in your recovery. My compliments. It was hard work."

"You got that right. I'd be lying if I said this was easy," Vanessa said. "But I'm getting used to the prosthesis and can wear it for longer stretches. April's here and the weather is nicer, so I've started taking short walks outside. And Tony's been a wonderful physical therapist. Well, most of the time." She thought about the first weeks when she wanted to punch him for his insistent pushing. She had stuck out her tongue on more than one occasion. Tony ignored her frustration and continued challenging her. "He's helped a lot."

"Are you taking care of your leg as we've taught you to prevent skin irritation and breakdown, and infection? Wearing the stump sock and/or pads?"

"Yeah. Adjusting the pads is a pain in the you know what. I wear long pants. I guess I'm self-conscious, but with matching shoes, the prosthesis is not so obvious. I don't like the slight limp though."

"Make an appointment for three months from now. I'll determine if any adjustments are necessary. Then you won't need to come in except for occasional checkups. Unless something unforeseen occurs."

Vanessa rose and shook the doctor's hand. "I appreciate everything you and Tony have done for me."

"Thank you. And speaking of the devil," Dr. Hutchinson chuckled as he departed.

"How's my favorite patient today?" Tony asked.

"I'll bet you say that to all your patients," Vanessa said.

"Does it work?" He grinned, assisting her onto the examining table. "This is it, my dear. Our last therapy appointment."
He and Vanessa had built a friendly rapport after the initial few weeks. Like they'd been best buddies forever. Tony often talked about his wife, a teacher, and his two adopted sons.

"What a coincidence," Vanessa said. "I was also adopted and I'm a teacher too, but not teaching for now."

"Do you ever wonder about your bio parents?" Tony ventured.

"Hell yes! You can't imagine. I didn't find out till I was twenty-four. Talk about a shock. I've done gobs of searching for answers."

"Not to be disrespectable of the dead, but your father should have told you. We plan to tell the boys when they're old enough to understand."

"You're doing the right thing."

"How is your search progressing?"

"Terrible. I keep running into a bunch of dead ends. I'm frustrated. It's on hold for now."

Tony placed his hands on his hips. "You've been a model patient and I'll miss your charming personality."

"And I'll miss hearing about your sons' escapades. But not your relentless pushing me to perform those annoying exercises."

"Are you going to resume teaching?"

"I'll have to renew my certificate, but I hope to."

Tony ran his fingers over his bald head. "And if I may be so bold as to ask. Why isn't an attractive woman like you married? Hard to believe."

"I was engaged, but it didn't work out. Greg, my former fiancé, didn't support my search. He called it an obsession."

She stared at the ceiling, sighing. "That was an enormous factor in our breakup."

"Sorry to hear that." Tony glanced at the clock. "I'm late for my next appointment. I wish you well." And shaking his finger at her, he ordered. "Continue the exercises. That's an order. You've made significant progress. Don't relapse. Call me anytime. Good luck with your quest." He sprinted from the room.

Outside, the April sunshine greeted Vanessa. She sat on a bench, soaking in the sun's warmth. A couple strolled by, arm in arm, gazing at one another, oblivious to their surroundings. The man's rugged features reminded her of JP. She thought about him more often than she would admit. She yearned to hear from him and considered trying to locate him. But abandoned the notion. *Who am I kidding? If he wanted to contact me, he knows where I live.* She bent over, concealing her face behind her hands.

Chapter 19

———◆———

In late June, Vanessa arranged a surprise party for Stephanie's sixth birthday. Melanie and Jason brought three-week-old Dylan to his first outing. The girls doted on the baby, finagling to hold him, and argued about feeding him.

"I'm nursing," Melanie told them.

Stephanie adored Dylan and appointed herself his big sister.

Vanessa lit the six candles on the princess-themed chocolate cake. Everyone sang an off-key rendition of *Happy Birthday*.

"Now make a wish," Ellie said.

"I wish for a mom." There was no hesitation as her eyes focused on Vanessa. Vanessa couldn't hide the smile on her face. Mrs. Steiner shot her a "too soon" look.

"You're not supposed to tell us what you wished out loud," said Kevin, "or it won't come true."

"Is that so?" Stephanie asked Mrs. Steiner.

"Well…"

"I don't care. That's what I want." She blew out all the candles in one breath. Everyone applauded. Melanie clapped sleepy Dylan's hands together.

"It'll come true because I blew them all out the first time!"

"No, it won't," Wayne said.

"Yes, it will!"

"What a dumb wish. Who's gonna give you a mom?"

Stephanie glared at Wayne, and as he opened his mouth to speak, her fist pulled back. She didn't get any further. Vanessa trapped it in her hand. She leaned down and whispered, "We don't hit. Remember?"

Stephanie froze, her lips pressed into a thin line. Vanessa watched as Stephanie's body relaxed and her hand dropped to her side.

"Time to cut the cake. And there's chocolate ice cream," Mrs. Steiner said.

"This is the best birthday ever," Stephanie whispered to Vanessa when she finished ripping open all the presents.

"I'm glad you enjoyed it. You got a lot of gifts. I love those new books. I'll bet Nancie would enjoy reading them."

"Yeah, I like them. But I don't want to share them." Stephanie hid them under the sofa, then moved away to a group of children nearby playing a board game.

Vanessa didn't think Stephanie was selfish or a mean child. Was she afraid to acknowledge anything was special in case it was taken away? She knew that feeling herself.

The children laughed and kidded with one another. Wayne accidentally knocked over a glass of punch. It splattered into Stephanie's lap. "My new dress is wet!" She pummeled him.

Vanessa reached for Stephanie and wrestled with her to stop the punching. She lost her balance and tripped over a chair, landing on the floor.

"It's not my fault. You grabbed me and that's why you fell."

"Stephanie, I'm fine. I don't want you fighting. I don't want you to think you can settle everything with your fists."

Vanessa used the chair for leverage and pulled herself into the seat.

"Wayne deserved it. Look at what he did to my dress." Her jaw jutted out and her eyes narrowed, looking at Vanessa. Wayne turned away, hiding a quivering lip and rubbing his eyes.

Vanessa lay her hand on the girl's shoulder. "Stephanie, apologize to Wayne. He didn't mean to spill the punch."

Stephanie backed away. "I'm not listening to you! Or obeying you either."

"You shouldn't say that to Vanessa." Nancie admonished Stephanie.

"Yeah," chimed in Lilyrose.

Stephanie glared from one girl to the next. Both girls backed up, aware of Stephanie's ire.

"Apologizing is the right thing to do," Vanessa said.

Stephanie whirled to face her new accuser. The girls' comments and Vanessa's stern expression lit a fuse in Stephanie. She kicked a chair and yelled in a shaky voice, "You're all against me." With venomous little eyes, she bellowed, "You're not my mother! You can't tell me what to do!" Stephanie smashed her palms into the leftover cake. With dramatic flair, she smeared the crumbs and sticky frosting on the linen tablecloth. Melanie, Jason, and the children stared wide-eyed at the hysterical girl as she fled the room.

Vanessa remembered her own words to her father. Had they hurt him as Stephanie's flareup pained her now? Her eyes moistened in response. With an effort, she stood and waved Mrs. Steiner away. "I'll go to her." She made her way to the foyer where she saw Stephanie headed. She sat on the wooden window seat thinking about how to approach the emotional child.

Vanessa lifted her head as a sniffling moan drifted from behind the staircase. Vanessa ambled toward the sound and lowered her body. Stephanie sat curled farther back under the staircase, her head resting on her bent knees, and frosting smeared on her dress. *I have to talk to her.* She crawled to Stephanie.

"Go away."

"I can't. I'm here now, and I want my effort to join you to pay off. Besides, I'm feeling teary-eyed too."

"Why?" Stephanie peeked up.

"Once, when I was about your age, I talked to my father mean like. I thought he was impatient and mean with me when he tried to teach me how to ride my bike without training wheels."

"What did you do?"

"Same as you. I got mad and ran into the garage and hid. My dad found me and got down beside me and held me."

"Did you feel better when he showed up?"

"Yes. I knew he was trying to help me, but I got frustrated and blamed him."

"Was he mad at you for yelling at him?"

"I don't remember exactly. He never raised his voice or scolded me."

Vanessa wrapped her arms around Stephanie. The girl rested her head on Vanessa's chest. "I don't know why I did what I did. I'm sorry."

"I know you are. We have to own our mistakes. Now, you need to change out of the dress and apologize to Mrs. Steiner for soiling her tablecloth and to Wayne too."

Stephanie jerked her head up, but Vanessa emphasized again. "It's the right thing to do." Vanessa waited while Stephanie thought about what she said. Shortly, the girl cupped her fingers around Vanessa's ear and whispered. "You're my favorite person in the whole world, and I wish you were my mom."

Vanessa squeezed the child against her chest, wanting to hold her forever. "Me too."

For the rest of the summer, Stephanie and Vanessa took excursions to the beach, the park playground, the library, and the zoo, occasionally accompanied by the other children. Scattered between these outings, Vanessa spent hours on the internet, hoping to discover info about her mother. No success. She'd re-read the note Rosey had written to her father a bazillion times. She tried to imagine what her mother looked like. *Do I resemble her? Or my bio father?*

THE LAST WEEK OF AUGUST, MRS. STEINER CONSENTED to let Stephanie spend a few days at Vanessa's helping babysit Dylan. "We'll take good care of him while you're gone," the young girl assured the apprehensive mother.

"I'm sure you will, but this is the first time I'll be away from him for more than a day," Melanie said. "I'll try not to worry." She checked the mountain of supplies she'd brought to Vanessa's. "I hope I pumped enough milk. What if you run out?"

"I've got the formula," Vanessa said. "He'll be fine."

The last Thursday before school started, Vanessa took Stephanie and Dylan to Oaks Amusement Park. As a kid, she and her father relished many outings to this popular fun spot. She closed her eyes and took a deep breath as a wave of nostalgia overtook her. The Ferris wheel had been her favorite. She never left without consuming a cone of pink cotton candy and a large Pepsi to wash the sticky concoction down.

On the drive to the park, Stephanie asked, "Do you think my birthday wish for a mom will come true?"

The question caught Vanessa off guard. "Why do you ask such a question?"

"All the other kids in my kindergarten class last year had a mother. Except for Jackson. He only has a father. His mother died. They make fun of me because I don't have a mother."

The lump in Vanessa's throat was acute. She patted Stephanie's thigh. "Kids can be cruel. What do you do when they tease you?"

"It makes me mad and I want to kick them. They want me to get into trouble."

"They keep on teasing you because you give them the satisfaction of reacting. If you want it to stop, change how you respond. Even when it hurts, don't show it."

"Hey, why don't you marry some guy? I'll bet Mrs. Steiner would let me live with you and him."

"I'm not planning on any wedding bells any time soon. I don't even have a boyfriend."

"I'm going to find you one."

Dylan cooed from his car seat as though voicing his approval.

Vanessa smiled at Stephanie's innocence. Routine activities presented challenges like the time she slipped off the folding bath bench. Lifting her body off the slippery shower tile required a Herculean effort. But she would not become dependent on any male. Yeah, no marriage in her future. She would remain single. Anyway, she had no desire for a romantic relationship. *Yeah, right,* mocked her mind.

Stephanie headed toward the ticket booth, eager to get in line. Vanessa bought a wristband allowing Stephanie unlimited rides. "Whee!" Stephanie squealed as she went round and round, up and down many times. After a while, she asked if she could go on the big people's roller coaster.

"No."

"How come?"

"You're not tall enough to go alone. You'd have to an adult with you and I can't bring Dylan on it."

She stomped her right foot. "That's not fair." She folded her arms across her chest.

"Your attitude is unacceptable." Vanessa's tone was firm. "If you're going to act this way, we're leaving."

"Sorry. I'll go on the kiddy one again. It's my favorite."

An hour later, Vanessa said, "We've been here long enough. We need to eat and then head home. Dylan's getting fussy. One more ride. No begging for more."

Fanning herself, Vanessa lowered the stroller's cover over Dylan to shade him from the sun. The three waited in line to buy lunch. Stephanie pointed to a row of cotton candy hanging inside the concession stand. "I want a pink one."

"Nope." Vanessa prided herself she avoided junk food. But how could she deprive the child just this once from consuming a treat she always enjoyed at this park? She caved. "Okay. The small size."

At the picnic table, Vanessa pulled several handy wipes from Dylan's diaper bag and handed them to Stephanie. Remnants of the cotton candy covered the girl's lips and chin. What a mess! Vanessa laughed. "Let's wipe your sticky face." Job completed, Vanessa announced it was time to head home. She cleared the clutter, and Stephanie tossed the trash into the garbage.

"Aw, do we have to?" Stephanie whined. "One more time on the roller coaster?" She flashed her most convincing smile and put her hands together.

"I told you no begging. Dylan is almost asleep and I want to get him into his car seat before he's completely conked out." She wiped a bead of perspiration from her forehead.

Vanessa removed sleepy Dylan from the stroller and secured him in the car seat. She folded the stroller, but jerked up as Stephanie shrieked, "Eek!" and darted into the driving lane. Vanessa spotted a car traveling toward the girl at a rapid speed. "Stephanie!" she screamed. "Stop!"

Stephanie froze in the path of the approaching car, paralyzed by fear. The driver slammed on his breaks, but the car skidded straight toward the child. Blood rushed up the back of Vanessa's neck, pounding at the base of her skull. Icy needles prickled up her spine. Out of nowhere, a man's figure appeared, snatching the frightened girl to safety. Vanessa inhaled sharply, her trembling body leaning against the trunk.

"What the hell?" the driver yelled, stepping out of his car. "Suddenly, there she was. Are you all right, kid?"

Shaken, Stephanie ran to Vanessa. They squeezed each other tighter than a vice. "Why did you run out into the driving path?"

"I saw a yucky snake in the grass. I got scared and ran."

Vanessa eyeballed the girl's rescuer. He stood several car lengths away, his back to her. He shook his finger at the teenage driver. The guy ran his fingers through his shoulder-length greasy hair, nodded, then entered his car. As he passed Stephanie and Vanessa, he stuck his head out the window. "Sorry, kid." He drove much slower toward the exit.

As Vanessa loosened her grip on Stephanie, she noticed from her peripheral the man leaving. "Thank you!" She yelled the heartfelt words. Recognition closed her throat to any additional utterances as the man turned around and she locked eyes with JP.

Chapter 20

Several moments passed before Vanessa could speak. Finally, above her hammering heart, the sound of JP's name escaped from deep within her throat.

"JP!"

JP's staring eyes were as immobile as the rest of his face and body, a statue.

"Do you know this guy?" Stephanie's voice broke the silence.

Vanessa blinked as though coming out of a trance. "Yes, but…" Words failed. Vanessa blushed, and with a quick and nervous motion, touched her hair to tidy it.

JP gained his senses and addressed Stephanie. "Are you sure you're OK, young lady?"

"I guess so."

JP cleared his throat. "Are you okay, Vanessa?"

Vanessa swallowed the lump in her throat. "I'm fine now. Quite a scare."

"What are you doing here?" Both adults asked at the same time.

"Jinx!" shouted Stephanie.

The two grownups smiled at her.

"I believe an ice cream cone is in order. Any objections, Vanessa?"

"Say yes, pleeease!" Stephanie gave her best pleading expression. A cry from the car interrupted them.

"The baby!" Vanessa whipped around and rushed to the car as fast as her foot allowed. Her heart pounded as thoughts of Dylan inside the hot car or someone kidnapping him whirled in her mind. It would be her fault if that happened. She thrust open the door and removed Dylan from inside. JP followed and took the infant from Vanessa's arms. He examined him for any signs of distress. The entire scenario had lasted a mere five or six minutes. Dylan was fine. JP recommended getting him out of the heat. He offered to take them home. "We can go in my car."

"No. You don't have a car seat."

"I can transfer it."

"Thanks, but no thanks."

"I'll drive your car to your place and phone my mother to come and get me. Then she can bring me back here to get my car." He snapped his fingers. "Won't work. I'm supposed to pick her up at her garden club meeting."

Vanessa reached for Dylan. "I'm fine. I'll manage."

Vanessa secured the baby in the car seat while JP put the stroller into the trunk, then helped Stephanie inside and fastened the seatbelt. "Allow me to introduce myself. I'm JP Monroe. And you are?"

"Stephanie. This is Dylan. He's almost three months old. I'm helping take care of him, except for his poopy diapers."

"Pleased to meet you," JP said, shaking her hand. "You too, Dylan."

JP walked around to Vanessa. "Dylan is a cutie. How thrilling for you and Greg."

Vanessa started the car and turned on the air conditioning. No need to correct JP's assumption.

"Who's Greg?" Stephanie asked.

JP hemmed and hawed. "Aren't you and Greg married?"

"Ah, no."

"Not married?" He looked at fussy Dylan. "What about the baby? Is he yours?"

"Not now. I want to get Dylan home. I'm out of diapers, and he's no doubt ready for a bottle."

"Hey, what about the ice cream?" Stephanie yelled from the back seat.

JP leaned down to Vanessa's eye level. "How about you head home? I'll drop by *Dairy Queen,* then bring the treat to your house. Still living in the same place?"

"Yes."

Vanessa traced the path of JP's eyes as he focused on the dangling handicap placard. And he couldn't have missed the car parked in a handicapped space. She knew he no doubt had a ton of questions. To her relief, he didn't ask any, at least not now.

"Okay, young lady. Chocolate or vanilla?"

"A chocolate milkshake."

"You got it. How about you, Vanessa? Want anything?"

Yes. An explanation of why you left. "No, thanks."

During the fifteen-minute drive home, Vanessa pondered what she should do when JP arrived. Invite him to stay? Or would he want to take off without visiting? She hoped not. A million questions spun in her mind about his whereabouts for the past two years. She had to prepare for JP's certain questioning about Greg, the two children, and the handicap placard.

When they entered the house, Vanessa turned on the air conditioning. Less than twenty minutes later, JP tapped on the front door. She had expected him to take longer to arrive. She wanted more time to freshen up and figure out how to answer the questions she was positive JP would ask.

Stephanie pulled JP inside, eyeing the milkshake.

JP handed the treat to the eager girl. She wasted no time slurping the cool, thick chocolate drink through the straw.

JP surveyed the living room. Everything was as he remembered it. Except for the playpen and an assortment of children's toys stashed in the corner.

"I'm going to change Dylan's diaper and then get his bottle ready," announced Vanessa. "Stephanie, how about entertaining JP until I return?" She studied his face for his reaction.

Stephanie grabbed a book. "I'm a wonderful reader. Do you want me to read a story to you?"

"You bet."

They settled on the couch.

Stephanie's animated voice drifted into the bathroom between sips of the milkshake. The corners of Vanessa's mouth turned up into a pleased expression.

Stephanie slammed the book shut when finished and ran her fingers along the cover. "Books about animals are my favorites. Vanessa and I take turns reading to each other."

"Does your father read with you too?"

"No, I don't have a dad. Well, I did, but he's dead. So is my mom. But I wished for one on my birthday. It'll come true because I blew out all six candles!"

JP rubbed his chin. Confusion reigned.

When Vanessa re-entered the room, she noticed JP watching her every step. She sat opposite him in the lounge chair and gave a bawling Dylan the bottle. "Hope you enjoyed Stephanie's reading." She spoke without voicing what was on her mind. *Why did you leave?*

"Yes, I did. She reads well." JP smiled at the proud child. "What grade are you going into?"

"First."

The ringing of JP's cell phone came from inside his T-shirt pocket. He pulled out the device, along with his sunglasses. He placed them on the coffee table. "Excuse me. My mother. I'll bet she's calling to remind me to pick her up from her garden club meeting. This won't take long."

While JP chatted with his mother in the foyer, Vanessa directed her eyes toward him. Two years since she'd last seen him. Her heartbeats increased. He was as handsome as she remembered. She guessed he still pumped iron because of his bulky bicep muscles. He was tanner and his hair a tad longer. He had a couple of days' worth of stubble. JP finished the conversation and turned his head toward Vanessa. She bowed her head, staring at Dylan.

JP placed the cell phone into his pocket and checked the time. "I'll have to leave in about a half-hour."

Vanessa told Stephanie to finish her clay figures in the dining room. She didn't want Stephanie blabbing about topics she didn't want mentioned. Like her amputation.

"Do I have to?"

Vanessa shot her a stern look. "Scat."

Vanessa pulled the bottle from Dylan and began burping him. Pretending her full attention was on the baby, she tried to figure out a subtle way to ask him questions. In a nonchalant voice, she inquired, "So, what brought you to the park today?"

"Thought while I was in town, I'd say hi to an old high school buddy. He owns the on-site roller-skating rink at Oaks. Believe it or not, I used to skate. Got quite proficient. I won a few competitions." He chuckled. "Now I'm rusty. Fell several times."

"Ah, where have you been the past couple of years?"

"I settled in Idaho and found a job working on the police force in a small town called Rathdrum. I'm here visiting mom. Have to be back at work in three days."

Vanessa hid her disappointment. So, he'd been living in Idaho. "Is this the first time you've returned since you left?" Before she could stop herself, she revealed, "I couldn't believe you left without a goodbye, nothing. Especially after you said you loved me."

"It was wrong of me, but I, well, you know. I couldn't remain here under the circumstances. There was no hope for a future with you. So," he leaned forward, "you're not married to Greg. What happened? You were adamant about marrying him." Her bare ring finger caught his eye.

As if on cue, formula oozed from Dylan's mouth, soiling his bib and outfit. Vanessa rose, excused herself, and carried the baby into the bathroom.

JP followed Vanessa. Stephanie ran into the room, holding up a clay puppy. "See what I made for you." She thrust it into JP's hands.

"Thank you. I like puppies." He put the crude sculpture on the coffee table beside his sunglasses. "This was nice of you." They sat side by side. Stephanie yapped about starting first grade next week and the other kids at the foster home.

Vanessa appeared and placed a drowsy Dylan in the playpen. She avoided mentioning Greg. "Thank you for saving Stephie. Once again, you were on hand for another rescue."

"Anyone would have stepped up to the plate. Now, where's Greg?" She was positive JP could see her tense muscles and flushed face.

"Stephie, honey, go back and make something else. Or color in your activity book."

"Is this Greg guy a boyfriend?" Stephanie didn't budge.

JP looked at the child, then at Vanessa.

Vanessa preferred not to discuss her former fiancé. She was more interested in JP's activities during the last couple of years. With two sets of eyes focused on her, she caved. "Remember, he got the coaching job in Hawaii? That's what he wanted more than me. He moved over there a week after you left. He's been there since."

"Why didn't you tell me?" His voice got louder as he paced the room.

Vanessa got loud back. "You didn't bother to tell me about your disappearing act. I called the precinct the morning after Greg and I broke our engagement, but you'd already resigned. I didn't know where you were all this time."

Dylan whimpered.

JP stomped to the playpen. "Who's *his* father?" His tone had a hard edge, daring her to deny an affair.

Vanessa opened her mouth to blast back but stopped. JP's annoyance became clear. *He thinks I'm an unwed mother!* "Dylan isn't mine."

"Huh?"

Stephanie tugged at JP's T-shirt. "Why are you shouting at Vanessa?"

JP inhaled and counted to ten. He knelt and placed his hands on the child's shoulders. "I'm sorry I lost my cool. Forgive me?"

"Hmmm." She tapped her finger against her lips and looked at Vanessa. She nodded. "Okay. But say you're sorry to Vanessa. It's the right thing to do, like when I apologized to Wayne."

Vanessa smiled, pleased her past words made an impression.

"I shouldn't have yelled." Pointing to Dylan, he asked, "Not your son?"

"Nope." She grinned as she saw his body relax. He cares, she thought. "Remember my friends Melanie and Jason? Dylan is their son. Stephie and I are caring for him while they're at a conference. They'll be back in a couple of days." She added, "Greg married Jason's sister."

JP stared at the ceiling. "He wasted little time."

Stephanie piped up. "Melanie lets me pretend I'm Dylan's big sister. I like to hold him and feed him a bottle." She walked to the playpen and stroked Dylan's bald head.

JP had to leave. He took Vanessa's hands in his. "I'm sorry for what happened between you and Greg, and I apologize for yelling at you." He looked down at her with that smile. The one making her heart pound like it was doing now.

JP took a chance. "Before I return to Rathdrum, how about going to Papandrea's?"

Vanessa's mind wrestled with her emotions. Her heart ordered her to accept the invitation. Her head said forget it. It was clear there was no point in reviving their relationship if he was leaving again. He hadn't given her any sign he wanted to resume so much as a friendly connection. Much to Stephanie's disappointment, she declined. "Sounds tempting, but no thanks."

"You sure?"

"Yes."

"Got a piece of paper and pen? I'll jot down my and Mom's cell numbers in case you change your mind."

After scribbling the numbers, he proceeded toward the door. "By the way. Did you find out anything about your bio parents?"

"No. Nothing more than the note you saw and my birth certificate. I've spent gobs of time searching, but not lately."

"How come? You were so determined."

"I've been busy with…other things."

"Talked with your aunt?"

"Ah, no." She picked up a restless Dylan, then joined him at the door.

"Now, young lady," JP squatted to Stephanie's eye level, "look both ways before running out where cars drive. Promise?"

"Yes, sir." She saluted him. "I like you except when you yelled." She scrutinized JP. "Hey, you could be Vanessa's boyfriend."

Vanessa stood frozen. Her body radiated enough heat to fry an egg. She wanted the earth to open up and swallow her whole.

JP made no move to acknowledge the comment. He faked a cough. "So long, ladies. You too, Dylan." As Vanessa watched him walk down the path, she kicked the door. *Why did I turn down his invitation?* She stepped onto the porch, watching his car until it turned the corner. She shut the door and leaned against it. Not until Dylan squirmed did Vanessa emerge from her numbness.

JP was silent with his mother. Concentrating on his driving proved difficult.

"What's wrong?" Barbara Monroe inquired.

"Nothing."

"This is your mother speaking. You don't fool me."

"Mom, she never got married! I—"

He slammed the brakes. A car traveling through the intersection blasted his horn, giving him the one finger salute. JP looked both ways before proceeding and steered to the curb. He inhaled, closing his eyes and leaning his head against the headrest. "Sorry, Mom. You okay?"

"Yes. Who never married?"

"Never mind."

"You're sweating." She opened the glove compartment and looked for a tissue. A small photograph fell onto the mat. She wiped the beads of perspiration from JP's forehead, then bent to retrieve the picture.

A woman with a blonde ponytail and lovable dimples sat on a bleacher bench grinning. She held up the snapshot. "Who's this?"

He stared at the photo. He'd forgotten he'd stuffed it in there. "Vanessa."

"She's attractive. Seems like a wholesome young woman. When was this picture taken?"

"A teammate's wife snapped a bunch of pictures the summer Vanessa's dad died, two years ago. She attended a few of my softball games."

Mrs. Monroe connected the dots. "This is the woman you mentioned, isn't it?"

JP grabbed the snapshot and shoved it back inside the glove compartment. He checked for oncoming vehicles, then inched back into traffic.

"I spent two years trying to forget Vanessa. Then today I find out she never married the bozo. Thank God she came to her senses."

"Head back to her house after you drop me off at home. Offer to take her out to dinner. McDonald's, Papandrea's, or a swanky restaurant. It doesn't matter."

"I already invited her to Papandrea's. She turned me down." He sighed as he reached to increase the air conditioning a notch. "I lost my cool, Mom. I yelled at her and upset Stephanie."

Mrs. Monroe patted her son's right thigh. "Who's Stephanie?"

"A young girl who seems very attached to Vanessa."

"I wish you'd move back to Milwaukie. I socialize with my garden club friends and my bowling league, but I'm lonely since your father's passing. And I never told you this but, damn it, JP, I was angry when you took off with no explanation. You didn't consider how leaving would affect me."

"Sorry."

"Ah-ha! Vanessa's the reason you left."

JP's resigned expression confirmed his mother's conclusion.

"Sweetie pie, I—"

"Mom." He leaned toward her, touching her arm. "Stop calling me that."

"If you insist. Anyway, I hate seeing you in misery. Like when Cheryl…" She bit her lip. Cheryl was a taboo subject.

"It took me well over a year before I didn't think about Vanessa daily. I didn't even glance at another woman let alone date one."

Mrs. Monroe prodded him to follow through on her suggestion. "Offer to take her and the young girl to dinner. Who knows? She may accept."

JP turned toward his mother. "Based on her less than enthusiastic response to me, forget it." A grin appeared. "Stephanie acted eager to go. Can you believe she wants me to be Vanessa's boyfriend?"

"Ha! She's got good taste," Mrs. Monroe said. "You're thirty, JP. I want grandchildren before I'm too old to spoil them."

His mother's remark prompted him to tell her he was ready to settle down. "I'd like to oblige you, Mom. But no prospects. And I assure you, I'll marry the gal first."

"I knew I raised you right," she said, reaching over and rubbing his shoulder. "I hope you try to reconnect with Vanessa, though. Could be Miss Right."

"Not in the cards. Guess I'm unlucky in love."

Mrs. Monroe took a risk. "How do your feelings for Vanessa compare with how you felt about Cheryl?"

"Mom, I asked you to never mention her name." He focused on his driving, trying to hide the sadness in his eyes as he flashbacked to the shock of that day six years ago. He had swallowed a sob and tried to keep his composure when Cheryl told him she loved someone else and handed him the engagement ring. There'd been no clue this bombshell was coming. His heart shattered into tiny pieces. It took several years to piece it together. It broke again when Vanessa refused to let him into her heart. So, he bolted…to put physical distance between him and Vanessa.

"You didn't answer my question," Mrs. Monroe said.

"Not to be disrespectful, Mom, but MYOB."

"Your attitude says it all. You love Vanessa more intensely than you did Cheryl. I'm right, aren't I?"

JP's expression verified his mother's astute observation.

"I insist you call her," Mrs. Monroe pressed.

"Forget it. I gave away my heart twice, only for it to be broken both times. I can't go through that again. Besides, I didn't get any encouragement from Vanessa today. She's not interested in me." As an afterthought, he said, "But I'd sure like to know why she has a handicap sign in her car. And she limped. And Stephanie? How'd she enter Vanessa's life?"

"More reasons to phone her."

"Hey, Mom," he said, staring at her head. "Did you color your hair? I like your new hairdo. With the gray gone, you appear younger than your fifty-nine years."

"Don't change the subject. Call Vanessa."

JP stated with conviction, "I'm heading back to Rathdrum tomorrow."

"You're making a stupid choice. Again."

Chapter 21

"Stephanie, where did you get those sunglasses?" Vanessa asked, laughing at the specs perched loosely on her face. "They don't fit you, silly."

"They were on the coffee table," replied Stephanie. "JP forgot them. If he doesn't want them, can I keep them to play with?" She held up the clay puppy. "He didn't take this either."

Vanessa hadn't noticed the sunglasses after JP departed yesterday. She removed them from Stephanie's face. *Michael Kors*. An expensive name brand.

"He'll no doubt want them back. We should try to contact him at his mother's and tell him they're here."

"Can I invite him over for dinner? He was a nice guy except when he yelled at you."

Vanessa liked the idea. She'd lain awake the night before, frustrated at her refusal to accept JP's invitation. She pounded her fists against the bedroom wall. Now, this spotless pair of sunglasses she placed on the bridge of her nose for a moment presented the ideal excuse to see him again. *The invitation would be from Stephanie, not me. Perfect!*

She located the sheet of paper with Mrs. Monroe's number written on it. Vanessa put the phone on speaker and watched Stephanie press the keys.

"Hi. Can I talk with JP, please? He left his sunglasses and I want him to come to eat pizza with me and Vanessa."

"Who is this?" Barbara Monroe asked.

"Stephanie!"

"Oh. You're the young lady JP mentioned. Hello."

"Is he there? I want him to come over here."

Mrs. Monroe switched the phone to her other ear, asking to speak to Vanessa.

In her most pleasant voice, Vanessa greeted Mrs. Monroe. "I hope we're not bothering you. We wanted to return JP's sunglasses. Also, Stephanie thought it'd be nice to invite him for dinner."

The lie slipped out, smooth like sugary syrup, running off a pile of pancakes. "JP's boss called him back to work. An emergency."

Vanessa plopped onto the sofa, bowing her head.

"I'm sure he would've accepted Stephanie's invitation," Mrs. Monroe assured her.

"I'll tell Stephanie. Thanks."

"Wait!" Mrs. Monroe said. "Let me give you JP's cell number and address. Stephanie *or you* can give him a buzz about his sunglasses. I'm positive he'd love to hear from you."

"I already have it. Take care." Expressing herself in what she hoped came across as nonchalant, she told Stephanie JP had returned to Rathdrum.

"Shucks." She eyed the sunglasses. "Can I keep them?"

Vanessa placed the spectacles inside the hallway desk drawer. "Leave them here for now along with his phone number. I don't think he'll miss them." *Like he won't miss me.* "Steph," she pushed her left ear lobe forward, "Dylan is fussing. Go check on him. I'll be there in a few minutes, and we'll start packing his stuff so he's ready when Melanie and Jason return tomorrow."

Stephanie skipped into the bedroom.

JP's second departure without a goodbye pained Vanessa. She opened the desk drawer and withdrew the sunglasses, holding them close to her chest. She felt like someone had pumped cement into her gut. She figured after two years JP's professed love for her died and was buried, never to resurrect. *It's clear where I stand.* She tossed the glasses into the drawer and slammed it shut. Stephanie's giggles drifted from the other room. She forced a smile and joined the children.

———— ✦ ————

THE FOLLOWING AFTERNOON, MELANIE AND JASON rushed straight from the airport.

Melanie cuddled Dylan and smothered him with kisses. "I didn't believe I would miss him so much. I couldn't wait to hold him in my arms." She added, laughing, "My boobs are full of milk. Need to nurse him. Soon!"

"My turn," Jason said, taking a contented Dylan from Melanie. "I missed him too."

"We enjoyed his company," Vanessa smiled. "As his godmother and 'sister' we expect you to let us take care of him whenever you need us. Are you ready to return to teaching next week?"

"It'll be hard," Melanie answered, staring lovingly at her child. "Thanks for the offer to babysit, Vanessa. Between Jason's flexible hours and his mother, I've got the days covered. But if I ever need you, trust me, I'll call."

"I want Dylan to stay," Stephanie chimed in. "I enjoy helping with him. And holding him. We even took him to the park. I went on a bunch of rides and JP grabbed me before I almost got hit by a car."

"JP?" Jason and Melanie asked in unison.

"He was a neat guy," Stephanie said. "He bought me a chocolate milkshake. Do you know him?"

"I've met him," Melanie answered.

Vanessa saw the expression on her friends' faces and knew they wanted an explanation. "Steph, how about going outside and running through the sprinkler?"

"Nah."

"How 'bout if I take you to *Dairy Queen* for an ice cream cone or milkshake as a reward for taking such good care of Dylan?" Jason suggested. "We'll be back in about a half-hour."

Stephanie headed toward the door.

"Thank you," Vanessa mouthed to Jason.

Melanie sat on the sofa, bouncing Dylan on her lap. "Okay, girl, start talking."

Vanessa explained what occurred at the amusement park and then at home. "Thank God JP rescued Stephanie or…It was a terrible moment. If for no other reason than that, I was glad to see him."

"And I'm the pope," Melanie laughed. "Do you expect me to believe you? Tell the truth, Van. You're fonder of JP than you're letting on. I can understand not admitting your feelings initially because you were engaged. Once you and Greg broke up, why didn't you try to find JP?"

"I guess I believed he no longer wanted me in his life. He didn't bother to say goodbye. If only he'd waited one more day. Then I had my accident, recovery period, Stephanie, and my search. JP wasn't in the mix anymore."

"It's comical he thought Dylan was your son," Melanie said, tilting her head back. "At least you set the record straight." Dylan showed a toothless grin as Melanie held him up and puckered her lips toward him. "Why didn't you tell him about your amputation and Stephanie?"

"He gave no indication he wanted to resume our friendship, and he's returning to Rathdrum, so I guess I figured why bother. And he raised his voice at me when he assumed I had an affair and Dylan was illegitimate. It upset me." A deep sigh escaped as Vanessa recalled the moment. "If not for Stephie's near miss, we wouldn't have crossed paths. He didn't make any effort to contact me even though he was in town."

Melanie slapped her knee for emphasis. "You don't get it, do you? It bothered JP thinking you were intimate with another man. Trust me. He still cares."

A grin appeared at the prospect "Then why no contact from him?"

Melanie placed her finger on her forehead. "Think, my dear, the last thing JP knew, you were going to marry Greg and live in Hawaii. Duh."

Of course, the plausible explanation.

"What are you going to do now?" Dylan fidgeted, and Melanie reached for his pacifier.

"Nothing. He left without—"

"Why wouldn't he? You didn't encourage him, did you?" Vanessa shook her head.

"Vanessa, call him," Melanie insisted. "You need to find out once and for all where you stand. Tell him everything that happened to you. Fess up, Van. You like the guy."

Vanessa stared at the floor. "I admit I think about him once in a while."

Melanie's roar of laughter startled Dylan. "Who are you kidding? I'll bet he's on your mind every day and also your dreams." She nudged Vanessa, winking.

Vanessa ignored the statement. "I guess I can understand why he never contacted me thinking I married Greg and moved to Hawaii."

"You have his cell phone number, don't you? Use it."

"He now knows I'm still single and available. Seems he isn't interested anymore. I doubt he wants to talk with me." She looked at her friend and shrugged. "Stephanie is a blessing and I've adjusted to my prosthesis. I'm content with my life except for finding about my bio parents. I'm going to resume my search."

Chapter 22

———————◆———————

Leaves carpeted the yards and plugged the street drains as Thanksgiving approached. Fruitless searches for the past few months and now three continuous days of rain dampened Vanessa's spirit. She'd visited every pertinent agency. Nothing but dead ends. Greg was right. She should shelve this nonsensical quest.

Two days before turkey day, Vanessa dusted the furniture in her father's bedroom. She saw a corner of the envelope peeking out of the top drawer. She sat and placed it on her lap, rehashing the unanswered questions haunting her. What relationship did Rosey have with her father? Why didn't she want me? Who was/is my bio father? Why did Lyle end up adopting me? She jerked up. Aunt Helene! She was the key to the mystery. Time to put aside her harsh mindset and locate her aunt. Right after Thanksgiving.

Vanessa persuaded Mrs. Steiner to allow Stephanie to spend the Thanksgiving holidays with her. "I need an extra pair of hands to help prepare the feast for you, Ellie, the children, Melanie, and Jason. First time I've cooked for this many people. Stephanie will love being my assistant."

"You don't fool me, Vanessa," Mrs. Steiner said, grinning. "It's an excuse to have Stephanie with you."

"I confess."

"I suppose if you're still planning to adopt her, spending more time at your house is a good idea. It'll help you determine if you can cope with being a full-time mother."

"I'm committed to becoming her mother. I decided to start the process on Monday."

On Wednesday Vanessa dropped by Mrs. Steiner's to pick up Stephanie's clothing and toiletries before picking her up from school. "See you and the kids tomorrow. Bring your appetites."

Students filed outside and darted to waiting cars or the bus when the dismissal bell rang. Stephanie slammed the car door shut, shaking the raindrops from her head. "Four days with you. Yea!"

Stephanie's enthusiasm melted Vanessa's heart. "We're headed to the grocery store. I still need some raw veggies, mayonnaise for the deviled eggs, and of course, a couple of pies." She laughed. "No homemade desserts by me. Everyone would gag."

"Mrs. Steiner's favorite pie is pumpkin. And don't forget the whipped cream," Stephanie said.

"Remind me at the store."

Vanessa and Stephanie dashed into Safeway. In the produce section, Vanessa grabbed several plastic bags. She crammed them full of fresh carrots, celery, and broccoli, then squeezed the tomatoes. Don't want them too ripe.

Vanessa examined a few Gala apples, looking for the right ones. Spotting several smooth ones, she leaned over the display to grab them. The weight of her body dislodged the pile. An avalanche tumbled off the table. Vanessa's arms flew in all directions while trying to prevent the apples from falling. Losing her balance, she fell, exposing her prosthesis.

A woman filling a plastic bag with sweet potatoes witnessed the mishap. She dropped the bag into her cart and rushed to Vanessa's aid. She extended her hand but pulled it back. Her hand covered her wide-opened mouth. "What, what is…?"

"Her fake foot," Stephanie blurted.

The woman regained her composure and offered to help once again.

Vanessa refused. "Thanks, but I'll manage." She looked around at a few shoppers staring at her. A teenage male stepped forward, extending his hand, but she gave a dismissing wave of her hand. She grabbed the edge of the apple display and hoisted herself upright. Flushed cheeks were one thing, but Vanessa was positive her face became brighter than the red apples scattered on the floor. She moistened her lips with her tongue, trying to make light of the awkward situation. "I only wanted a few apples, not the whole dang bunch." She smoothed her pants and straightened her coat.

Stephanie knelt and slid up Vanessa's pants leg, pointing an accusatory finger at the prosthesis. "Bad, bad pros… prosth… Oh, heck, bad fake foot!"

The child's serious yet lighthearted scolding eased Vanessa's humiliation. A grin appeared. "My prosthesis is not at fault. I lost my balance. I'm not as agile as I used to be."

"What does agile mean?" Stephanie asked as she removed her hand from the pants and stood.

"I can't move as fast as I use to." Vanessa smiled at the woman and thanked her. "Now, Steph, let's pick up these scattered apples."

"Don't bother," the woman said. "I'll find an employee to clean up." The woman creased her forehead, concentrating on Vanessa. "You look familiar."

Vanessa shrugged.

"Have a nice Thanksgiving." The stranger turned to glance at Vanessa as she rounded the corner, accidentally bumping into a potato chip display.

Vanessa and Stephanie finished selecting the pumpkin pies and an apple pie for Jason, his favorite. They headed to grab the whipped cream when they encountered the woman again.

"Are you sure you're okay?" she asked.

"Yes, I'm fine."

"Pardon me for asking, but is your name Vanessa?"

Vanessa's jaw dropped. "Ah, yes. How in the world do you know my name or is this a lucky guess?"

"Do you know JP Monroe?"

Stephanie perked up. "Yeah. I like him."

At the mere mention of JP's name, Vanessa's heart rate increased. She had succeeded, well, almost, to erase him from her thoughts. Now this stranger brought him to the forefront of her mind. "Who are you?"

"I'm Barbara Monroe, JP's mother."

Vanessa's mind went blank and her eyes wide as she studied the woman. Yep, an uncanny resemblance. She swore she was staring at a female JP. She opened her mouth to speak, but her voice went AWOL. Stephanie spoke the words she couldn't express.

"Is he here?" Stephanie turned her head, surveying the length of the aisle.

"No, he had to work. And you must be Stephanie."

Stephanie eyeballed Mrs. Monroe. "Who told you my name?"

"JP."

"Did he tell you I like to read?"

"How do you know who we are?" Vanessa asked.

"I recognized you from a photo. I wasn't sure it was you, but I took a chance."

Mrs. Monroe's eyes glanced at Vanessa's left shoe. "I'm sorry about your injury. How did it happen?"

Vanessa didn't want to rehash the ordeal, especially to a stranger. But this lady standing so close was JP's mother... the person who raised the man whom she longed for yet continued to hold at a distance. She wiped her clammy palms on her coat before launching into the explanation. "A year ago, in October while on a hike, I lost my footing and tumbled down a hill. A log rolled onto my foot and crushed it beyond repair. Amputation was the only choice. I have my moments, but I've accepted my fate. With my prosthesis or crutches, I function well."

Mrs. Monroe clasped her hands together. "No wonder JP mentioned you were limping and had a handicap placard in your car. It makes sense now."

"He did?"

"Yes, when he picked me up the day he rescued Stephanie last August. We discussed several things he couldn't quite understand. Your limp was one of them. And your non-marriage." She put a finger to her mouth. "Is that even a word? So what? Did you call him about his sunglasses?"

"No. Ah, how is he?"

"He's doing fine. Loves the small-town life, but I can tell he's lonely. A mother knows these things. I'm trying to talk him into coming back home."

"No friends?" *Girlfriend?*

"I don't think so."

"Does he mention me?" How the question escaped from her, Vanessa knew not. "I mean Stephanie."

"Ah, once or twice since he left."

Not the answer Vanessa hoped for.

Stephanie leaned over the grocery cart, tapping her foot and exhaling an impatient sigh.

"I'll let you finish shopping. Nice meeting you," Mrs. Monroe said.

"Wait!" Vanessa yelled before Mrs. Monroe reached the end of the aisle. The women met halfway.

"Please don't mention my disability to JP."

"Why not?"

Although JP expressed his love for her ages ago, she convinced herself that was no longer the case. She concocted a plausible reason. "Because JP wouldn't want to hang around a handicapped woman."

"JP is not a superficial person. Your disability won't faze him."

"I still prefer he doesn't find out," she said, her stubborn streak surfacing.

"I disagree with you, but I'll honor your request."

"Thank you." Vanessa stared at Barbara Monroe until she reached the end of the aisle. She dismissed the slight twinge of jealousy enveloping her. JP was fortunate to have a devoted mother. If only she'd been so lucky.

<hr />

THE THREE-DAY DELUGE OF RAIN FINALLY CEASED, AND the sun peeked through the clouds in time for the Thanksgiving feast. The aroma of the nineteen-pound turkey roasting in the oven blanketed the house.

"My compliments to the chef," Jason said, patting his belly. "I ate enough for a horse."

"Me too!" Alana said.

"Dylan liked the mashed potatoes I fed him. He didn't spit any out," Stephanie said.

"Thank you." The kudos pleased Vanessa. She had worried her first solo Thanksgiving meal might be a disaster.

"The deviled eggs were delicious," remarked Wayne, reaching for the last two.

"Hey, I want one," said Kevin, grabbing one egg.

"Boys," Mrs. Steiner said. "You can each take one." Standing, she began clearing the table and coffee trays. Melanie pitched in.

"Leave the dishes, ladies," Vanessa ordered. "They can wait till tomorrow."

"We'll at least carry everything into the kitchen," Mrs. Steiner said, stacking a pile of plates and utensils. "Kids, help clear the mess."

Melanie removed the soiled tablecloth. "Children, let's play some board games. Which one would you like to play first?"

"How 'bout Candy Land?" Stephanie suggested. She ran to fetch it from the corner.

Fourteen-year-old Wayne looked at the clock. "It's four. The Seahawks are playing the '49ers. Should be a cool match-up. I'd rather watch football. How about it?"

Jason motioned to the boy to join him and a cooing Dylan on the sofa. "I'm a step ahead of you, buddy. Already got the game on."

"All right!" Wayne said, pumping his fist. "Hope Seattle wins."

Several hours later, an excited Wayne jumped up and high-fived Jason. The Seahawks won with a last-second field goal. By then everyone had devoured the pies, homemade cookies, and applesauce cake Mrs. Steiner had baked.

"Time to head home," Mrs. Steiner said. "Thank you for a wonderful meal." Ellie and the children each hugged Vanessa.

"See you Sunday, Stephanie. Help Vanessa," Mrs. Steiner said.

"I will."

Jason filled several containers with leftovers while Melanie changed Dylan's diaper and dressed him in his snowsuit. "Are you sure you don't want help?"

"Positive." She looked at Stephanie. "It'll give her something to do tomorrow."

The youngster swiveled around in the chair, squinting her face. She sprang up to kiss Dylan on his head.

"Thank you for inviting us," Melanie said. "I enjoyed getting more acquainted with the children."

Stephanie parked herself on the floor in front of the TV to watch an animated holiday special. Vanessa relaxed her exhausted body on the sofa for a few minutes of rest. She plunked her feet on the coffee table and closed her eyes. Within moments her head drooped downward and rhythmic, soft breaths escaped. A half-hour later, the ringing phone awakened her.

"I'll get it!" Stephanie said, running to grab the device. When Stephanie's voice yelled JP's name, Vanessa sat erect, wide awake.

Chapter 23

Vanessa strained her neck to hear Stephanie's side of the conversation. She tried to get her attention. Too late. Stephanie disconnected. She didn't want to appear too eager. In a subdued tone, she asked, "What did JP want?"

"He's coming tomorrow for his sunglasses." She headed to the bathroom.

Vanessa tapped her right foot, waiting for Stephanie to return.

"Come sit beside me." Vanessa patted the cushion. She wanted Stephanie's undivided attention. "Now, tell me what he said. Did he ask to speak with me?"

"Nah. All he said is he'll be here tomorrow to pick up his glasses and the clay puppy I made him."

"You mean he's in town?" Every nerve in her body electrified, and her heart skipped a million beats.

"I guess so."

"What time is he coming?"

"Didn't say." Stephanie stretched herself on the carpet and resumed watching the show.

Vanessa leaned back on the sofa. Her lips curved into a pleasant smile. She thought about what she'd wear. My red pullover sweater or a festive Christmas blouse she'd bought for half price last year? And what about makeup and jewelry? She didn't want to overdress. Better to keep her appearance causal. Vanessa ran her fingers through her hair, trying to remember if JP preferred it pulled back behind her ears or cascading loosely along her face.

"Can I stay up a little later tonight?" Stephanie asked, interrupting Vanessa's musings.

Vanessa blinked. "I suppose so."

The next morning, Vanessa boiled water for the umpteenth time. Wired with caffeine from green tea, Vanessa busied herself tidying the house. She eyed the phone as if she could bully it to ring and hear JP's voice greeting her. The doorbell was also on her radar screen.

"Hey, can JP stay for dinner?"

"Are you sure he said he's coming?"

"Yep."

By six with no word from JP, Vanessa figured Stephanie misunderstood. She'd put her nerves through hell for nothing. She changed into comfortable sweatpants and a sweatshirt. Sighing, she removed the locket and earrings, then microwaved the leftovers. "Steph, set the table."

After dinner, Vanessa stepped outside to empty the wastebasket. She didn't hear the rat-a-tat-tat on the front door. Stephanie opened it in a flash, greeting JP. She grabbed his hand and pulled him inside to the kitchen. "He's here!"

Re-entering the kitchen, Vanessa dropped the wastebasket when she saw JP watching her. Something fluttered in her stomach. She didn't know what that feeling was.

"You okay?"

"I'm...I'm fine." She puffed her hair and smoothed the wrinkles from her sweatshirt. "I'm surprised you're here. When I met your mother at the grocery store, she said you had to work."

"I got a few days off and surprised Mom last night. She suggested—and I agreed—it was a good chance to come over and retrieve my sunglasses." JP plucked a clean plastic trash bag from under the sink and lined the basket. He smiled at Stephanie. "If you want the sunglasses, they're yours."

"All right! Don't forget your clay puppy."

"I won't this time." He rubbed his palms together. "Where are your coats? Mom said you planned to attend the Christmas tree lighting festivities at Pioneer Square. How about I accompany you two charming ladies?"

Vanessa knew she hadn't mentioned the ceremony to Mrs. Monroe. *Hmmm…*

"Can we? Please," Stephanie begged, climbing on a chair and bouncing up and down.

"Get down before you fall," Vanessa said.

Stephanie jumped off. "Well, can we?"

Two sets of eyes focused on Vanessa. "It's chilly tonight."

"Stephanie and I won't take no for an answer." JP winked at the excited child. "Bundle up. Put on your heaviest coat."

Stephanie wasted no time pulling her hooded jacket off the hanger.

"I can't go looking like this." Vanessa touched her drab sweatshirt and sweatpants.

JP glanced at his watch. "We need to leave. The lighting starts in less than an hour."

"I'll freshen up a bit."

"You're gorgeous as you are."

Vanessa's heart fluttered. "Steph and I'll use the bathroom first, and I need my gloves," Vanessa said. "Be back in a jiffy."

A myriad of twinkling stars dotted the clear sky. The moon resembled a smooth pearl, illuminating the earth.

But as they neared the ceremony site, ominous gray clouds appeared.

"I hope the rain holds off until we're on the way home," Vanessa remarked.

Parking spots close to Pioneer Square were non-existent. They parked several long blocks away.

Vanessa wrapped her wool scarf around her neck and nudged her gloved hands inside her pockets. She fell in step behind JP and Stephanie, her gait faltering and uneven. She struggled to keep pace with them.

JP slowed his stride to match hers. "Are you okay? You're hobbling a little."

"I'm all right."

"It's her—"

"Look, Stephie," Vanessa interrupted. "A person dressed as a Christmas tree with sparkling lights. How neato. Don't you agree?"

"Yeah." Then, looking up at JP, Stephanie said, "I'm glad you brought us here. Thanks."

JP took Stephanie's left hand and swung it back and forth as they walked. "My pleasure."

Vanessa's rapid heartbeat settled down. She'd dodged a bullet, at least for now.

Mirthful folks of all ages jammed Pioneer Square. The exciting atmosphere seeped into Vanessa. She tingled from head to toe. She reminisced about the times her father had taken her to witness this annual ritual. This ceremony had always fascinated her.

The crowd listened to short speeches by local dignitaries, sang Christmas carols, and then the countdown "… three, two, one!" everyone shouted in unison. A bazillion-colored lights twinkled on the seventy-foot Douglas fir tree.

Stephanie was giddy with exhilaration. "Boy, oh, boy!" she exclaimed, jumping up and down. "What a gigantic tree! Neat star on top." As Stephanie's squeals got louder, Vanessa's grin grew wider. There is something intoxicating about an excited child. She was having an enjoyable time. She glimpsed in JP's direction. *Is he?*

The festive event concluded, and the trio headed toward the car. Vanessa pulled her knitted hat from her coat pocket and placed it on her head, covering her ears.

JP spotted a vendor selling coffee and hot cocoa. "How 'bout a cup?"

"Yeah!" Stephanie darted right in front of Vanessa, causing her to lose her balance. She tumbled forward onto the cement sidewalk. Her loafer shoe slipped off, and the prosthesis scraped against the hard surface. Vanessa could tell by the look of mild shock on the child's face she hadn't meant to cause the mishap. Her immediate concern, though, was to conceal the exposed prosthesis. She reached for the shoe. To hell with her embarrassment and skinned right knee.

With three quick strides, JP was beside her. "Are you okay?" He extended his hand.

Vanessa waved him off. "I can manage. Thanks." She tried to stand but failed. "I guess I'll need help after all." She stretched her hands upward. JP pulled her up. They were face to face. Vanessa turned her head and backed away, but staggered as she put weight on her left leg. "Sorry," she said as she grabbed JP's jacket.

Stephanie lifted Vanessa's sweatpants, exposing the misaligned prosthesis. "Look, JP, her fake foot." She laughed. "She's bionic."

JP's jaw dropped. Without a word, his arms moved to scoop up Vanessa.

Chapter 24

Vanessa clung to JP as he hurried to the car. Even on this chilly evening, warmth from JP's caring eyes reached into her soul and flamed her heart. She buried her face in his chest, keenly aware of his rapid heartbeat.

"I'm taking you to emergency at Providence." He started the engine and inched into the street, then accelerated beyond the speed limit.

"No, don't," Vanessa said. "There's nothing they can do. My stump doesn't hurt. I'll take off the prosthesis and call Dr. Hutchinson on Monday. He'll fix or replace this one. In the meantime, I'll use my crutches."

"Are you sure you want to go straight home?" JP turned his head and stared at Vanessa. A loud honk startled him as he drifted into the next lane. He swerved to avoid a collision, then eyeballed Stephanie in the rearview mirror. "Are you okay?"

"Yep."

"And you, Vanessa?"

"Fine." She stared forward, avoiding eye contact. She breathed a sigh of relief as JP slowed the car, and so did her heartbeat.

"I suppose you're wondering what happened." Vanessa broke the tense silence. She expected JP to blow a gasket because she'd hidden her injury from him. But his calm demeanor after the initial shock relaxed her.

Stephanie chimed in from the back seat. "She rolled down a hill, and a log ruined her foot."

JP touched Vanessa's shoulder.

"When we get to the house, I'll explain." She pointed to Stephanie.

JP nodded. "I get your drift."

JP steered his car into the driveway. He carried Vanessa to the front door and set her down. She leaned against the house as she pulled the door key from her coat pocket and unlocked the door. Settling Vanessa on the sofa, he helped remove her coat.

Stephanie yawned and rubbed her eyes.

"Young lady," Vanessa said, "past your bedtime. Say goodnight."

Running to Vanessa, she asked, "Are we going to read tonight?"

"How 'bout if I do the honors this time?" JP volunteered. "But let's make it a quick story. I want to make sure Vanessa is okay."

"Skip reading tonight. We'll read two stories tomorrow," Vanessa said.

Stephanie didn't argue. She hugged Vanessa and JP too, then scurried upstairs.

"Brush your teeth," Vanessa reminded her.

JP sat opposite Vanessa in the lounge chair. He crossed his legs, moving his left foot up and down. "I'm ready."

Vanessa wanted JP to stay, but she wasn't in the mood to discuss her accident. "I'm tired myself. How about you come tomorrow, and I'll explain everything?"

"I'm not budging until you tell me what happened. I'll

stay all night if need be," JP said, half-serious, half-kidding.

Of course, he would want an explanation…now, not tomorrow. "All right. But first I need to take off my prosthesis." She pointed to her crutches standing against the wall. "Would you bring them to me?"

JP handed them to Vanessa. "You need my help?"

"Nope." She grinned. "I've done this a million times by now. Be back in a flash."

Vanessa entered the downstairs powder room and lowered herself onto a wooden chair. She slid her leg out of the socket and removed the liner. Closing her eyes, she tensed her body and inhaled several deep breaths. She glanced at her image in the mirror. She reached for a hairbrush and ran it through her hair and pinched her cheeks. *Here goes!*

From the comfort of the lounge chair, JP observed Vanessa as she returned. She sat on the sofa opposite him, the sweatpants leg now flat.

"Are you going to be okay until you see the doctor?"

"Yes." She shot him a don't worry expression. "Now, about what happened." She cleared her throat. "I'm sure you recall how distraught I was about my father's sudden death. Then I called off the wedding—"

"I've been wondering what happened. About Stephanie too."

"Why?"

JP sat back, uncrossing his legs. "Who wouldn't be? A broken engagement? A young girl devoted to you and vice versa?" He pointed to her left foot. "Three surprising, unexpected events. At least to me."

Vanessa recounted the accident and amputation. "…next thing I knew I woke up in the hospital. While I was out of it, the doctors decided they had no choice but to amputate to save my life. Gangrene had set in."

"I'm so sorry." He moved across the room and sat beside her on the sofa. "Wish I had known."

"And if you did?"

"Would you have wanted to see me?"

Yes! Yes! She screamed to herself. But she couldn't admit it out loud.

"Well, would you?" JP pressed.

"I lost my father and Greg. Then you leave without a word. Except for Stephanie and the other foster kids, it's been a tough couple of years. Everyone close to me was gone."

"Did that include me?"

"I considered you a special friend. You made me feel alive again and were supportive and helpful. You were more than willing to help me find info about my adoption. I was appreciative."

Did she see hope fade from his eyes, or did she imagine it?

JP didn't look at her but brushed imaginary lint from his jeans.

Vanessa yawned.

He rose. "I can take a hint. I'm sorry about your foot, but you appear to be functioning well. Working?"

"Not yet. I'm planning to resume teaching in the next year or two. Meanwhile, my priority is Stephanie. I want to adopt her."

"Speaking of Stephanie, how did you meet her? And what happened between you and Greg? All I know so far is he's coaching in Hawaii."

"Not now, JP."

"How about if I come by tomorrow and take you bowling?" He covered his mouth. "Oops. How about lunch? You can tell me all the details then. By the way, I'm assuming you haven't found out anything more about your mother. How about your aunt? Located and contacted her yet?"

"No."

"Why not? She no doubt has all the answers."

"Later."

"Okay, but this inquiring mind wants to find out everything before I return to Rathdrum on Sunday."

He's leaving again. No intention of pursuing a relationship. She declined his invitation.

"I'll tell you what," he said, forcing enthusiasm. "Tomorrow's Saturday. My last full day before I leave. I'll come around noon with lunch. Pizza? Hamburger? Or how about stir-fry? Your favorite."

He remembers. "Ah, why not?" It would be the last chance to see him. Vanessa stood and positioned the crutches under her armpits. She followed him to the front door.

"I wish I could persuade you to explain everything tonight. I doubt I'll sleep well." Opening the door, he turned around. He cupped Vanessa's chin in his hand. His eyes met hers. He seemed to ask permission for his next move. Vanessa didn't push him away. Her fingers loosened their grip on the crutches as his lips covered hers in a fleeting kiss. He was out the door, running to the car as one crutch landed on the tile entrance with a bang. He glanced backward before he bolted inside his vehicle as the threatening clouds began drenching the landscape.

Vanessa had delayed closing the door. She watched as he exited the car and ran across the lawn toward her. The beat of her heart was louder and faster than the falling rain. He stepped inside and pulled her into his embrace. Warm lips pressed against hers. He deepened the kiss, igniting a burning sensation cruising from her head to her toes. His grip squeezed her tighter. She urged herself to pull away, but her body refused.

"Oh, Vanessa," JP whispered. Never had her name sounded so wonderful.

He picked up the crutch, and as sudden as he had appeared, he departed, leaving Vanessa in a daze.

As Vanessa lay in bed, she traced her finger along her lips. She savored the brief yet passionate kiss. A pleasant smile lingered.

"WHEN YOU DO SOMETHING, YOU GO ALL OUT, MOM," JP kidded. "You sure did a number on your ankle." He reprimanded her. "Carrying too many of your garden supplies down the slippery stairs was dumb."

"Yeah, yeah. I learned my lesson," Mrs. Monroe said, wincing at the pain in her swollen ankle.

"I'll make you comfy," JP said, fluffing a pillow. "Plan on staying off your foot. Can I trust you after I return to Rathdrum? Will you follow the doc's orders?"

"I'll be fine. Don't worry."

"I don't like being so far away, especially now with your injury."

She pummeled her fist on the couch cushion. "Then move back home!"

"I can't quit my job."

"Nonsense. You quit Milwaukie PD without warning," she reminded him. She reached for the latest issue of *Homes and Gardens* magazine. "By the way, didn't you mention something about seeing Vanessa today?"

"I was going to bring her lunch, but it's too late now." He glanced at his watch. One o'clock. "I'll stay here with you. I'll call her in a bit and tell her what happened. She'll understand." He grabbed the remote and turned on the

Oregon State football game. They trailed as usual.

Putting down the magazine, his mother seized the opportunity to knock some sense into her son. "Just because Cheryl burned you, doesn't mean you can't give love another shot. I will not let your fear of another rejection rob you of a chance to win Vanessa's heart. Go fight for her."

"I'm not convinced I can break through her barrier. I'm not encouraged she hid her injury from me. Why didn't she tell me about it last August?"

"I believe she was afraid you'd reject her. Vanessa has feelings for you. Strong ones."

Cheers coming from the TV drew JP's attention. Oregon State scored a touchdown. They now led. But there was still an entire quarter remaining.

"JP, forget the game," Mrs. Monroe said. "You want to be with Vanessa, not babysitting me. You care more for her than you ever did for Cheryl. Tell her."

"You're right," he admitted. "If you don't mind, I will head over there. Also, I'm curious what happened between her and Greg."

"You haven't left yet? Vamoose!"

He paused for a moment to watch the replay of Oregon State fumbling the football on their six-yard line. He turned off the TV.

"Put the crutches close to me." Mrs. Monroe motioned with her hands for him to leave.

He kissed his mother's cheek. "Call if you need me. I'll be home—"

"Late tonight? Or better yet, tomorrow morning," she said, cracking a smile.

When the doorbell rang, Vanessa grabbed her crutches and shuffled to the door. JP greeted her with an apologetic smile. "Sorry I'm late. I should have called." He held up a container of stir-fry. "A packet of extra soy sauce included. And an order of mac and cheese for Stephanie." He placed the containers on the coffee table. "My mother fell and sprained her ankle. I had to take her to emergency."

"How is she?"

"She'll be on crutches for a few days."

Vanessa held up a crutch, grinning. "I can relate."

"Ready to eat?"

"I already ate when you didn't show up. Put it in the kitchen. I'll warm it up for dinner."

"Where's Stephanie?"

"At Melanie's visiting Dylan. She loves spending time with him. She's his 'big sister' after all. Melanie's bringing her back any time now."

As the two approached the sofa, JP noticed the damaged prosthesis lying on the lounge chair. "I'm impressed how you've adjusted to your 'fake' foot as Stephanie calls it." He laughed.

"At first everything was tedious and cumbersome but I'm now used to the process."

"Do you sleep with it on?"

"No. I remove it every night."

"Is it hard climbing the stairs?"

"I struggled at first, but I've developed a method. I considered moving to a one-level house or apartment, but,"—she looked around the room with a sentimental twinge—"this is my home. Anyway, I'm seeing Dr. Hutchinson Monday. I learned to deal with periodic mishaps. How about something to drink?"

"No thanks." JP sat on the opposite end. He crossed his legs and leaned forward, resting his chin on his fingers. "I don't want to beg. Tell me about Stephanie and Greg."

It was time. He'd waited long enough. Vanessa told him how Stephanie entered her life. "We both needed someone to love. I am so grateful fate brought us together. Stephanie helped lift me out of my misery. She's my savior and I'm so blessed she's in my life. I've applied to adopt her."

"It's obvious you two adore each other," JP commented. "You'll be a wonderful mother. Does she know about her parents?"

"She knows they're dead, but not that they both died of drug overdoses. In due time, someone will tell her. I hope it's me. Based on my experience, the truth is the best policy. I don't want her to go through what I did, finding out about my adoption at twenty-four. I wish someone had told me much earlier."

The elephant in the room loomed. JP broached the topic. "And now, how about the breakup details?"

"Okay, okay. As you may recall, my search bugged Greg. He called it an obsession. And when they offered him the job in Hawaii, he accepted without discussing it with me. I guess you could say we each had our agendas, and neither of us would budge. Both stubborn. There was no room for compromise...here or Hawaii."

"Do you think you genuinely loved him, and him you?"

"Yes, but he changed. I realized he was arrogant and self-centered and wanted the coaching job more than he wanted me. It was difficult, but I ended the engagement." A scowl appeared as she reflected on the day she had thrown the ring at him and his harsh reaction.

JP slid closer and rubbed the back of Vanessa's neck.

"Jason told me his sister, Alicia, and Greg are happy. They both love Hawaii and his coaching is doing well."

"If only you'd told me you called off the wedding."

"You left with no warning, no goodbye, nothing. I had no idea where you went."

JP stood and placed his hands on his head, pacing. "I was a dodo brain. Two years," he said, his mouth tight and grim. "I spent two years assuming you married Greg. I ached for months trying to forget you."

"Well, if you hadn't rushed off, you would have found out." She wasn't about to take the blame. "I told you I called the precinct the morning after Greg and I split. If you'd waited one more day...I wanted—no, needed—your comfort." She waited for his reaction.

JP inhaled a deep breath and moved even closer, so close their thighs touched.

"I loved you more than life itself. I realized you were engaged, but I sensed you felt something for me. More than a casual friendship. Tell me I'm wrong," he challenged.

Vanessa bent her head down, staring at the carpet.

The ringing of JP's cell phone interrupted the moment. He stood, pulled the device from his jeans pocket. Caller ID showed the police chief. *Damn!* His sense of duty prevailed.

"Monroe here."

JP frowned and shook his head as he shoved the phone into his pocket. "A menacing gang of troublemakers from around the area is threatening to create havoc in town. They've already vandalized the town's Christmas tree. Folks are worried it could escalate into violence." He rubbed his chin, shaking his head. "Thought nothing like this would happen in a small town. The county sheriff has ordered all law enforcement to report for duty. No exceptions. The chief wanted me to fly, but agreed to let me drive back if I leave right now."

Vanessa broke eye contact with JP. Her head sagged down to her chest, her eyes shutting. She would say nothing now…wouldn't let JP see any sign of disappointment in her. Arranging her face into something she hoped appeared casual, she asked, "Will you be at risk?"

"I'll be fine." He sat and wrapped his arms around Vanessa, pressing his forehead against hers. "I want to stay. I need to explain why I left two years ago so you'll understand why I did."

"I'm all ears." She wished JP had let the call go to voice mail.

"No time now. But I'd move back here in a heartbeat if you encouraged me there's a chance with you. Do I leave a happy camper, or should I walk through the door and out of your life forever?"

Chapter 25

Vanessa looked at JP, wishing she could blurt out, "I love you!" The thought seemed so real she expected him to answer, but she hadn't expressed it out loud. Instead, she said, "You realize I'm handicapped. I'm damaged."

JP's eyes widened. "Your foot isn't an issue." He leaned closer and smiled. "You aren't just a leg. You are the person...I like."

Vanessa thought about the hesitation she heard before he said, *I like.*

He turned Vanessa's head to face him. "Are you trying to discourage me?"

The front door slammed against the wall. "JP!" Stephanie shouted. She ran to JP and wrapped her arms around his waist. "I'm glad you're here."

JP picked up the excited child and twirled her around. "Me too."

"Are you staying for dinner?"

Looking into her eyes with a serious expression, he said, "I'd like to, but I have to leave. I was just saying goodbye to Vanessa." JP acknowledged Melanie as he set Stephanie on the sofa.

"Where's Dylan?" Vanessa asked. She loved cuddling her godchild as often as possible.

"Home with Jason."

Stephanie's smile turned into a frown. "Humph. Why can't you stay?"

"Believe me, young lady, I want to hang around, but there's trouble brewing in Rathdrum. The chief ordered me back to work."

"Tell him you don't wanna leave," Stephanie said.

"I wish I could." JP glanced in Vanessa's direction. He couldn't linger any longer. It was a seven-hour drive to Rathdrum. "Give me a goodbye hug, kiddo." Stephanie jumped off the couch into JP's arms. The cop and kid embraced.

Then he approached Vanessa and pulled her up so close their noses almost touched. Warmth cruised throughout her body. She bowed her head, but not before she saw the pleading expression on JP's face. Her voice betrayed her. No words came forth.

Whispering, JP said, "I'll be waiting to hear from you… but not forever." He eased her back onto the sofa.

JP's car door slammed shut. An invisible force tugged at Vanessa. *I must go after him!* Positioning the crutches under her armpits, she hurried to the door. By the time she reached the porch stairs, his car turned the corner out of sight. Vanessa launched a futile yell. "JP! Don't leave! Please come back!" She leaned against the railing and thumped her crutches up and down. *I'm a stubborn, stupid fool!*

Melanie stepped outside. She put her arm around Vanessa. "He isn't coming back today." Vanessa nodded as she followed her friend inside. She plopped onto the couch, allowing the crutches to drop. She stared at the ceiling as if in a trance. A single tear squeezed out.

"Does your leg hurt?" Stephanie stroked the leg.

Vanessa shook her head as more tears flowed.

"Why are you crying? Are you sad 'cause JP left?"

"Steph," Melanie pointed to a box of Kleenex, "bring it to me."

"He's gone. Gone without me telling him what he wanted to hear," Vanessa wailed.

"What do you mean?" Melanie leaned closer.

Stephanie handed Vanessa a tissue. "Don't cry. I'm here and I love you."

The child's sentiment comforted Vanessa, but not enough to halt the streams of tears. "Steph, honey, how about doing your homework or creating another clay masterpiece?"

"I want to stay with you."

"I'm fine," Vanessa said. "I'd like to talk with Melanie alone."

Stephanie's lips jutted out, and she made no move to leave.

Melanie took the girl's hand. "How about some—"

"Ice cream!" Stephanie withdrew her hand from Melanie and took off for the kitchen. "I'll dish myself up."

"Rinse the bowl and spoon when you're done and then make something Christmassy with the clay. Or read." Vanessa called out to the departing youngster.

Melanie sat next to Vanessa. "What happened?"

Vanessa looked into Melanie's questioning eyes. "He asked me if I wanted him in my life, but I didn't answer."

"Why not, Miss Stubborn?"

"I guess I'm afraid he'll tire of me because of my disability. Or we'll disagree where to live like Greg and I did. Crap. I don't know why!" She plucked a tissue from the box and blew her nose. "I drove him away. I'll never see him again."

"What did you say to him?"

"Instead of telling him my genuine feelings, I reminded him of my handicap. He asked if I was discouraging him."

"It sounds as though you can't say the words he's longing for."

Vanessa's lungs struggled for breath. Failure to express herself to JP was one of the dumbest blunders she ever made.

"You are so pigheaded," Melanie said, smiling.

"Dad accused me of the same thing on more than one occasion."

Melanie handed the phone to Vanessa. "Miss Stubborn, start pressing those numbers and tell JP the truth. It'll make his long drive more tolerable."

"I can't. Not now. He's no doubt heading to his mother's to get his stuff and say goodbye. I'll call him tomorrow."

"Promise?"

"Yes."

Melanie stood, putting her coat on. "I'll hold you to it." She shook her finger at her friend before leaving.

<hr/>

"You were quite fortunate, Miss Cox," Dr. Hutchinson said. "Your prosthesis needs only a minor adjustment. It'll take a few moments. How was your Thanksgiving?"

"We had a great time. Thanksgiving with all the trimmings. I never laughed so much. Then this." She pointed to the leg. "Talk about ruining the holiday weekend."

The doctor chuckled. "Would you like a hairy leg? I had a guy who changed his mind. I can give you one for half-price."

Vanessa laughed. "That would be a conversation starter if I wore shorts or a dress. Sorry, not this time."

The doctor shrugged. "Your loss. It might be a good spare." He handed the prosthesis to Vanessa. "All done! Put it on and make sure it's a proper fit and feels okay."

Vanessa smoothed the liner and slipped her leg inside

the prostheses. She walked around the office several times. "Everything seems fine. Thank you, Dr. Hutchinson."

"You're welcome. See you in a few months." He paused at the door. "Enjoy the holiday season."

Melanie was waiting for Vanessa in the lobby area, grading homework assignments. "Looks like the doc repaired your fake foot," Melanie observed.

"Yep." She tossed the crutches into the back seat.

On the ride home, Melanie asked in a lighthearted tone. "What did JP say when you called him?"

Vanessa stared through the window at the bright Christmas lights adorning several businesses.

Melanie forged on. "Have you called him as you promised?"

Yes, she'd kept her promise. Well, not exactly. She phoned him twice but hung up before the first ring. "He didn't answer," she fibbed.

"Did you leave a message?"

"No."

Melanie shook her head. "For Pete's sake, Vanessa. Must I call him for you? Leave a message next time if he doesn't answer." She shot a glance in Vanessa's direction. "Stephanie and I may have to join forces. She's determined to make JP your boyfriend." With a sly grin, she added, "I'm inclined to help her."

"You are cunning, my dear friend." Vanessa patted Melanie's thigh. "Don't give her any ideas."

Melanie grinned like a Cheshire cat.

Chapter 26

———◆———

Five days later, on Saturday, Vanessa picked up Stephanie for the weekend. Stephanie's upbeat Christmas spirit was infectious. Once home, Vanessa didn't waste any time pulling out the boxes of decorations from the garage. Stephanie dived right in, arranging the assortment of figures, artificial garland, and candles. Vanessa offered to help her display the nativity scene.

"I can do it all by myself." She began unwrapping the figurines. She put a lot of effort into displaying them in perfect order and gave special care to baby Jesus.

Vanessa opened a tote container filled with ornaments. Lying on top was a silver box lined inside with green velvet. She pulled out an ornament wrapped in red tissue paper. *Baby's first Christmas, 1986.* The angel's wings still shined with gold glitter, but there was a tiny chip above one eye. Vanessa held the angel in her hand, brushing her fingers over the surface. She placed it against her chest, soaking in the memories of her father lifting her onto his shoulders so she could place it near the top of the tree. This angel was a bridge back to happy times when she was a carefree youngster cloaked in the love of her father. A small whimper escaped.

Stephanie stepped back to admire the nativity scene. The satisfaction on Stephanie's face evoked a smile from Vanessa.

"Am I interrupting anything?" Melanie asked as she walked inside.

"Heck, no," Stephanie said, grabbing her arm. "Look what I did!"

Melanie eyeballed the decorated living room and nativity scene. "You've been busy. Quite a cheery sight. My compliments."

"Where's Dylan?" Stephanie asked.

"At his grandma's. I'm on my way there to fetch him. I thought I'd stop by for a short time to say hi. Vanessa told me you're spending the weekend."

"Can we get a tree now?" Stephanie stood in front of Vanessa.

"Too soon. It's only December first," Vanessa answered.

"So what?" Stephanie said, her eyes pleading.

"All righty. We'll go to the church lot this afternoon and choose one."

"I want a gigantic tree with a twinkling star on top." Stephanie stood on her tiptoes and twirled around, reaching for the ceiling.

"Not too tall. I don't think we can handle a large tree by ourselves."

"Let's ask Jason to help us. Or I know! How about JP?"

Melanie flashed her eyes toward Vanessa to see her reaction.

"He lives too far away," Vanessa said, wishing that weren't true.

"But he likes me." Stephanie placed her hands on her hips and puffed her cheeks out.

Vanessa rose, kissing Stephanie on the head. "Fun's over for now. Homework time. Might as well tackle your math problems." Addressing Melanie, she said, "Hey, teacher with superb talent, you can help get her started while I take the empty boxes into the garage. I'm going to give the shelves a quick dusting."

"Take your time." She held out her hand to Stephanie. "Come on. Show me how your addition and subtraction are improving." Moments later, Melanie swung into action. "Quick, Stephanie. Do you know JP's cell phone number?"

Stephanie darted to the hallway desk and opened the drawer. She pulled out a piece of paper and handed it to Melanie. They headed to the kitchen.

"I'm sure Vanessa didn't call JP as she promised. So, you call him and ask him to come help with the Christmas tree. But don't tell Vanessa. It'll be our secret."

The girl's eyes lit up. She grabbed the phone and pressed the buttons as Melanie spoke each number.

Stephanie counted six rings before JP picked up.

"Hi. It's me, Stephanie!" She greeted him in a sing-song tone. "What took you so long to answer?"

Panting and wiping away sweat, JP answered. "Hi, young lady. I'm in the middle of my workout."

"Guess what? We're getting a Christmas tree. I want a tall one, but Vanessa says we'll have trouble carrying a heavy one. Could you come to help us?"

"I'd love to, Stephie, but I can't."

"Shucks. We'll ask Jason then. But we'd rather you help."

"We? Does Vanessa want me to come?"

"She said you live too far away."

"How…how is she?"

"Okay, but she bawled a bunch when you left."

"She did?"

"Tell JP Vanessa wants him to come back," Melanie whispered.

"She misses you and wants you here."

"Hmmm. Then why hasn't she..." his voice trailed off. "Does she know you're calling me?"

"Nah. She's in the garage. Would you...Uh oh. Gotta go." Click.

———— ❖ ————

THE FOLLOWING EVENING VANESSA RELAXED IN THE lounge chair, munching on a Santa-shaped sugar cookie. She had invited the children over to help decorate the tree and frost the cookies. Her heart warmed as she watched the delighted children wrap strings of blinking lights and the handmade green and red paper chain around the branches. Wayne got the honor of placing the twinkling star on top. She hung her first Christmas angel ornament on the highest bough. Crumbs and paper scraps dotted the carpet. But she didn't care. Clean up could wait till tomorrow.

Vanessa leaned against the headrest, closing her eyes. Her mind wandered off, thinking about JP. She wanted to talk with him, to resume their interrupted conversation. She scolded herself for discouraging him and failing to contact him as she promised Melanie. What held her back?

The doorbell rang. Her eyes shot open. She wasn't expecting anyone.

When she opened the door, Vanessa's face washed blank with confusion. Her brain couldn't register fast enough her Aunt Helene stood inches from her. She stared, motionless, at the woman, oblivious to the nippy air drifting inside.

Chapter 27

———◆———

"Are you going to invite me in?" Helene asked.

"Ah…ah, of course," Vanessa stammered, stepping aside.

Helene shed her coat, gloves, and wool hat, draping them on the lounge chair.

An awkward silence dominated the reunion. Vanessa stared at the woman whom she blamed for her father's death. She had no contact with her for almost two-and-a-half years. And now, over time, her hostility toward her aunt had thawed.

The pair sat side by side on the sofa. "I completed my latest assignment, and I decided it was about time I find out how you're doing. I wish I'd contacted you sooner, but I was afraid you'd still reject me. You were quite mad at me at Lyle's funeral." Her hands covered Vanessa's. She got right to the point. "I'm so sorry I divulged your adoption in the manner I did." She looked at Vanessa with pleading eyes. "I'm hoping you'll forgive me, and we can establish a relationship."

"I over-reacted. Guess it was the double whammy of finding out Dad was not my biological father and his death." Stroking her aunt's coarse hands, Vanessa continued. "You're my only relative. Nothing gained by holding a grudge. Besides," her lips curved into a wily grin, "I'm counting on *you* to tell me all the details about my adoption and mother."

Staring at the tree, Helene commented, "I like the handmade decorations. Did your class make them?"

"No. I volunteer at a foster home. The kids made them. We had a decorating party earlier today."

"Are you still teaching fifth grade?"

"Not now. I've taken time off."

"I'm surprised. Why?"

Vanessa steered the conversation back to the only topic open for discussion. "I've spent many hours searching for information. So far, I found my birth certificate naming Rosemary Peterson as my mother. She died in a fire when I was about six months old. I also found a note written to Dad signed by Rosey saying she wants nothing to do with the baby. That baby was me, wasn't it?"

Helene stared at the floor, loosening her collar.

"Well?"

"Yes, it was you."

Vanessa leaned against the sofa back, staring straight ahead. Her aunt confirmed what she'd suspected. She sat there, her heart cracking like glass and lips quivering.

Helene touched Vanessa's knee. "I understand your desire to find out the truth, but I'm concerned about your reaction. Let's talk about something else. Where's your hubby? Greg is his name if I recall."

Vanessa waved her index finger back and forth. "No changing the subject. I've waited too long. If only I'd let you tell me after Dad's death instead of chasing you off."

Her aunt hesitated. "It's best you never know the circumstances."

"How bad could it be? I can handle whatever." At least she hoped so.

"The truth is unpleasant." She looked down the hallway toward the kitchen. "I need a drink. Have any coffee?"

Vanessa stood. "Where are my manners? I only have instant. Are you hungry?"

"I'm famished."

"Don't think I'm letting you off the hook." They proceeded to the kitchen. "You like meatloaf? I added chopped onions."

"I'll eat anything," Helene said. "You wouldn't believe the local cuisine I tasted in some foreign countries." She shook her head, sticking out her tongue. "Ever try fried tarantulas? In Vietnam, I ate cobra heart."

"Ugh."

Helene sat at the table while Vanessa warmed the meatloaf, mashed potatoes, and green beans. Looking around the kitchen, Helene noticed Lyle had updated it since her last visit eons ago. A shade of bright yellow covered the walls, matching the sunflower café curtains. An assortment of hand-painted plates of various flowers hung in a random arrangement on one wall. She smiled when she recognized her mother's 1950s era Betty Crocker cookbook standing upright on the granite countertop.

Without warning, pain cut deep within Vanessa's stump, throbbing and burning. She bit her lip to keep from crying out. She grabbed the corner of the countertop, clutching her left leg.

Helene leaped from the chair. "What's wrong?"

Vanessa had no choice but to disclose her handicap. "It's phantom pain from my stump. I experience it now and then."

"Phantom pain? Stump?"

"I had an accident over a year ago in October. A log crushed my left foot. The doctors amputated it. I now have a fake foot as Stephanie calls it." She pulled up her pant leg, revealing the prosthesis.

Helene gasped and put her hands over her lips.

"Right now, I need to sit and massage my stump. The pain should subside soon. Most of the time it's mild. I don't take medication." She walked at a snail's pace into the living room.

"I'm so sorry. If only I'd known, I would've flown here right away." Helene approached her. "Lean on me and I'll help you to the sofa."

"Thanks, but I can manage. I'm used to these occasional bouts." She sat on the couch. Removing the prosthesis, she began massaging the stump.

Helene sat beside her. "Why didn't you notify me?"

"You never told let me where you were. And at the time of my accident, I still blamed you for Dad's death." A few minutes later, she rested against the armrest. "Better now."

Helene's tense muscles relaxed. "Appears you've adjusted to your handicap."

After the initial anger and self-pity of the first few months, Vanessa had accepted the card dealt to her. It pleased her she had adapted to the lifestyle dictated by such an injury.

"Is there anything I can do?" Helene asked.

"Yes, tell me about my birth parents." She leaned forward, wide-eyed. "You and Dad became estranged because you wanted him to tell me the truth when I was old enough, and he wouldn't. Right?"

Helene nodded. "I'm still convinced you shouldn't know everything. Keep the thought your dad kept your adoption a secret out of deep love for you."

"Too bad you never reconciled before he died." Vanessa exhaled a deep breath, thinking about her father. She still missed him.

"I regret that, and it has weighed on my mind all this time. I loved my brother. He was a good man. Our disagreement cost us the relationship we enjoyed before your adoption."

At that moment Vanessa understood the siblings' bitter disagreement had adversely impacted Helene. She raised an imaginary white flag. "Thanksgiving has passed, but I'm thankful you've re-entered my life," Vanessa said, her tone sincere. "Let's put the past aside and start anew."

"Thank you, dear. I'm happy and relieved. And now," she sat erect, "I'm eager to hear about Greg. It would have delighted Lyle you two settled in this house. I'm relieved you didn't move. Would've been harder to locate you."

"I'm not married."

"Whoa, Nellie. I hope there are no more bombshells. You mentioned Stephanie. Who is she?"

"A young girl I plan to adopt, God willing. She's one of the children living in the foster home. She and the other children decorated the tree today. I hope you can meet Stephie. Are you planning on spending a few days here?"

"I do if you'll have me."

"Of course." She dangled her left leg over the armrest. "I acknowledge you want to know about Greg and me. But I don't want to wait any longer for an explanation about my birth. Tell me first, then it'll be my turn."

"Pain gone?"

"Yep."

Helene stood. "Well, before I start, I need a bathroom break and then I'm going to get the food you dished up. The growl you heard is my empty stomach begging for nourishment." She walked a few steps down the hall. She stopped, turning toward Vanessa. "Are you sure you want me to tell you every detail? Ignorance is bliss as the saying goes."

"Yes! The whole truth. I want you to disclose everything. How terrible could the truth be?"

Helene shook her head as the corners of her mouth turned down.

Chapter 28

Helene returned, carrying a plate heaped with warmed-up food. She took a few bites. "Mmmm. Yummy. Tastes like the meatloaf Mom made."

"It should. I followed your mother's recipe. Dad made meatloaf two, three times a month. He experimented with additional ingredients. Never put in jalapeno peppers." She chuckled, recalling running to the sink to spit out the first bite and sticking her mouth under the faucet. "I should copy the recipe onto a fresh card. It's faded and has ketchup smudges."

Helene puffed a pillow and leaned against it. Lyle's portrait stared at her from above the fireplace mantel. She faced Vanessa. "It's fitting, I guess, seeing Lyle looking down on us as though he's permitting me to tell you everything."

Vanessa blew her father a kiss. "Now, no more stalling. Please start talking." She wouldn't wait a second longer to learn what she searched and obsessed over for two-and-a-half years.

"Here goes." Helene glanced at her brother's cheery face. "When your father was sixteen, a family moved in a few doors down the block. Their only child, Rosemary— everyone called her Rosey—was a year younger than Lyle.

They developed a close friendship and became inseparable. I guess you could call them a couple." Helene smiled, but her expression soon soured. "For some incomprehensible reason, during her senior year, Rosey did a one-eighty. She started hanging around with an immoral, despicable crowd. She dropped out of school, began drinking, smoking, and became promiscuous. Her parents and your father tried everything under the sun to change her behavior. Nothing worked. Rosey rebuffed their 'meddling' as she called it, and left home at eighteen, estranged. She broke her parents' hearts. Lyle continued for years to convince Rosey to abandon her lifestyle. She rejected all his efforts. It tortured him. Mom and Dad tried to persuade him to get over her and move on with his life. He paid no attention. To this day I'm convinced Rosey had a mental disorder."

Vanessa leaned forward, resting her chin on clenched fists. "Did Dad love her?"

"He said he cared about her. I believe he loved her but wasn't *in* love with her. Your father seemed obsessed. Like he was under her spell." Pausing, Helene took another bite. "Yum, this is so good."

"So, how did I appear in this picture?"

"Rosey," Helene paused, "got mixed up with a rotten son-of-a-bitch pimp. She fell under his influence, prostituting herself. That's what bothered your father the most. He still wouldn't abandon her throughout his college years, even after he landed his first job. When she was twenty-three—" The sound of Vanessa's phone ringing startled them.

"Go on." The last thing Vanessa wanted was an interruption.

"Aren't you going to answer the phone?" Helene asked. "Could be important."

"No. What happened?"

"She became pregnant. My brother, still fixated on her—but why, God only knows—persuaded her to have the baby, *you*." She ate a few more mouthfuls of food. "Rosey told Lyle she regretted letting him talk her into carrying the baby. She wanted an abortion. But she did cut way down on her drinking and smoking. Thank God you were born healthy."

"I'm numb," Vanessa said. "This news is nothing I expected. I can't figure how a decent person like Dad remained involved with this Rosey person, my mother."

From the time she learned of her adoption, Vanessa speculated about her birth. "I considered all the usual suspect circumstances. An unwed teenager. Two teenagers ill-equipped to raise a child. The girl forced to give up the baby. Or the mother died in childbirth." She waved her hand to dismiss the idea. She leaned closer to Helene and lowered her voice. "I'd even thought about rape. But I never imagined it was a sexual encounter for money. A business arrangement. Offspring of a prostitute. Rejected." The words bounced inside her mind. Vanessa's brain scrambled to make sense of it all. Her earlier enthusiasm evaporated. The throbbing pain in her head felt like someone stabbed her skull with a sharp knife. She rested her head against the sofa back, squeezing her eyes shut. She massaged her temples, willing the aching to go away.

"I hope you now understand why your father didn't want to reveal the origins of your birth. He tried to protect you."

Vanessa's moist eyes blurred her vision as she stared at her father's portrait.

It was done. Helene had revealed the cruel truth. She pulled Vanessa to her and massaged Vanessa's back as Vanessa rested her head on her aunt's ample bosom. The tears dampened her khaki shirt. "I regret telling you. I'm sorry."

Vanessa lifted her head. "Why do you think Dad wanted to raise me?"

"Who knows? I suspect since you were Rosey's child, Lyle thought he could remain connected to her. Despite the circumstances of your conception, you were lucky Lyle adopted you. Can you imagine her as a mother? You've got to admit Lyle was a damn good father."

"True. What about Rosey's parents? The baby, *me*, was their granddaughter."

"Rosey made it clear she didn't want them to raise you. Also, Lyle feared they might want to claim you in the future. He didn't want them in your life. In my opinion that was a mistake. They relinquished any rights to you. I was sorry for them. They lost their daughter to that repugnant lifestyle and then her death. A wasted life. They moved to Arizona."

"Are you positive?"

"Yes, they told me." She eyed Vanessa. "You aren't thinking about trying to find them, are you? They were in their early fifties in 1986. Twenty-six years later they'd be in their late seventies if they're still alive."

Her maternal grandparents, not fighting for and never contacting her, further dismayed Vanessa. "I'm tempted, but no."

Vanessa leaned back, processing the ugly truth. "How did you, Grandma, and Grandpa react to Dad's decision?"

Helene hesitated for a moment. "Your grandparents and I opposed the whole idea of the adoption. But Lyle was unwavering." She clasped her hands on her head and stretched her legs. "He considered himself fortunate to adopt you. He never complained about the sacrifices he made. I wish he would've found some lucky lady to marry."

"Did he encounter obstacles adopting me? A single father?"

"He met with resistance, but the court granted the adoption. You were about eight, nine months old. If they denied his petition, he would have fought for you with every means at his disposal. He adjusted his entire life to raising you. Our parents and I eventually accepted his decision. We grew to love you." Her warm smile convinced Vanessa. "We also promised to keep the secret. We agreed to tell you your mother died when you were still an infant."

"Why did you agree?" The deception bothered and saddened Vanessa. Her grandparents and Helene were complicit in perpetuating the lie.

"Speaking for myself, I maintained your father should be the one to tell you the truth. But when he continued to refuse, I finally demanded he tell you. Not all the details. Just the adoption part, but Lyle figured you'd be curious and ask questions. He didn't want you to find out you were unwanted. He wanted to spare you."

Unwanted. The word seared in Vanessa's mind.

"I felt you had a right to know Lyle wasn't your biological father. I was afraid the truth might come out someday, causing you anguish. Remember how you reacted the day in the hospital? I imagine it's been difficult for you living over two years with so many questions."

"How right you are." The note from Rosey popped into Vanessa's mind. "I want you to read what Rosey wrote to Dad. Hope you can make sense of it." She reached for her prosthesis.

"No, sit there. I'll get it."

"Go to Dad's bedroom and look inside the desk's top drawer for a white envelope."

Helene headed upstairs after bringing Vanessa a glass of water.

"Here we are." Helene waved the wrinkled paper like a rally towel at a sports game.

"Read it out loud," Vanessa said.

Helene sat, smoothing the paper.

"Lyle,

There's no way I want to keep the child and I don't want my parents raising her. I don't think they want to anyway. Since you're willing and already caring for her, she's yours. I'm relinquishing my parental rights. I'll sign whatever documents so you can adopt. I know you'll raise her well and give her the love she deserves. Are you crazy? No way would I marry you. I made a mess of my life. You deserve better. Don't contact me or bring the baby near me. Thanks for everything.

So long and take care. Rosey"

A deep sigh escaped from Helene as she silently re-read the note. "Looks like Rosey had a smidgeon of remorse. Hard to believe. She had no intention of changing her lifestyle. Seems she had no qualms allowing him to adopt you. The only honorable thing she did." She set the paper on the coffee table, stifling a yawn. "I've told you enough."

Vanessa sensed Helene was ready to end the emotional conversation, but she pressed on. Despite the ugly truth, Vanessa wanted every sordid detail. "And my bio father?"

"Let's drop this conversation," Helene said.

Vanessa insisted. "What could be worse than what you've already told me?"

"All right. Might as well get everything out in the open." She took a sip of the instant coffee. "Rosey refused to divulge the father's identity. We suspected a local public politician or prominent business executive."

"Why?"

"Rosey's clientele was upper class. No average dudes or slimeballs for her. After your birth, she bragged to Lyle about a hefty sum of money she received. No doubt hush money. She went on a shopping spree."

"The pimp?"

"He took his cut."

"So, my bio father is unknown?"

"Yes."

Another harsh blow.

Helene reached for her purse and pulled out a faded piece of paper. "Here's a snapshot."

Vanessa studied the two smiling figures standing in front of a stone fireplace. The man sported a white tuxedo with a red cummerbund and bow tie. The woman wore a floor-length red gown with a bodice sparkling with sequins. A three-bud, white rose corsage adorned her left shoulder strap. Vanessa recognized her father at once. But more intriguing, the young woman was a mirror image of herself. She looked at her aunt.

"Yes, that's your mother."

Vanessa's eyes refused to stray from the picture. "She doesn't seem like an awful person." A momentary pang of sympathy struck her. Then her tongue slithered between her lips, aimed at the individual who had given her birth… the mother she was obsessed to find.

"Dad snapped the picture the night of the prom Rosey's junior year. What a perfect couple." Helene sighed. "No one ever dreamed she'd change so drastically."

Although his intentions were admirable, she wished her father had told her everything. Vanessa ran her fingers along the edge of the snapshot, wrestling with her desire to keep it versus her compulsion to rip it to shreds. Vanessa stuffed the photo inside her pants pocket.

"Greg and several other people told me I should forget about finding out about my birth mother. They said the truth could be worse than not knowing. They were right," she admitted. "But I would always wonder. You understand, don't you?"

"Yes." Helene wrapped her hands around Vanessa's.

"By the way, what about the fire?"

"Rosey fell asleep in bed with a lit cigarette. A blanket ignited. Her death devastated your father. He said Rosey was at peace now. Her parents decided on cremation." Helene clasped her hands together, sitting erect. "Now, your turn. No marriage to Greg? What happened?"

"If you don't mind, can we wait till tomorrow? I don't feel up to talking about anything else right now." A yawn escaped. "I'm emotionally exhausted."

"Understandable."

"I doubt I'll be able to sleep. This was quite a revelation." Vanessa slid to the edge of the couch. "Would you hand me the crutches?" As Vanessa gripped them and stood, she lost her balance. Helene grasped her and pulled her close. Vanessa hugged her aunt, all traces of animosity replaced by a budding closeness. Her aunt had re-entered her life, and they made peace. Even the sudden ringing telephone failed to tear them apart.

Chapter 29

S till awake long after midnight, Vanessa turned on the lamp and reached for her pants. She pulled the snap-shot from the pocket, staring at the smiling couple. She ran her fingers over and over on the faded surface. Finally, a yawn escaped. Vanessa opened the nightstand's top drawer and dropped the picture inside. A single tear trickled down her cheek as she curled into the fetal position, drifting to sleep.

A few hours later, Vanessa's eyes blinked open. She stretched her body, then leaned against the headboard, contemplating Aunt Helen's revelations. She wished they weren't true. At least she now had a modicum of closure and realized the depth of her father's love and devotion. The illuminated clock showed six-ten. Too early to get up, but going back to sleep would not happen. She took a quick shower, careful to keep any noise low. Refreshed, she put on her prosthesis and clothing.

The aroma of pork sausage invaded Helene's nostrils as she entered the kitchen.

"Smells scrumptious," she said.

"Good morning, Aunt Helene," Vanessa said. "I'm fixing blueberry pancakes and sausage."

Helene began opening drawers and cupboards, looking for the dishes and utensils.

Vanessa pointed to a cupboard above the dishwasher. "Plates in there, silverware in that drawer."

"How did you sleep?" Helene asked as she set the table.

"Not well. I kept thinking about everything you told me last night."

"Now that you've learned the truth, I hope you can come to terms with it."

"I find comfort to know how much Dad loved me. If not for him, I wouldn't be—"

"Bottom line, Lyle wanted to protect you. His love for you was all-consuming," Helene said.

"I'd be lying if I said it doesn't bother me my birth mother was a prostitute who didn't want me. Hard to stomach she conceived me as a business arrangement." She stirred the pancake batter and added the fresh blueberries. "If only I hadn't been so pigheaded and angry. I made an idiotic choice to drive you away after Dad's death. I would have known everything over two years ago."

"Don't be so hard on yourself. How about telling me what happened between you and Greg?" Helene asked as she put a cup of instant coffee into the microwave.

"Not much to tell," Vanessa shrugged. "Let's just say we didn't have the same goals. It came down to did I love him enough to uproot myself and sacrifice my career?" She flipped a pancake and turned to Helene. "I came to realize I didn't and ended the engagement. He's married now to my best friend's sister-in-law."

"I'm sorry. Sounds like you had a tough couple of years."

"I couldn't agree more. There is one bright spot though."

"Let me guess," Helene said, tapping her finger against

her chin. "A young girl named Stephanie?"

"When I saw Stephanie peek out from behind Ellie, I was drawn to the shy girl. I decided to make her my special friend." A satisfying grin appeared. "We've helped each other deal with our troubled emotions. I consider her my savior. And the teacher in me is glad she loves to read." Vanessa shook her head, thinking about the child's traumatic past.

"You're a positive influence in her life. Be proud of yourself." Helene patted Vanessa's hand.

Pride is okay if you earned it through hard work, or dedication, or love. Vanessa gave her heart and soul to this young girl. She considered Stephanie her daughter. "She knows her parents are dead, but not that they were drug addicts and they rejected her. If I'm lucky enough to adopt her, I plan to disclose the facts at the appropriate time. I don't want her surprised like I was. Do you agree?"

"One hundred percent. You've experienced firsthand what consequences can happen from withholding the truth." Helene took a sip of coffee. "It's been well over a year since your broken engagement. No guy smart enough to date you this past year?"

"Stephanie is determined to find me a boyfriend." She laughed at the idea.

"Good for her. You could use a little nudging. You're what? Twenty-five? Six? Time's ticking."

"Look who's talking Miss Old Maid. For now, Stephie is my focus. Couldn't bear it if I lost her. There was a close call in August when a car almost hit her. Thank God JP rescued her."

"JP?"

A slight sparkle flashed on Vanessa's face without her permission.

"Tell me about this JP."

"He's the guy who saved Stephanie from the near-miss."

Vanessa cut another bite of pancake, hoping her aunt wouldn't see the flush creeping across her cheeks.

Astute Helene noticed Vanessa's reaction. "This JP isn't a mere casual acquaintance. Is he?"

Vanessa dipped her chin and stuffed another bite into her mouth.

Helene rested her chin on her left palm. "I'm waiting."

"Oh, all right." Vanessa gave her aunt the *Reader's Digest* version of how she met JP and his help with the search. "When he took off over two years ago, he assumed I was going to marry Greg. We had no contact until almost four months ago at Oaks Park, so he never knew I called off the marriage. But he knows now. He hasn't bothered to call since he returned to Rathdrum. I'm beginning not to care."

Helene's howl of laughter bounced off the walls. She fought for balance to prevent herself from falling off the chair, sprawled on the floor. "You don't fool me for a nano-second. Why don't you call him?"

Vanessa stacked the dirty dishes.

Helene wouldn't let it rest. She leaned across the table and removed Vanessa's hands from the plates. She focused on her eyes. "You're in love with him, aren't you?"

Vanessa neither confirmed nor denied the assertion. She wouldn't divulge how often her mind allowed JP tenancy. And how his mere touch sent tingling sensations cruising through her veins.

"Vanessa Rosemary Cox," Helene addressed her with a serious expression. "You want to see him and don't deny it! Contact him. There's nothing to lose."

"Okay, I admit I want him to see him, but I can't bring

myself to make the first move. What if he doesn't want to hear from me?"

Helene's tone became serious. "A piece of advice, dear. Act on your feelings. Don't choose to sacrifice a loving relationship or marriage as your father did. You deserve happiness with someone who loves you."

"Humph," grumbled Vanessa. "Now, what are your plans?"

"I can take a hint to change the subject." She brought the dirty dishes to the sink. "I've got to be at headquarters in Seattle a week from today. I'm applying for a desk job. The novelty and excitement of trekking all over the globe no longer exists. I'll leave Sunday to get settled in my apartment. Can you stand me for another six days?"

"You're welcome here as long as you want. I'll take you to Mrs. Steiner's so you can meet Stephanie and the other children." A pleasant feeling flowed through her body. "Steph's spending next weekend here. You can become more acquainted."

"I'm looking forward to meeting this young lady. Sounds like a delightful child." She did a quick rinse of the dishes and loaded them into the dishwasher. Vanessa covered the leftover sausage patties with plastic wrap and placed them in the fridge.

"I'm thankful we've reconciled," Helene said.

"Me too." They wrapped their arms around each other in a tight bear hug.

VANESSA PICKED UP STEPHANIE ON SATURDAY MORNING. Stephanie's frequent visits made Vanessa more determined than ever to adopt the child. Their bond was unbreakable.

"I know I promised to take you to the mall today," Vanessa said, "but I don't relish battling the crowds. How about we bake Christmas cookies instead, right after lunch?"

To Vanessa's surprise and relief, Stephanie didn't protest. "Okay, I guess. Can I bring some to the other kids?"

"Of course."

Stephanie wanted to show off her reading skills to Aunt Helene while Vanessa gathered the ingredients for sugar cookies.

"I'm glad to share this time with you, Stephanie," Helene said. "Vanessa told me how well you read and how much she loves you."

"I want her to be my forever mom." Her tone exhibited uncertainty mixed with hope.

Stephanie ran to the bookcase and chose a book about a mischievous puppy. Three pages into the story, the doorbell rang. Stephanie plopped down the book, running to the door. "JP!" she yelled.

Chapter 30

———◆———

Stephanie stepped onto the porch and thrust her petite frame against him in a tight hug. He twirled her around several times. Helene wasted no time joining Stephanie. She extended her hand toward the unexpected visitor.

"I'm Vanessa's aunt. Do come in."

JP entered, shaking off the chill.

Helene lifted her head to stare at JP's clean-cut face.

Turning to Helene, he said, "You must be the aunt Vanessa told me about. I'm glad to meet you, Ms…"

"Call me Helene."

"He's the guy who saved me from getting hit by the car and bought me a chocolate milkshake." Stephanie remained close by his side.

"I heard about the episode. Thank the Lord you appeared," Helene said.

"Yeah. I…" he stopped as his eyes focused on Vanessa entering the room. A small smile played on his lips as he saw the shock on Vanessa's face before she could hide it. For a split-second, Vanessa's expression turned blank before a grin crept onto her face. It soon stretched from one side to the other, showing her picture-perfect aligned teeth thanks to the braces her father insisted she needed.

Never one to let an opportunity go to waste, Helene spoke up. "We were just going to bake Christmas cookies. How about joining us? You can be the official taster. I'm sure Vanessa and Stephanie won't mind."

"Yeah," Stephanie answered for both.

JP removed his bulky jacket and tossed it on the lounge chair armrest. Helene entwined her arm around JP's. Side by side, they proceeded into the kitchen.

"So, what gives us the pleasure of your company?" Helene asked as she greased the baking sheets.

Vanessa perked up, eager for the answer while she showed Stephanie how to cream the sugar and butter.

"I got a phone call about ten days ago from a young lady asking for help with a Christmas tree. Looks like you managed without me." JP winked at the youngster.

"You told her I called!" Stephanie scolded him, cracking an egg. Vanessa removed a few pieces of shell from the batter.

"I phoned here twice last Sunday, but no answer. I decided to drop in while I'm in town to see the decorated tree."

"Hmmm," Helene said. "I'll bet those were the two calls the night I arrived. Didn't I tell you the first time it could be important?"

"You know why I didn't want to take the call," Vanessa said.

"You were here and didn't answer?" JP asked.

"We were having a serious discussion. I didn't want any interruptions," Vanessa answered.

JP scraped a fingerful of the cookie mixture. Helene slapped his hand, grinning. "Don't eat raw dough."

"What? Doesn't everyone?" He dipped his finger again and made a production licking the sweet dough.

Helene looked at Stephanie, now spotted with specks of flour on her face. "Have you visited Santa yet?"

"Nah."

"Not yet? A little over two weeks to put your order in. I'll finish the baking while JP and Vanessa take you to visit Santa. You can frost the cookies after you get home."

"I don't like crowds," Vanessa said. Stephanie's expression changed from happy to disappointed. "On second thought, I think I need some Christmas spirit." She glanced in JP's direction.

"I'm game."

"All settled." Helene helped Stephanie wash the flour from her face and hands. "Head to the bathroom while I get your coat and hat." Shortly, Helene shoved the trio out the door. "Stop for dinner on the way home. Don't hurry back." She flashed a devious smile and crossed her fingers.

The prospect of holiday discounts and finding the perfect gift lured hundreds of folks to the Clackamas Town Center mall. Shoppers flocked in and out of the decorated shops, carrying packages or dealing with cranky toddlers.

Stephanie sniffed and pointed. "Yum. Pizza! Can I have a piece?"

Lines in the food court stretched five, six persons deep in front of an assortment of fast-food vendors. JP squatted at eye level with the girl. "Tell you what, young lady. On the way home, we'll stop at Papandrea's."

"Goody. Can I order pepperoni?"

"Any kind your heart desires."

The trio strolled toward Santa's Village, dodging several inattentive shoppers texting on their cell phones. Stephanie joined giggling children waiting their turn to chat with Santa. The traditional fourteen-foot-high noble fir tree dominated the area behind Santa's red velvet throne. Blinking multi-colored lights illuminated heart-shaped ornaments inscribed with cancer victims' names, red for survivors, white for deceased. Vanessa said a silent prayer.

Stephanie's turn came. She sat on Santa's lap, tugging at his long beard. "This is soft. Is it real?"

"Ho, ho, ho," Santa blurted. "Of course. Your name is…?"

"Stephanie. I want a Barbie doll and books. I like to read."

Santa smiled at Stephanie as she leaned closer and whispered into his ear.

Santa looked over at Vanessa and then at JP. His lips curved. "Smile at the elf now." He handed her a candy cane then whispered louder, "I will do my best to grant your wish."

Santa gave her an extra hug.

Vanessa held Stephanie's hand. "What did you ask Santa for besides the books and Barbie doll?"

Stephanie smiled a secret smile. "Wait and see."

Everyone gathered in front of the TV watching *Rudolph the Red-Nosed Reindeer*. Stephanie, with Helene's encouragement, begged JP to stay and help frost the sugar cookies. Vanessa welcomed his presence.

"Stephanie, what'd you tell Santa you wanted?" Helene asked.

"A Barbie doll and books."

"Excellent choice," JP said.

"A mom and dad too."

An icy chill cruised through Vanessa's spine. The silence lingered in the air, thick and heavy like a blanket.

Vanessa broke the stillness. "Your wish might be hard for Santa to fulfill."

"He said he would try. Santa wouldn't lie," Stephanie said with conviction. She reached for another cookie.

Snuggled next to JP, she asked, "Hey, JP, you aren't leaving again, are you?"

"I need to return to Rathdrum, but I'm planning to come back at Christmas unless the chief denies my request for time off."

"Goody. I like you visiting us and so does Vanessa."

Vanessa gave Helene a quick look to see a thin edge of a grin on her lips. She wondered what her aunt was thinking.

When the credits began running on the TV screen, Vanessa stood. "Time for bed, kiddo. Choose a book."

Stephanie didn't argue as usual about going to bed. She showed her selection to everyone. "This story is about baby Jesus."

"Say goodnight to Aunt Helene and JP."

Stephanie ran and hugged them both. She did not conceal her yawn.

"You're in love with Vanessa," Helene stated as she watched JP staring at the two climbing the stairs.

"Huh? What'd you say?" He turned his attention to Helene.

"I see the way you look at her. I only met you a few hours ago, but I can size up people well. I repeat. You're in love with her."

"Obvious, huh? I won't deny it," JP said. "I only wish she reciprocated."

"She does. She's too stubborn to admit it." She shook her head.

"A couple of weeks ago, after Thanksgiving, I told Vanessa I'll wait for her to phone me. I hoped she'd call me, but she didn't. So here I am, using Stephanie's phone call as an excuse to drop by." The sigh was resigned and weary. He began confiding in Helene. "I was in love before and engaged. But the gal dumped me for another guy. It took me quite a while to get over the heartache. I didn't date, afraid if I fell for someone, the same thing would happen again. Dumb, of course. Then Vanessa came into my life. I was hooked. Never looked at or wanted another woman. What I felt for Cheryl doesn't compare to how I feel about Vanessa. I'm on an emotional roller coaster."

"She'll come around. Trust me."

"Hope you're right. By the way, I'm assuming you told Vanessa about her birth parents."

Helene nodded.

"I'm glad you told her. She was determined to find the truth."

"If she so chooses, I'll let her tell you everything," Helene said.

"You going to stay here for a while?"

"Need to report Monday to headquarters in Seattle. I'm done traveling all over the globe. Besides, now that Vanessa and I reconciled, I plan to involve myself in her life."

Upstairs, Stephanie finished the story. Vanessa tucked her in and kissed her forehead. "Goodnight."

"I wish you would marry JP. We could all live together. I'll bet Mrs. Steiner would let me."

Words failed Vanessa. She stared into Stephanie's blue eyes, bright with hope. Her heart fell silent, and her lips refused to move. She flipped off the light and closed the door. Vanessa joined JP on the sofa, a cushion apart from him.

Helene stood and stretched toward the ceiling, faking a yawn. "I need my beauty sleep." She shook JP's hand, winking. "Nice meeting you. Goodnight, Vanessa."

Vanessa wondered why Helene winked at JP.

"Quite a lady," JP said.

"A little pushy today, but I'm happy she's here. We've reconciled, and my search is over. She told me everything." The sordid reality of her conception was still fresh. She picked up the remote and turned off the TV.

"My birth mother was a prostitute." The words cut through her like a knife. "She refused to identify the father."

JP scooted next to Vanessa as she began telling JP every rotten detail.

There are no magic wands for deep pain. JP looked at Vanessa, his eyes filled with empathy. His hands entwined hers, holding them and squeezing firmly. "Wow. A lot to absorb."

"I'm glad I learned the truth about everything and have a bit of closure. I never considered anything so…so sickening. But now I understand why my father was unwilling to tell me what happened. Aunt Helene insisted he should. That's what caused their estrangement." She chuckled. "Do you realize all the sleuthing we did was unnecessary?"

"Yeah, I kept telling you to get a hold of your aunt. I figured she'd be the key to the mystery. You—"

"Shush." Vanessa put a finger on his lips. "Don't rub it in how driving Aunt Helene away was a foolish thing to do. I regret it." She leaned back, her yawn long and audible. "I'm exhausted."

"I'm not ready to leave yet. Unless you're planning to kick me out."

"Tell me why you came by today."

"When Stephanie called,"—he glanced at Stephanie's picture on the fireplace mantel—"she wanted me to come right away and help with the Christmas tree."

"The sneaky kid. I didn't know."

"She also said you were sad and bawled when I left. True?"

Vanessa couldn't bring herself to admit she'd cried. "So, you're here because of Stephanie?" *Not me?*

JP placed his hands on Vanessa's shoulders and turned her toward him. "I got tired of waiting for your call."

"I phoned you twice. Before the first ring both times, I chickened out and hung up."

"Why?"

"I guess I hoped you'd make the first move. Then I'd know for sure you wanted to talk with me."

JP leaned back, slapping his knee and laughing. "I felt the same way." He wrapped his hands around hers. "I know as sure as a dime is worth ten cents you have affectionate feelings for me. What's holding you back from admitting it, Miss Stubborn?" A chuckle surfaced. "That should be your middle name. I won't release my hold until you answer."

She leaned away from him and took a deep breath. "You've only known about my amputation for about a couple of weeks."

"So?"

"You haven't seen my bare stump. Think you can deal with it?"

"Is a forty-pound robin fat?"

Vanessa pulled up her pants leg and removed the prosthesis. JP stroked the stump, showing no signs of repulsion or rejection. "Not an issue. There's no way I will ever let your handicap affect my feelings."

Relief enveloped Vanessa. *He's not bothered.* That fear debunked, she broached another matter. "Why'd you leave the first time?"

"I was engaged six years ago." JP cleared his throat. "She fell in love with another guy and dumped me."

Vanessa's mouth fell open, her fingers touching her

parted lips. Her brain formulated no thoughts other than to register stunned surprise.

"It broke my heart. I convinced myself if I ever fell in love again, the same thing would happen. So, I stayed clear of women…until I met you. And boy, did I fall hard. But again, my heart broke. I left because I needed to put distance between us to eliminate the temptation to see you, knowing I could never have you in my life. Stupid move." He cupped Vanessa's cheeks within his hands. "Leaving didn't help." He touched his lips to her forehead. "Vanessa, I've never stopped loving you, although God knows I tried. For the last two years, I thought about you daily and wondered if you were happy with Greg."

Before she could stop herself, she admitted, "I thought about you quite a bit. I longed for your presence."

"How about telling me the words I want to hear?" He leaped through the air, mimicking a clumsy ballet dancer.

"Stop!"

"Not until you let me steal into your heart."

"Stealing is a crime, Mr. Cop."

"If loving you is a crime, I'm guilty every time."

She motioned with her index finger for him to return to the sofa.

With two long leaps, JP was at her side. They laughed at their corniness. He leaned closer. Vanessa felt a fiery breath on her neck, then a gentle brush of lips. A hand slid around her waist, pulling her close to JP's Irish Spring soap-scented body. His kisses were now on her lips, becoming harder and more urgent. Goosebumps lined Vanessa's arms, not the kind from being cold, but the kind one gets when awakened by passion. Her resistance collapsed. There was only one desire, only a matter of time before the deed happened.

"Let's head upstairs to your boudoir," JP said, bending to lift her.

Vanessa voiced no objection.

As JP stepped onto the landing, the flushing toilet interrupted the silence. The bathroom door opened and Stephanie emerged. Spotting the pair, she asked JP, "How come you're carrying Vanessa?"

Chapter 31

Without missing a beat, JP asked. "You didn't expect Vanessa to hop up the stairs on one foot, did you?" Vanessa played along, wiggling her left leg absent the prosthesis. "I took it off to show JP my stump before I headed to bed. He offered to carry me upstairs."

JP advanced toward the bedroom, making a big deal about how his arms were tiring of holding Vanessa. He kidded Vanessa about losing several pounds.

"Vanessa's not fat," Stephanie pointed out.

Vanessa assumed JP's remark was to lighten this untimely and embarrassing interruption. At least she hoped so.

Stephanie followed them into the bedroom. "Stephie, time to head back to bed," Vanessa said after JP placed her on the bedspread.

Despite yawning and rubbing her eyes, Stephanie protested louder than necessary. "I'm not tired."

Vanessa tapped the child's lips with her finger. "Shush. You'll wake up Aunt Helene."

JP lifted the youngster and positioned her over his right shoulder. He galloped to the bedroom across the hallway and tucked her in. "Sweet dreams."

JP stopped outside the door as Stephanie's voice floated

to his ears, wishing out loud he was her dad.

Vanessa sat on the bed, her legs dangling over the edge. In a sheepish whisper, she asked, "Do you think we were convincing? Stephie's quite perceptive."

"Yep." He lowered himself next to Vanessa. "I don't want to leave." He leaned toward her and began running his hand along her thigh.

Vanessa pushed it away. Stephanie's appearance had spoiled the certain intimacy. The moment had passed. "I'm sorry."

"Don't be. Bad timing, but I'll be back tomorrow evening." JP kissed the top of her head. He inched away backward and stopped at the door, blowing her a kiss.

"Wait," Vanessa said.

In two leaps, he stood in front of her.

"I…I, um. Would you bring me the crutches and prosthesis before you leave?"

VANESSA SAUNTERED INTO THE KITCHEN WEARING JEANS and a bright red Christmas sweatshirt. The aroma of the sizzling bacon drifted into her nostrils. She bent her head over the frying pan, licking her lips.

"I poked around in your fridge. Scrambled eggs with sauteed green peppers, onions, and cheddar cheese coming up. Or would you prefer an omelette?" Helene continued stirring.

"Scrambled. My favorite besides blueberry pancakes."

Her niece's dreamy expression caught Helene's attention. "JP on your mind?"

Vanessa blinked. "Ah, no."

"Did he profess his undying love for you? And you the same?" Helene wasted no time soliciting details about last night.

"Aunt Helene, or should I call you Miss Busybody? I'll just say I enjoyed his company."

"Did you tell him how you feel?"

"How come you're so interested in what did—or didn't—happen?" Vanessa poured a glass of orange juice and washed down her daily vitamin pill.

"I want you two together. Sooner than later." She put a couple of slices of bread into the toaster. "Trust me, he loves you. And vice versa. When are you going to admit it?"

"Thanks, Dr. Helene, for that insightful analysis."

"You didn't tell him, did you? You are so stubborn!" Helene added a pinch of salt to the mixture. "Call him right after breakfast and invite him for dinner. Say Stephanie wants to see him again if that will make you more comfortable. I'm sure he'll accept."

"You're playing Cupid." Vanessa laughed at her aunt's meddling. "Where's your bow and arrow?"

"You caught me red-handed."

"Cool your jets," Vanessa said. "He's coming over tonight."

"Alleluia! Lucky for you, I'll be gone and so will Stephanie. Take advantage."

"He kissed me." The words tumbled from her mouth. Now Helene would gloat. Sure enough.

"What'd I tell you? I'm right, aren't I?" With a cocky grin, she added, "You liked it."

"Liked what?" Stephanie entered the kitchen carrying a hairbrush and bands. Vanessa untangled and braided the child's long tresses.

"JP kissed Vanessa."

"Did JP go back to your bedroom after he tucked me in? Did you kiss him back?"

"He was in your room?" Helene perked up. "This has got

to be good. Tell me what I missed. I must have slept through all the commotion." She turned off the burners and dished up the eggs and crisp bacon onto a platter.

"JP carried Vanessa upstairs 'cause her fake foot was off." Stephanie giggled. "He said she was heavy."

"No biggie," Vanessa said. "I took off my prosthesis to show JP my stump. He carried me because it made no sense to put it back on only to take it off minutes later."

"Humph. And I'm the queen of England." Helene's smug smile convinced Vanessa she hadn't fooled her aunt.

"Why'd you let him kiss you?" Stephanie asked.

Vanessa pooh-poohed the kiss. "People give friends and relatives hugs and kisses all the time. It was a quick smooch," she fibbed. "Nothing more happened." Reaching for the platter of scrambled eggs, she piled several spoonsful on her plate. "Let's eat."

"I'M GOING TO MISS YOU, YOUNG LADY," HELENE SAID. "I'M so happy I met you and am looking forward to spoiling you."

"Can't you stay longer?" Vanessa asked.

Helene glanced at her watch. Three fifteen. "I'd love to, but I planned to leave earlier. It's a three-hour drive to Seattle. I planned to get there before dark, but won't make it now."

"When are you coming again?" asked Stephanie.

"I'll be back for Christmas." She addressed her niece. "I hate leaving you so soon. We've just got re-acquainted. Goodbye, my two dears." Helene hugged them both. "I'm so thrilled and grateful we are a family again. Stephanie, come with me. I have several items for you in the car."

Stephanie slipped on her coat and followed Helene. Scattered snowflakes fluttered to the ground.

"Snow!" Stephanie shouted, reaching to secure a few flakes in her hands.

Helene tilted her head upward. The flakes wouldn't stick. She reached inside her compact vehicle and removed a small bag, handing it to the eager child. Stephanie opened it and pulled out the contents.

"What are these?" She wrinkled her face.

"Arrowheads. Ancient cultures and American Indians attached them to arrow shafts. They aimed at animals to kill them for food, shelter, and clothing."

"You mean like a bow and arrow?"

"Yes."

Stephanie held an artifact close to her chest, examining it. "Thank you, Aunt Helene." Stephanie pressed her frame against the woman.

"I enjoy being your unofficial aunt. Now Stephanie, call me anytime. My phone number is in the address book." She planted a subtle suggestion into the girl's mind. "I know JP would like a call from you now and then when he returns to Rathdrum. You can tell him how you and Vanessa are doing and how much Vanessa misses him. Try to talk him into moving back here."

"I wish they would get married. They can be my parents."

"I do too. Keep bugging them. But don't tell Vanessa I told you to. This will be our secret."

Stephanie put her finger up to her lips. "I didn't tell anyone about mine and Melanie's secret."

"I know I can trust you. Bye for now. Keep up your reading."

Vanessa appeared. She wrapped her arms around her aunt, melting into her form. Tears for the missed years she'd never make back dripped unchecked, washing a path onto her aunt's wool scarf.

Chapter 32

———◆———

"Are you packed and ready to go back to Mrs. Steiner's?" Vanessa asked after they stepped back inside the house. "She's expecting you by five. And I need to get back here before JP arrives."

"JP's coming? Goodie! Please let me stay another night. You can bring me to school in the morning." Stephanie knelt, pressing her hands together. "Pleeease."

Vanessa wouldn't mind Stephanie staying another night, of course. But she wanted to be *alone* with JP. She'd put the onus on Mrs. Steiner to decide. "You'll have to ask Mrs. Steiner's permission."

Stephanie grabbed the phone, thrusting it into Vanessa's hand. "Here!"

Moments later, in a resigned tone, Vanessa said, "You can stay here one more night. You'll have to go to bed early, though. School's tomorrow."

"All right!" She raised her arms in triumphant.

When JP arrived, Stephanie pulled out a couple of board games. "Bet I'll beat ya both!"

"Bring it on," JP said, rubbing his palms together.

Several victories later, Stephanie announced she was going to prepare her favorite dish for dinner.

"Fine," Vanessa said. "But first pick up the pieces and put away the games."

Stephanie dominated the conversation during dinner. Vanessa smiled at the camaraderie between the two.

"Thanks for the delicious mac and cheese," JP complimented Stephanie. "It was one of my favs as a kid. Now, let's give Vanessa a break from doing the dishes." JP opened the dishwasher. Stephanie placed the plates inside without complaining.

Wow, thought Vanessa. JP has a way with Stephanie. Impressive. You'd think she enjoyed helping with this chore.

At bedtime, Stephanie insisted she read the nightly story to JP instead of Vanessa.

Vanessa shooed them upstairs.

JP hefted the young girl onto his shoulders. He galloped around the room a few times before ascending the stairs. He listened to Stephanie's flawless reading of a story about a kitten and puppy who became best friends.

"Great story. Goodnight," JP said, kissing the top of her head.

"Vanessa likes you, but don't tell her I told you."

"It'll be our secret. I like her quite a bit too."

"Can you marry her?"

JP grinned and turned out the light. He beelined to Vanessa. He noticed the prosthesis leaning against the sofa and Vanessa massaging the stump. "Are you okay?"

"Yes. A small amount of pain. Gone now."

"Good. Stephanie loves to read, doesn't she?"

"Yeah, she excels in reading. Math, not her forte."

Vanessa knew what JP had on his mind. For whatever stubborn reason, she needed a wee bit more time to express her love for him. She challenged him to a game of *Battleship*.

She recalled the first time they'd played the game. While both crawled on all fours to retrieve the scattered pegs, he'd kissed her for the first time.

"Okay," JP agreed, "But only one game."

JP lost again.

"Hey, no fair, you cheated so I would win, didn't you?" Vanessa grumbled.

"I admit it. I wanted to finish quicker." JP slid next to her, facing her so close their noses almost touched. "Are you ready to let me steal into your heart?"

"I…I," she stammered.

His fingers stroked the nape of her neck, delicately, like butterfly wings. JP's lips brushed Vanessa's. They were warm, and the scent of mint from the gum he'd chewed earlier wafted to her nostrils. JP showered her with tender kisses. Her brain lit on fire, and warmth cruised throughout her entire body as the kisses deepened. The fragrance of her sweet pea perfume and the touch of her skin flooded JP's senses. He removed his tennis shoes and tossed his shirt onto the floor. He reached to unbutton Vanessa's blouse, then stopped. "Let's head to your bedroom."

Vanessa knew it was coming. "I'll need my crutches."

"Forget them." He reached to lift her.

From the landing upstairs, Stephanie stood spying on the two. She leaned over too far and lost her balance. Her body thudded downward and her limbs tumbled over one another, hitting against the stairs' edges. Her agonizing screech reverberated throughout the house. High pitched, the scream had an intensity smacking of urgency and desperation. It bypassed Vanessa's logical thinking and went right to her emotional response. This wasn't just any scream. It was Stephanie's. Vanessa was sliding off the sofa before JP could hold her back.

"Stay here!" JP ordered. He dashed to Stephanie, now lying at the bottom of the staircase. He bent over the moaning child, assessing the situation. At first examination, he saw no signs of visible injury other than a trickle of blood on her left knee.

"Steph! Where do you hurt?"

Vanessa stared at the child with wide, alarming eyes. Her hand covered her mouth to muffle her shriek. Adrenalin kicked in, propelling Vanessa to hop on one foot to Stephanie. She sat on the bottom stair and reached to hold the whimpering child.

"Don't move her." JP's body stung with nerves as he leaned over Stephanie, but he remained calm.

"My hand hurts," Stephanie moaned, tears flowing.

"What's wrong with her?" Vanessa expected an immediate diagnosis.

JP examined the left hand. Swelling and bruising. "Can you move your wrist or fingers?"

"No. It hurts bad. Can you make it stop?"

JP looked at Vanessa. "We should call 911."

She didn't have insurance to cover the cost. It didn't matter.

"Never mind. We'll take her to emergency. I'm confident there are no internal injuries. I suspect a broken wrist." He grabbed his shirt, ripping it as he pulled it over his head, and shoved his feet inside the shoes.

Stephanie cried louder. "I don't wanna go to the hospital."

"Everything will be fine." JP comforted her. Vanessa watched JP quiet Stephanie's crying with superb tenderness. Numb with worry, she couldn't speak.

"Here. Put on your prosthesis," JP said as he handed it to Vanessa before heading to the kitchen for ice. When he returned, she hadn't made a move.

"Vanessa!" JP's voice shocked her into action.

Vanessa battled with her trembling hands to put on the prosthesis, delaying their departure. At last, JP sat behind the steering wheel, zooming the four miles toward Providence Hospital. Vanessa sat in the rear, holding Stephanie on her lap. The girl's eyes closed in a grimace, her skin pale. Guilt pestered Vanessa. *It's all my fault we're not at the hospital yet.* They could have left sooner if she hadn't taken so long to put on her stupid foot.

"Are you authorized to allow any medical treatment?" JP asked.

Vanessa hadn't thought about that. "No."

"Call the foster mother," JP said.

Her shaky hand fumbled with the cell phone. She pressed the wrong speed dial number. The second attempt succeeded. "I'll meet you there," Mrs. Steiner said. She raced down the hall to tell Ellie.

The staff took Stephanie in minutes before Mrs. Steiner arrived. She completed the medical forms before a nurse brought her to join Stephanie.

"Stephie will be fine," JP said, pouring himself a cup of complimentary coffee.

Vanessa gave him a grateful look, thankful he'd taken charge. She'd been no help. She clenched her fists, digging her fingernails into the palm of her hands. The only thing she was aware of was her heart pounding against her chest. A life-size painting of Jesus hung on the pastel green wall. She laced her hands together and prayed.

An eternity later a nurse emerged, pushing a weary Stephanie in a wheelchair. Vanessa was resting her head on JP's shoulder, eyes closed.

"Vanessa! Look what I got!" Stephanie held up her wrist, grinning. "A white cast!"

Vanessa leaped from the chair. "Let me be the first to sign it." She rummaged through her purse and pulled out a blue ink pen.

Stephanie looked at her funny-like. "You can write on this?"

"Of course."

"I'll bet the other kids will want to draw something on it. Wayne will want to draw a stupid basketball."

All three adults autographed the fresh cast. Vanessa added a heart with an arrow through it. "Because I love you," she said.

The clock inched toward midnight. "It's been a long evening," Mrs. Steiner said. "Even though I'm going to keep Stephanie home from school tomorrow, she needs her sleep."

"Please, let me stay at Vanessa's one more night," Stephanie begged.

Vanessa and Mrs. Steiner exchanged glances. "I'll bring her home first thing tomorrow morning," Vanessa promised.

Mrs. Steiner patted fingers against her chin, deep in deliberation. Finally, she said, "All right, but I'll be expecting you to head on over as soon as Stephanie wakes up." She bent eye level with the drowsy youngster, hugging her. "See you in the morning, my dear. Sleep well."

Stephanie mumbled goodnight, struggling to keep her eyes open.

Arriving at Vanessa's, JP carried the child to her bedroom after Vanessa gave her a firm goodnight hug. In a matter of minutes, a man's silly laugh drifted to Vanessa's ears. She retreated to the sofa, pulling off her coat in a huff. Was Stephanie shifting her affection to JP? Nonsense. Their bond was strong.

Vanessa leaned back, closing her eyes, anticipating JP's return and the words she planned to tell him. No more delays. Stephanie's accident tonight was the spark she needed to tell JP she was more than ready to let him steal into her heart. She couldn't imagine life without him. She loved him. With genuine love, you feel like the other person is the reason your life is wonderful. It's when you think about him all the time. It's when he tells you "Everything will be all right. I'm right here by your side."

After fifteen minutes elapsed, impatience overtook her. *What's taking him so long?* She climbed the stairs. Stephanie's giggles grew louder as she approached the door. When she poked her head inside, Stephanie covered her mouth with her right hand, stifling a snicker.

"What are you two up to?" Vanessa forced a cheerful demeanor. She suspected they had a secret she wasn't privy to, and it bothered her.

"Ah, nothing," JP answered. He stood, pulling the blankets over Stephanie. He bent to kiss her forehead and Stephanie whispered too loud, "Can I tell Vanessa?"

"Tell me what?" Vanessa asked.

Chapter 33

In two long strides, JP was beside Vanessa, nudging her into the hallway.

"What's going on?" Vanessa stared into JP's eyes.

JP silenced her with a quick peck on her lips as his muscular arms snatched her up and he descended the stairs. Her heart thumped against her caged chest.

He placed Vanessa on the sofa, noting the yawn she tried to suppress. He glanced at the mantel clock. One fifteen.

"I don't want to, but I should let you get your beauty sleep, although you're lovely already," JP said.

"No! You can't leave," Vanessa blurted out. "I want to tell you…I mean…"

In a voice barely above a whisper, she uttered, "I love you." *There. She'd said it.*

JP plunked himself beside Vanessa. His eyes wandered toward the stairs as though he hadn't heard what she'd said seconds ago. "I guess Stephanie won't mind if I tell you what we discussed." He gave her a sly look. "We've decided…" He interrupted himself, turning his torso toward Vanessa. "Wait a second." He wiggled his ear lobes. "Did you say the words I've longed to hear since forever, Miss Stubborn?" He cupped her chin within his hands.

"Yes. I love you. I'm sorry I chose to take so long to express my genuine feelings for you."

JP lowered his face to Vanessa's, and their lips met. The kiss was gentle, yet fervent. As they parted, Vanessa saw the sparkle in JP's eyes and his lips curve into a smile. She couldn't help but smile back.

"I don't want to be in love with anyone but you ever again," JP said.

"Ditto."

He pulled Vanessa close. "Stephie and I decided I'm going to be her dad."

Vanessa sat erect. "You what?" She expressed her opposition. "You can't," she emphasized. "*I* applied to adopt her." There couldn't be a competition. She wouldn't allow it. "Is that what Stephie wanted to tell me?"

"Yes. And also—"

"You're single," she interrupted him, voicing the first objection popping into her mind. Vanessa's jealousy alarmed her.

Placing his forehead against hers and looking deep into her eyes, JP said, "We also decided I'm going to marry you. How does a honeymoon in Denali sound?"

"Denali? Honeymoon?"

"I'm proposing."

Vanessa stared at JP. "As in *marriage?*"

"Of course."

Vanessa realized her jealousy was foolish. There was no reason Stephanie couldn't love both her and JP. She thought about the time he rescued Stephanie at the park. And how excited the child was every time she saw him. And the way he'd comforted the youngster tonight after the accident. She couldn't imagine a more fitting, loving father.

Vanessa wrapped her arms around JP. She couldn't say yes fast enough.

JP twirled her.

"Put me down, silly," Vanessa said.

"All righty," JP said, then whirled her around the room in a clumsy waltz. Fred Astaire and Ginger Rogers they weren't, but neither cared. Vanessa's "fake foot" didn't hinder her. She floated on a cloud of sheer ecstasy.

Breathless, they plopped on the sofa. "Let's go tell Stephie," Vanessa suggested.

"Don't disturb her. Wait till morning. I want to be alone with you for now."

"Hey, where are we going to live? What about your job in Rathdrum?"

"I'll resign. I think I can get my job back here if there's an opening. If not, I'll apply elsewhere."

"Does that mean you're moving back to Milwaukie? You'll thrill your mother."

JP squeezed his lips together in an agreeable grin. "No doubt."

"What about this house? Do you want to—"

"A one-level house might be more suitable for you, but you decide. I don't care where we live as long as we're together." He planted a long smooch on her lips. "Now pick a date. The sooner the better. A quick ceremony at the courthouse is fine with me."

Vanessa teasingly slapped his hand. "No way. We can't deprive Stephanie, Aunt Helene, and your mother of the pleasure of a wedding. It'll be simple, I promise."

Vanessa stared at the Christmas tree. She calculated in her mind. "It's after midnight. Monday, the tenth now. Christmas Eve is two weeks from today. I can put together a small, intimate wedding with Melanie's help."

JP didn't wait for any other possibilities. "Christmas Eve it is."

After more than two years of trauma, peace embraced Vanessa. She snuggled against JP's chest, lulled by the rhythmic beat of his heart. She closed her eyes, saying nary a word, content to remain within JP's embrace all night.

JP had another idea. "How 'bout we pick up where we left off before Stephanie's tumble?" He lifted Vanessa into his muscular arms and headed upstairs. She pictured Rhett Butler carrying Scarlett up the red-carpeted stairway in the Southern mansion. In her case, she welcomed JP's action and offered no resistance. She was beyond ready to give her heart and soul to the man she loved. To become one. JP's foot pushed the door closed and he locked the door.

———◆———

VANESSA, JP, STEPHANIE, AND MRS. STEINER TALKED IN excited tones as they waited in the judge's small chambers. The older man arrived and sat behind an enormous mahogany desk. He opened the file, frowning at the papers.

Vanessa gripped JP's hand with sudden worry. Had there been a problem with the paperwork?

The judge looked up, and the frown changed to a broad smile revealing pearl white teeth. Vanessa sighed in relief.

Stephanie approached the judge, pointing to Vanessa and JP. "They're going to be my mom and dad!" Vanessa pulled the wiggling girl to her side, giving her a stare that settled the girl a tad bit. Vanessa smiled as she watched the happy child smooth the white dress and finger the red sash. She'd insisted she wear the flower girl attire she'd worn for Vanessa's and JP's wedding. "It's my special day."

Melanie, holding Dylan, stood beside Jason. The children jockeyed for front row positions around the desk. Ellie tried to maintain order while Aunt Helene snapped pictures. Barbara Monroe dabbed her moistened eyes.

The judge invited Stephanie to stand beside him. He admonished Stephanie this was a serious matter and asked her a few questions. Stephanie nodded and answered in the same manner. He smiled at her answers and signed and dated the document. He announced her new surname, shook her hand, and handed her the papers.

March 2, 2013. Vanessa's twenty-seventh birthday. She couldn't have received a better present. She was officially Stephanie's forever mother. Happiness seeped into her bones. The traumas of the past were mended. The future appeared promising with her new family. She closed her eyes, sensing her father's presence. She wanted this sensation to last into old age. Vanessa felt JP's arm encircle her waist, and she leaned against his strength. She smiled when he kissed the side of her forehead.

"Happy Birthday, Mom!" The moniker danced off Stephanie's lips as she ran from behind the desk and wrapped her arms around Vanessa's waist.

Mom, a name Vanessa already cherished.

Hand in hand, the brand-new Monroe family raised their arms in triumph. Cheers and clapping erupted. A beaming Stephanie smiled at her *parents* and announced. "Now I wish for a baby sister or brother. And a puppy."

THE END

ACKNOWLEDGEMENTS

I want to thank the ladies in the critique group, Chrysalis, for their blunt critiques/suggestions that deflated me in the beginning, but turned out most beneficial. I extend my gratitude to Mary Jean Rivera and Kaila Jacobs, thorough beta readers. Lastly, I want to acknowledge Christina Weaver, author and editor extraordinaire. Her invaluable help and encouragement propelled me across the finish line.

About the Author

Roseann Cotton lives in rural Oregon on a Christmas tree farm. She and her husband love the season and enjoy meeting people. They are both avid Oregon State Beaver fans.